CHICKEN SCRATCH

The Sisters, Texas Series

Becki Willis

Copyright© 2015 by Becki Willis
Clear Creek Publishers

ISBN: 1508530807
ISBN 13: 9781508530800

All rights reserved. No part of this book may be copied, shared, or reproduced without written consent of the author.

This is a work of fiction. All characters, businesses, and interaction with these people and places are purely fictional and a figment of the writer's imagination.

OTHER BOOKS BY BECKI WILLIS

He Kills Me, He Kills Me Not

The Girl from Her Mirror
(Mirrors Don't Lie, Book 1)

Mirror, Mirror on Her Wall
(Mirrors Don't Lie, Book 2)

Light from Her Mirror
(Mirrors Don't Lie, Book 3)

1

Finding a dead body was not a good way to start a new job. Finding the dead body of your newest client was decidedly worse.

Ten minutes after making the horrendous discovery, Madison Reynolds sat outside the commercial chicken houses, waiting for the police to arrive. She was still trembling, but the shiver working its own down her spine had nothing to do with the wind whipping around her. Never mind that she had spent the entire morning sweating profusely; thermostat-controlled heaters kept the inside of the houses at a balmy eighty degrees. The cold seeping into her bones now had less to do with temperature, and more to do with shock. She could still see his face, so gruesome and distorted in death. And with that chicken perched upon it so proudly, as if staking its claim...

Madison shivered again and forced the image from her mind. She considered calling her best friend for some much-needed support, but the wail of an approaching siren drew her attention. She struggled to her feet, found that her knees were too weak to support her, and fell sharply back onto her rumpus.

Less than a minute later, a fire truck arrived on the farm amid a swirl of white dust and red lights. Madison was thankful to the driver for turning off the siren and strobe lights as he approached where she sat in front of House 4.

The truck barely stopped before the driver opened the door and jumped out.

"Are you all right?" the man demanded immediately, his eyes already probing the area for potential danger.

Madison opened her mouth to speak, but no sound came out. With eyes that were large and swimming with sudden tears, she merely nodded.

The firefighter seemed to recognize her distress. The quality of his voice changed, as if he were speaking to a frightened child. He even crouched down in front of her to be at the same eye level. "You're Miss Bert's granddaughter, aren't you?" he asked.

Again, she could only nod. She thought she recognized the young man as one of Tug Montgomery's boys, even though his slim frame bore no resemblance to his father's famous 'tug-boat' build, the one from which Texas football legends were made. But he had Mary Alice's eyes and was certainly handsome enough to be the former beauty queen's son. She thought she recalled her grandmother saying something about one of their sons being on the fire department. Her guess was that this was little Cutter Montgomery, all grown up and setting women's hearts aflutter, with or without the uniform.

He confirmed her suspicions with a smile. "Cutter Montgomery." He extended a hand that was large and calloused.

Madison tugged off her filthy leather glove and placed her trembling hand into his. He immediately cocooned her icy fingers within the warmth of both his palms, his brows puckered in concern. "Are you sure you're all right, ma'am? I don't want you going into shock."

It took two attempts, but she finally found her voice. "I'm- I'm okay. It's not every day I find a ... dead body." In spite of herself, she shivered at the mere words.

"Would you like to sit in the fire truck, ma'am, until the police arrive? You might be more comfortable."

Madison shook her head. She looked over her shoulder, toward the long metal building that housed the body. "I feel like we should do something. The chickens are- are pecking at him." Again she shivered, this time in revulsion.

Cutter Montgomery rocked back on his heels and deliberated for less than a minute. "We need to preserve the scene," he acknowledged. "I don't want to disturb anything, but you're right, we need to stop the chickens from doing even more damage." With one smooth movement, he shot to his full height of just under six feet.

Madison's attempt was much less graceful. As she lumbered to her feet, she wavered for a moment like a leaf in the breeze. Squaring her shoulders and digging in her heels, she took on a battle stance as she made a brave offer. "I'll help."

"Are you sure?"

No, she was not at all certain, but she felt obligated to see the mission through. "It's the least I can do."

"What were you doing out here, anyway?" Despite his friendly tone, the first responder's eyes were speculative.

"Mr. Gleason hired me to walk his chicken houses for him this week while he was out of town."

Cutter Montgomery looked down at her with obvious surprise. His gaze flickered over her, as if noticing her attire for the first time. Hazel eyes took in the raggedy t-shirt streaked with dust and perspiration, the filthy jeans smeared with Heaven-only-knows-what, the plastic sleeves over muck boots at least a size too large, and the disposable respirator dangling from her neck. He bit back the smile, but amusement still sparked in his eyes as he questioned his hearing. "You?"

Madison lifted her chin defiantly. "Yes, me," she fairly snapped.

"Sorry, ma'am, I meant no disrespect," the younger man apologized. He reached around to open and hold the door for her. "I'm just surprised, is all. I didn't realize Ronny had hired anyone to work for him."

"He didn't, not exactly. I own In a Pinch Temporary Services," she explained. With a brave gulp, she stepped over the threshold and into the chicken house.

She immediately regretted the deep breath without interference from the respirator. The stench of twenty-five thousand chickens and high levels of ammonia burned her lungs and assaulted her nostrils. As her eyes adjusted to the dim interior, she quickly put the breathing apparatus back in place.

Cutter Montgomery murmured something as he backed out of the doorway and disappeared into the adjacent control room. Madison had a moment of panic at the thought of being alone with the body, but when the long barn brightened, she realized the firefighter was merely adjusting the lighting. Seconds later he was back beside her and asking which way to go.

Madison motioned to the fan end of the five-hundred-foot building. When he waited for her to take the lead, she reluctantly pushed forward, wading through the dense maze of white birds.

Less than one week ago, she joined Ronny Gleason on rounds through the houses where he grew commercial broilers for Barbour Foods. Although the houses were fully automated and run by a computer program, some things still needed personal inspections. He taught her how to 'walk' the houses, which entailed looking for trouble spots and picking up dead or inferior chickens. Water lines needed adjusting every few days as the chickens grew, and feed lines had to be free and flowing. The list of potential problems was overwhelming —everything from broken fan belts and stalled motors to leaking water nipples and disease among the chickens— but surprisingly enough, the massive process was generally smooth and trouble-free. The crash course in chicken growing taught Madison more than she ever intended to know about the feathered fowl, but at this point in her life, a job was a job. She needed the meager amount Ronny Gleason was paying her to tend his houses for the week.

To her chagrin, a sudden thought crossed Madison's mind. *Who will pay me now? Do I even still have the job?* She knew it was in poor taste to be thinking of a paycheck when a man lay dead just a few dozen feet away, but she had a lot riding on this job. It was her first 'real' service. Walking Glitter Thompson's dogs while she was out of town, carrying Leroy Huddleston back and forth to physical therapy in Bryan, and running small errands for some of her grandmother's friends were such meager jobs they hardly qualified; unless, of course, she was putting together a resume. In that case, her agency had experience in transportation needs, personal shopper assistance, and pet care.

Even though the odd jobs brought in a small amount of income, they were more like kid work than actual temporary services. She had not been blind to the evil looks ten-year-old Trey Hadley gave her at church last Sunday; after all, he usually walked the Thompson poodles when their owner was away. Madison found no pleasure in stealing jobs from the local youth, but she was just desperate enough to do it anyway.

That was why this job was so important to her. If Ronny Gleason gave her a good recommendation, other chicken growers in the community might call her when they needed help, and her agency would finally get off to a solid start.

The sickening sweet, rancid smell of death permeated the respirator as she approached the end of the house, reminding Madison that there would be no recommendation from poor Ronny Gleason. She stared at the mound of chickens that now roosted atop his prone body and was ashamed of herself for worrying about her own plight at a time like this. When her feet stalled, unwilling to carry her closer, Cutter Montgomery bumped into her from behind.

The first responder stepped around her and plodded forward. He shooed the birds away with sweeping movements of his arms. The action set off a flurry of noisy activity as chickens squawked and flapped and scurried away, but it cleared a direct path to the body. Stopping within a couple of feet of the dead man, the young fireman assessed the situation without touching any evidence.

He said something, but the words drowned under the noisy cluck of the disturbed chickens. Madison reluctantly stepped forward so that she could catch his next statement. "Looks like he's been dead several hours. In this kind of heat, though, it's hard to tell."

A shiver of repulsion shimmed through Madison. She had only been in the chicken business for one day, but she knew exactly what he was talking about. Even she had no trouble telling which chickens had died within the day and which ones had been missed on the last walk-through. The chickens could quickly deteriorate into a gooey, disgusting mess when left in these conditions; she supposed a human body would be no different.

As Madison bit back a gag reflex, Cutter looked around the huge building and continued to speak. "We need to section off this area to keep the chickens away. If you'll stay here, I'll move those divider fences this way."

"I'll help!" she said frantically. She wasn't about to stand there with the body.

"I know it's not pleasant, ma'am," he said, his voice gentle, "but you'd be more help standing here and keeping the chickens away."

"Oh." The flap of nearby wings swept the small word away.

Madison turned her back to the body as she shooed away the curious birds. She fought back a wave of panic as she watched Cutter move away from her, leaving her alone with the dead man. She was almost thankful when one feisty rooster pecked at her calf; the brief sting of pain gave her something else to think about, other than the fact that she stood two feet away from a grotesquely mutilated body, swollen by heat and ravished by a flock of chickens.

Low-to-the-ground grid panels were used as fences within the house to create distinct sections down the five-hundred foot corridor. The fences helped distribute bird density for more equal access to feed pans and water lines, while still being low enough for the growers to step over. With no heed now to unbalanced sections, Cutter Montgomery jerked holding stakes from the ground and began maneuvering the long panels amid the feathered sea of white.

He dutifully made his way back toward Madison, who was careful to keep her back to the dead man as she circled his prone form, flapping her arms to chase away chickens. If the situation had not been so dire, she might have laughed at the crazy sight she must make. When she made a round and saw Cutter just a few feet away, a sound that was half-sob, half-laughter escaped her scorched throat and she almost tripped on her own clumsy feet.

"We need to push all the birds forward," he advised. "Go to the back wall and start herding them this way."

Madison soon learned that herding several hundred chickens was about as easy as convincing a pair of petulant toddlers into doing something they refused to do. Every time she thought she was making progress in moving the mass forward, a half dozen birds slipped behind her. While she chased those birds down, another dozen or so decided to backtrack.

"This isn't working," Cutter announced after several minutes. Madison would have agreed, but she was too busy trying to get a deep breath, horrid odor and all. The combination of physical exertion and excessive heat zapped her energy and robbed her of air. Bent at the waist to catch her breath, she barely heard him as he planned their next course of action. "We'll just make a section here around the body. That will have to be good enough, at least until the police gets here."

Madison nodded incoherently. In retrospect, maybe getting her unruly twins into the bathtub hadn't been as difficult as she remembered; it was certainly easier than getting all these feathered fowl to move. Maybe she should take chicken houses off her list of offered services...

As Cutter Montgomery went to work erecting a triangular fence around the dead chicken grower, Madison shooed birds away and followed simple instructions. She held the panels as Cutter drove stakes into the ground to make them stay upright, careful to keep her eyes averted from the body. Bending to hold the low fences brought her closer to the cloying smell that permeated the air and turned her stomach, but Madison held her breath as much as possible. Even without the noxious fetor of death, the odor in the chicken houses was already so overpowering it was enough to make any sane woman run the other way.

Madison, however, had always found that sanity was overrated. Ignoring the bile that rose in her throat, she took tiny sips of air through her mouth and steeled herself to the task that must be done.

To keep her mind off the mutilated mass just feet away, Madison tried to concentrate on something else. She wondered what the twins were doing. It was still mid-morning, so they would probably be in their shared Science Lab about now, or maybe in their respective classes of English Lit and Algebra. Didn't Bethani have a math test today? Madison worried that her daughter's grades were slipping. The move had been hard on the fifteen-year-old, especially after losing the father she so adored. Blake seemed to be adjusting better than his sister was, but with boys, it was often hard to tell. Not for the first time, Madison felt the swell of insecurity wash over her, making her question herself and her decision to move back to her hometown.

"There, that should do it." The firefighter's satisfied grunt brought Madison from her musings and back to the situation at hand.

Without thinking, Madison glanced over at the body they protected. After so carefully avoiding the sight since her initial discovery —and even then she had not looked at his face— this one careless action was a brutal and cruel slap of reality that brought Madison up short. With no chance to brace herself to the sight before her, she was less than a foot away from the distorted flesh that slipped from Ronny Gleason's face. One unseeing eye stared straight up at the ceiling; the other had been pecked out by the chickens, leaving a bloodied, empty socket in its place. His mouth gaped open and was a festering place for dozens of swarming flies and beetles and maggots. The skin of his neck was ripped from a hundred sharp claws marching over it, and what was once his Adam's apple was now pecked clean.

Horrified, Madison jumped to her feet and whirled around. She slipped in the wet litter beneath her feet and went down amid the chickens. Scrabbling for traction, she used whatever she could find —chickens, the filth she lay in, a nearby feed line— to push herself upright and get her feet beneath her once again. She ran for the end door, stepping over and sometimes on the hapless chickens in her path. She wrestled with the door that stood between her and freedom, finding even the simple doorknob too difficult to manage in her hysteria.

When the handle finally turned, Madison burst out into the gloriously fresh air and gobbled it in with deep, greedy gulps. The cold air collided in her airway with remnants of her breakfast, on its way up from her queasy stomach. As

Madison choked and gagged and gasped for air, the police finally arrived on scene.

※

Brash deCordova pulled behind the fire truck, grateful that at least the VFD had responded to the call in a timely manner. With his crew of exactly three officers, himself included, the police department was stretched thin across the connecting cities of Juliet and Naomi, collectively known as The Sisters. The Volunteer Fire Department often filled in the gaping holes.

Okay, so maybe the term *cities* was a bit presumptuous, he acknowledged to himself. Even thrown together, the population of the two towns barely scraped two thousand. Admittedly, he was not chief of a thriving metropolis, but there were plenty enough residents to keep his job interesting and his hours long. And according to Vina, his ever-efficient clerk and the best department coordinator he had ever known, the arrival of the area's newest three citizens bumped the department into a new category that qualified them for additional state funding. The dream of having a fourth officer might finally become a reality and take some of the workload off his overstressed team.

Dreaming aside, Brash had work to do. Never mind that he worked last night's shift and should be sleeping right now. A minor wreck along the highway tied up Officer Perry, as well as most of the fire department. Officer Schimanski was responding to a report of a suspicious person lurking around The Gold and Silver Exchange. Which left him to respond to the report of an unattended death here at Gleason's Poultry Farm.

Just a few hundred feet to the north, he mused as he stepped into the dank and putrid interior of the chicken house. Then the farm would fall under the county's jurisdiction. But no, last year's re-districting of the Naomi city limits —a blatant and obvious effort to outrank their rival town's population— landed the farm within his responsibilities. So much for a nap.

Even with the lights turned up, it took a moment for his eyes to adjust to the interior lighting. Over the tops of fluffy white feathers and through the haze of dust that seemed to always inhabit the houses, Brash could see a figure at the back of the long structure. Judging from the rig outside, his guess was Cutter Montgomery. *A good kid,* the police chief thought, *always ready and eager to help. Let's see what he found this time.*

Halfway down the house, Brash decided being an overworked, under-paid, sleep-deprived public servant was still a far sight better than being a chicken farmer. Even without the smell, the noisy din of thousands of clucking birds was enough to drive him to drinking. A few more feet, and he got a whiff of another kind of odor. The undeniable stench of death immediately reminded him that his own career was hardly glamorous.

"What have we got?" he called out when he came within hearing range of the other man.

Cutter Montgomery turned to acknowledge the officer's presence. "Ronny Gleason. At least, I think that's who it is. Kind of hard to tell, considering."

Stepping over the fence with an easy stride, Brash deCordova crouched beside the badly damaged body. Using the antenna of his hand-held radio, he gingerly pushed and pulled at the dead man's shirt, trying to determine if there were any obvious signs of foul play. No bullet holes, but slashes from a knife could be easily confused with slashes from chicken claws.

"I'd say it's definitely Ronny," he agreed as he eyed the body. "Good idea with the fence, by the way, even though the damage has already been done. So who found the body?"

"New worker." With a thumb, he motioned toward the end door which still stood ajar. "Losing her breakfast, as we speak."

"Her?"

"Yeah, but to give her credit, she hung in there longer than I expected. She's been a real trooper, helping me section off this area and keeping the birds away. I know a lot of men who couldn't have done what she did."

"You'd need an iron stomach, that's for sure," Brash muttered. He lifted his wrist to his nose and breathed against it, hoping to dilute the reek of death laced with ammonia and wet litter. He could not recall ever smelling something quite so repulsive. Ignoring his own stomach's protest, he studied the body for a few moments longer. "As far as I know, Ronny was in good health. How old do you figure he was?"

The fireman shrugged. "I think he was younger than my dad, so late forties, maybe? About your age, I'd say."

Brash pulled to his feet and did his best to stare down at the younger man. Given the fact they were both within an inch of six feet tall, the attempt was not as effective as he hoped. He resorted to a glare. "Just how old do you think I am, boy?"

Unfazed, the younger man grinned cockily. "Old enough to consider me a boy."

"I don't even qualify for mid-forties," Brash grumbled. Forty-two was still the early forties, was it not?

"No, but I could still hear your knee pop, even over all this racket," Cutter quipped.

"Perils of playing football."

"I know. My old man pops the same way."

Brash pretended to scowl as he stepped over the fence. *And with no popping joints,* he was proud to note. "Don't forget your old man can still whip your ass, boy," Brash informed the younger man. He felt the need to defend the great Tag Montgomery. After all, Tag had been not only his hero, but also his mentor. Between the two of them, they still claimed most of the standing records for The Sisters Fighting Cotton Kings. For good measure, he threw out another warning. "And so could I."

Cutter Montgomery merely laughed. "I'll keep that in mind."

Exerting his authority, Brash got in the last word. "You stay with the body; I'll go talk to the witness."

But as the police chief walked away, the younger man called after him. "Fine by me," the fireman insisted affably. "I guess the smell doesn't bother the younger generation near as much as it does you old folks."

2

Madison swiped the back of her hand across her mouth as she knelt at the edge of the white rock road. Tears stung her eyes and her stomach burned, but she thought the worst of it was over. Surely, there was nothing left in her stomach to heave.

She heard the crunch of footsteps on the driveway behind her. Hurriedly wiping her face and righting her filthy and crumbled t-shirt, she struggled to her feet. The Montgomery boy had been more than tolerant of her so far, but she knew she had to pull herself together. The police would be here soon, but with any luck she would be long gone before the Chief showed up. She didn't want to see her high school crush for the first time in twenty years, looking like this.

"Ma'am?" That was not Cutter Montgomery's deep voice rumbling close behind her. "Ma'am, I understand you were the one to find the body. Could I have a few words with you?"

The police must have arrived. She hadn't heard the sirens because she was too busy purging her body of the lining of her stomach. Remembering the peppermint in her pants pocket,

Madison slipped the morsel into her mouth as she nodded and turned around.

She practically choked on the mint when she saw the man standing before her. As she sputtered and coughed ungracefully, Madison gazed into the soulful brown eyes of none other than Brash deCordova, the boy she had loved from afar in high school.

"Ma'am? Are you all right?" he asked in concern.

With her face so blotchy and red, Madison was grateful he did not recognize her. After all, he had hardly given her a second glance in school. Three years her senior, he was king of the high school when she schlepped in as a lowly freshman. Why should he suddenly recognize her now, after all these years?

Madison coughed one last time. "I will be," she insisted, her voice coming out ragged and hoarse.

"I'm Chief of Police deCordova, ma'am, and I'd like to ask you a few questions. Would you be more comfortable sitting in the patrol car?"

She managed a stiff shake of the head. "I'm fine."

Brash reached into his shirt pocket and pulled out a small notebook. Madison could not help but notice he had nice hands, fingers all long and lean. Always athletic in high school, he still had a good, solid physique, with no pudginess around the middle. His dark russet hair was as thick as ever, but there were now a few fine strands of silver woven in here and there. It gave him a distinguished look. *And my word!* The man was as good-looking as ever, maybe even more so now.

"Ma'am?" Apparently she had missed something he said, because he looked at her in concern, waiting for her answer to the unknown question.

"I'm sorry, what did you say?"

"I understand that you're a little shaken up, ma'am. I'll try to make this as brief as possible. Could you walk me through what happened this morning? How did you come to find Mr. Gleason's body?"

Madison pushed a limp strand of hair from her forehead, inadvertently leaving a streak of dirt or worse in its wake. Even before falling, she was covered in dust, grime, and questionable chicken substances. After the fall, there was little question as to what covered most of her legs from the knee down, one elbow, and patches of her sweat-drenched shirt. Even to her own nose, she reeked. What difference did a splatter or two of vomit matter at this point?

Yet as horrible as her own body smelled, she feared she might never cleanse the stench of dead flesh from her nose's membranes. Shivering, Madison pulled her thoughts together and began the arduous task of reliving her horrendous morning.

"Mr. Gleason hired me to walk houses for him while he was away this week. I came by a couple of days last week to learn the ropes before he left. He-"

"Excuse me. Hate to interrupt, but do you know where he was supposed to be going this week?"

"Uhm, deep-sea fishing. Out of Galveston, I think."

Scribbling in his notebook, he glanced up for only a second. "Any idea who he was going with?"

Madison shook her head. When she realized he had returned his gaze to the notebook, she verbalized her answer. "No idea."

"Okay, so you showed up today, ready to work. You knew where to find the keys?"

Madison frowned. "None of the houses were locked. The computers don't even have pass-codes on them. All I had to do was show up and go to work."

"Describe to me what you were hired to do."

"Walk houses." When he glanced up again expectantly, she expounded on her answer. "You know, make four rounds in each house, picking up dead chickens, looking for water leaks, that sort of thing. I have to record the number of dead chickens and throw them in the incinerator out back. I also have to record the levels of ammonia in each house, the gallons of water consumed, and check back-up temperatures."

The police chief flashed a smile that still had the power to set Madison's heart aflutter. "Sounds like you really did 'learn the ropes', as you called it. Have you done this sort of work before?"

"Hardly," she muttered. "There aren't many chicken houses in Dallas."

"Oh? Is that where you're from?"

"I've lived there for the past fifteen years." *And will be headed back there soon, with any luck.*

"When was the last time you spoke with Mr. Gleason?"

Madison's mind was reeling, bouncing back and forth along with the conversation. She supposed this was all part of the technique, intended to put a witness as ease. *Or to lull a suspect into admission,* a wicked inner voice whispered. Was she a suspect? The thought caused a new shiver to dance down her spine.

"He called me yesterday morning. He reminded me of a couple of things I needed to do and said he would be leaving by early afternoon."

"What were you supposed to do if you had any trouble?"

"He gave me his cell phone number, although he said he might not have service out in the Gulf. He also gave me the number for Barbour Foods' Poultry Division and for his Service Tech." A thought occurred to her. "Oh, dear. I suppose I should call them, shouldn't I?" She fished in her pocket for her cell phone, but the officer held up a restraining hand.

"Not yet. We'll take care of that in due time. I still have a few more questions."

With a worried glance toward the structure behind her, Madison asked a question of her own. "Is the fireman still inside?"

She wondered about the policeman's short but humorless laugh. "Don't worry about Montgomery. The kid apparently has an iron stomach. He'll be fine."

"Why did the fire department show up, anyway?" It just now struck her as odd.

"We do things a little differently in small towns than what you're used to in Dallas, ma'am." His drawled voice was openly condescending. "Our volunteer fire departments respond to a variety of emergency situations, not just fires. Most of the department is out on the highway right now, working a wreck and providing traffic control."

"He seemed very efficient," she murmured somewhat lamely.

"Be assured, Montgomery is one of our finest First Responders." Brash cleared his throat and pulled the conversation back to the victim. "You were telling me how and when you first discovered the body."

"Yes. Right. Well, I got here around eight this morning and started in House 6. It took me about an hour and a half to walk the first two houses. I had already made one round on the opposite end of this house and started down toward this end. I noticed several chickens were . . . taller than the others. I knew they sometimes ganged up on injured birds or stood on top of dead ones, so that's what I thought was happening. As I got a little closer, I noticed the smell. It was horrendous."

She stopped to clear her throat, trying, too, to clear her nose of the putrid memory. "It was worse than anything I had ever smelled before. I-I thought it must be a chicken that was several days old. There was a horribly messy one in House 6 that just . . . fell apart when I lifted it. I-I remember thinking this one would be even worse. And then- And then I saw it. Him. There was a - a rooster perched upon his chest, strutting about like he was king of the roost. It was horrible." Madison clenched her stomach, afraid she was going to be sick once more.

"I know this is difficult, ma'am. You're doing great. Just hang in here with me a little while longer, we're nearly done. By the way, I didn't catch your name."

He probably wouldn't recognize her name, any more than he had recognized her face. She took a deep breath and blew it out. "Reynolds. Madison Reynolds."

His russet head snapped up and he peered at her with new curiosity. "Maddy? Maddy Cessna, is that you?"

Brash stared at the woman before him. She was covered in filth and looked like death warmed over. At the beginning of the interview, her face had been bright red, all splotchy and mottled, but the color had drained slowly away as she recanted the day's events. She was now as pale as any ghost might be. He remembered Maddy Cessna as being a cute brunette with a straight, slim figure and killer long legs. In this garb, it was impossible to tell what kind of figure now hid behind the baggy shirt and tattered jeans. Even though he knew he wasn't catching her on her best day, he was guessing that the years had not been kind to the girl he once knew.

"It's Reynolds now," she said stiffly.

"I heard about your husband. Sorry for your loss." He offered the rote sentiment as he pushed the brim of his cowboy hat up with one finger.

"Thank you." She dropped her eyes as she murmured the weary reply.

Brash was an expert at reading people's expressions. It was necessary in his line of work. He watched as the emotions flickered briefly across Madison Cessna Reynold's grimy face. He saw sadness and regret, a touch of resentment, a lot of worry, but the one emotion he did not see was grief. He made a mental note to find out more about that later; right now he had more important things to worry about than whether or not she had been in a happy marriage.

"I heard you moved back," he said conversationally. "I know Miss Bert is glad to have you home."

Bertha Cessna, or Miss Bert as she was commonly known, was Madison's feisty eighty-year-old grandmother. She was a cornerstone of the community and more or less the matriarch of Juliet since the namesake's death in the early 1980's. Miss Bert only recently resigned as Mayor, saying the duties interfered with her love to travel. After all, she wanted to go as much as possible now, before she got too old to enjoy the sights, particularly those seen from behind the windshield of her brand new motor home.

For the first time, Brash saw a glimpse of the girl he remembered. A smile flashed across Madison Reynold's face, transforming her haggard features with the glow of genuine affection. "She's thrilled to have someone to fuss over again."

"And to cook for, I'm sure."

A grimace created new creases in her dirt-streaked face. "Except that she's on a new health-food kick. I made the mistake of giving her a juicer for Christmas, so now she's experimenting with a 'liquid' diet. Believe me, there are some foods that are not meant to go into a blender." As her shoulders shimmied with distaste, Brash could not help but laugh. He could only imagine some of the combinations Miss Bert would come up with.

A gust of wind whipped away his burst of laughter, rendering the atmosphere solemn once again. His next question was all business. "I don't suppose Mrs. Gleason has been down here this morning?"

Madison looked up in surprise. "I-I guess I didn't realize there was a Mrs. Gleason."

"And why is that?" Something in her expression set off warning bells.

Madison Cessna Reynolds shrugged. "He never mentioned a wife, for one thing. I got the impression there was no one else to walk houses for him when he was out of town."

Brash tried to imagine Ramona Gleason stepping foot in the chicken houses. It would be one of those high-heeled shoes, no doubt; hadn't Shannon called them stilettos? He had a mental image of one of those heels impaling a hapless chicken.

"You said 'for one thing'. What else?"

"Well, he was a little ... flirty," Madison admitted reluctantly.

Before he could stop himself, Brash dropped his gaze to trail over her, frightful clothes and all. Her face flamed in humiliation after his silent assessment, particularly when he questioned, "Flirty?"

Madison lifted her chin with defiance. "Yes, flirty." This time her voice held more conviction. Her hazel eyes flashed with irritation. "A true gentleman would never sound so surprised," she snapped.

Brash found her ire amusing. He even had the audacity to grin. "You knew me in the early days. Never claimed to be a gentleman," he drawled. When she merely sniffed in disdain, he returned to business once again. "I was surprised because he's married. Happily so, from all indication. And because you are newly widowed. I know these days that doesn't account for much, but I figured Ronny for the faithful sort."

She softened only a fraction. Her tone was still frosty when she spoke. "I said he was flirty, not that he propositioned me. And my marital status has nothing to do with it. I can assure you, I did not flirt back."

Brash waved a large hand with an air of surrender. "Never suggested you did, ma'am." It seemed safest to address her with the respectful —and less personal— title.

Now she huffed at him, still clearly agitated. "Are we through yet? I still have three houses to walk, and I would like to get out of these filthy rags before they start to set up."

Glancing over his notes, Brash checked out a few last details. "What did you do after you discovered the body?"

"I ran back outside and called 9-1-1. My cell phone was in the golf cart he left for me to use."

"Did you come back inside the house?"

She gave him a withering look that only mothers knew how to perfect. He vaguely recalled hearing she had twins, hence the three newest citizens to their community. "Not until the fireman arrived. And only then because it seemed the humane thing to do." Her haughty tone faltered as she added, "You know, with the chickens, and all."

Brash took mercy on her at that point. Most women he knew would have fallen apart long before now. Many men would have done the same. "I think that will be all for now, Maddy, but I may have more questions later."

She sighed wearily. "You know where to find me if you do." She turned to walk away, mustering as much dignity as possible when covered with chicken poop and vomit.

Madison went through the rest of her duties on autopilot. She numbed her mind to the images which danced through her head with alarming frequency. Each whiff of a dead carcass brought on a fresh wave of nausea, each sight of two or more chickens converging in a group filled her with dread. By the time she finished her rounds and threw the last of the dead birds into the incinerator, her nerves were frayed, her head was pounding, and her mind was no longer numb.

More officials had come and gone on the scene, numerous people were milling around the farm, and the county coroner's van was now backed up to the end of House 4, alongside another fire truck and several cop cars. She pulled the golf cart up next to the fire truck and got out. Her body was aching from all the walking and bending and, if possible, she now smelled even worse. If she never stepped foot inside another chicken house again in her life it would suit her fine. She was considering eliminating the versatile fowl from her kitchen, as well.

She caught sight of Brash deCordova's broad back and made her way toward him. As she approached, she heard a woman's high-pitched whine. "I just can't believe this! He can't be gone, he just can't!"

"There, there, Ramona." The police chief made a clumsy attempt to console the woman in front of him. He moved just enough for Madison to get a glimpse of bleached blond hair, a bright pink jogging suit, and the same neon pink and black designer sneakers her own teenage daughter had her heart set on. Mrs. Gleason, she presumed.

The woman clung to the officer, pressing her voluptuous body a bit closer than was necessary. Madison took an immediate dislike to Ronny Gleason's widow. She told herself it had less to do with the officer involved and more to do with the inappropriate spectacle she made of herself. Having had a recent similar experience herself, Madison certainly had not thrown herself at the man delivering Gray's death notice.

Madison hung back, but she suspected the odor emanating from her clothes announced her presence. Brash turned, looking so grateful for the interruption that she almost smiled. Almost. This was still a solemn situation.

"Ah, Miz Reynolds," Brash said, setting the weeping woman away from him. "Did you think of anything else that would be helpful?"

There was such desperation in his tone that Madison started to pretend she had recalled another tidbit of information, just to save him from the clinging widow. But her pride still stung from his earlier implied insult, and she had the distinct impression that Brash deCordova could handle himself in most any situation, particularly those that involved the fairer sex. Dashing his hopes of an escape, she shook her head. "No, I just thought I would let you know I'm heading home now."

"Are you- Are you her?" The simpering note in the other woman's voice was so exaggerated that Madison almost rolled her eyes.

Brash made the introductions, using the opportunity to move several feet away from the woman in pink. "Mrs. Gleason, this is Madison Reynolds. Madison, Ramona Gleason."

"I'm so sorry about your husband, Mrs. Gleason," Madison said with utter sincerity.

The blond sniffed delicately. "Thank you. I'm-I'm so sorry you had to find him like that. Oh, my poor Ronny!" Another wail of sorrow had her reaching for the chief's arm again.

An awkward moment stretched into two. Over the top of the crying woman's head, Brash sent Madison a beseeching look, silently begging her, *Do something!* Madison shrugged helplessly, which earned her an exasperated stare from the officer. She finally gave into the urge and rolled her eyes, then reluctantly moved forward.

Touching the other woman's shoulder, her voice was compassionate as she asked, "Mrs. Gleason, is there anything I can do to help?"

She pulled away from the broad shoulder she camped against. "Why, yes, yes there is," Ramona said unexpectedly. "Would you continue to take care of the chicken houses for me?"

Madison's jaw fell open in dismay. It was the very last thing she wanted. "I, uh, I'm afraid I don't know very much about them, ma'am."

"You were planning to work here for the week, weren't you?" There was something almost challenging in the question.

"Well, yes."

"Then I'll expect you to honor your commitment." For a grieving widow, her tone had the definite ring of business. "I trust that you and Ronny had some sort of contract?"

"Yes," Madison nodded reluctantly.

"Then it's settled. At least for the week, you'll honor your agreement with … my husband." Her voice crumpled on the last words.

Brash must have anticipated the fresh round of tears that was coming, because he quickly moved away and out of her reach. He turned his attention to the activity stirring at the door of the chicken house, where the coroner was leading the way out for the stretcher carrying Ronny Gleason's torn and battered body.

This time when Ramona Gleason wailed out mournfully, there was no one there to hold her.

3

A shower never felt as good as it did that day. Madison stayed under the spray until the water turned tepid and her freshly scrubbed skin began to pucker. Only then did she step from the shower stall and slip into gloriously fresh clothes that held no odor of chickens.

She considered burning the outfit she had worn that morning, but knew she would need them again, possibly even the next day. There was no need to ruin another set of clothes, after all. She used extra portions of detergent, but doubted the shirt and jeans would ever come truly clean; at the end of the week, she could drop them into the dumpster and be done with them.

Just as she slid into fresh jeans and a soft sweater set, Madison's cell phone rang. When she saw the number that popped up on the caller I.D. screen, she grabbed the phone and answered with an unsteady hello.

"Is it true?" Genesis Baker demanded. "I just heard the most horrible news!"

Hearing her best friend's voice was her undoing. The tears she held at bay sprang free, leaking from her eyes and streaming down her face. "Oh, Genny, it was- it was horrible!"

"Where are you? Are you all right?"

"I'm home. And I'm not sure I'll ever be all right," she admitted on a sob. "You can't imagine how he looked…"

"I'll be right over."

"You can't do that! You're at work!"

"Of course I can! I'm the owner, remember?"

Madison wanted to be brave and insist that she didn't need her friend to come, but they both knew it was a lie. She had to compose herself before the twins got home from school, and Genny was her best chance at doing so.

"If you're sure…" she whispered.

"Be there in a jiffy!" Genny promised. Before she hung up the phone, Madison could hear her friend's voice ringing out, "People, watch the café for me. Got a family emergency!"

Ten minutes later, Genesis Baker bounded up the steps of the three-bedroom craftsman-style home. She let herself in and found her friend in the kitchen, exactly where she knew she would be.

"Oh, honey, are you all right? You look terrible!" Genny said the words with love as she folded her best friend into her embrace.

"I've been getting that a lot today," Madison said dryly, returning the hug.

Genesis frowned and stepped back to examine her friend. "Who said such a thing to you?"

"Of all people, none other than Brash deCordova. Although in his defense, he didn't say the words out loud, and even if he had, he would have been right."

Genny gasped. "You saw Brash? On today, of all days?"

"Well, he is the chief of police, and I did find a dead body. The two sort of go hand-in-hand."

"Sit down and start from the beginning. I want to hear everything." Genny deposited a white sack onto the table and drew out two of her signature Genny-doodle cookies, the same delectable treats she sold at her newly opened café and bakery in downtown Naomi. Before joining Madison at the table, she poured them both a cup of coffee as if they sat in her own kitchen.

Madison relived the gruesome morning once more, instinctively knowing this would hardly be the last time she was asked to do so. Genesis interrupted her story more times than Brash deCordova ever dreamed of doing, but she found her friend's questions far less disruptive. When she finally got to the end of her tale, she sagged in exhaustion and watched Genny's eyes fill with sympathetic tears.

"You poor thing! I'm so sorry you had to see that!"

"I have a feeling I'll be seeing it again tonight in my sleep. And I doubt I'll ever get that stench from my nostrils." She sipped at her coffee, needing the warmth it provided. She was still chilled to the bone.

"Well, at least you don't have to go back."

"Didn't I tell you? Ramona Gleason wants me to complete the week. In fact, she insisted that I do."

"She would, that peroxide floozy!" There was uncharacteristic disdain in her friend's normally cheerful voice.

"I was a little surprised when I saw her," Madison admitted. "In fact, I never even suspected that Ronny Gleason was married. He actually made a pass at me the first day I went to his farm. After seeing his wife, I can't imagine what he thought he saw in me." Madison frowned into her coffee mug as she cradled it with both hands.

"Oh, please, not that again!" Genny rolled her eyes in exasperation. "You really do have to buy yourself a mirror, Maddy, and not one of those ripply ones that comes out of a carnival. You've always been gorgeous. And unlike Ramona Gleason, your beauty is real. Hers comes from a bottle." She grinned from behind her own coffee mug, displaying her trademark dimples as her sense of humor returned. "Well, actually, I hear that her boobs came from a clinic down in old Mexico."

"They did seem a little too perky to be real."

"I heard she's had plastic surgery so many times she hardly looks a thing like she did when they married ten years ago."

"Wouldn't all that be expensive? Ronny didn't seem to be exactly rolling in money," she said, thinking of his tattered clothes and hair that needed trimming.

"Oh, please, did you see the house they live in? And the vehicles they drive? The man owns six chicken houses. Do you have any idea how much money those things rake in each year?"

"Not really," Madison admitted. "The way he negotiated down my contract price, I got the impression he was barely scraping by."

"He was going deep-sea fishing for a week. That had to cost a small fortune in itself."

Madison frowned. "I guess I was so excited to make the deal, I never thought about that."

"I doubt you have to honor the contract, you know. If Ramona's name wasn't on the dotted line, she really can't hold you to it."

"I know. And as much as I dread the thought of having to go back —dead body or no dead body— the fact is, I need the money."

Genesis shook her head in sad wonder. "I still can't believe Gray left you penniless." They had been over the same road a hundred times, but the destination was always the same.

"I know." Madison's sigh was glum. "But he did, and I need what little money this job will bring in. I was originally hoping it would also bring in more business, but I don't think I'm cut out to be a chicken farmer, even for a week or less." She crinkled her nose derisively.

"If I hadn't already spent most of my inheritance, you know I'd give it to you." Genny's blue eyes were soft and earnest.

"In a heartbeat. But I can't think of a better way for you to have invested your money, than in your very own café. You're a natural, Genny girl." Madison's smile was proud as she beamed at her friend.

"You can still come to work for me full-time. The offer stands."

"You're the best friend a gal could ever have, and I do appreciate the offer. But friendship and business just don't mix, and we've been friends for too long to mess things up between us now. You go live your dream, and I'll live mine."

"That's the thing, Maddy. I've always dreamed of owning my own bakery and I'm finally getting to live out my fantasy. But I know running a temp agency has never been your life-long goal. It doesn't seem fair that I get to have so much fun, and you have to work in chicken houses, of all places." She crinkled her nose as she mentioned the smelly profession.

"Like I'm always telling the kids, life is not always fair. And to be honest, I don't know what my dream job is. Maybe working at a variety of professions will point me in the right direction."

Genesis's eyes danced with amusement as she sat up straighter in her chair. "Oh, do tell!" she gushed dramatically. "So far you've been a chauffeur, a gofer, a dog-walker, and now a chicken farmer. Which of these glamorous professions do you prefer?" She batted her eyes with feigned fascination.

Madison laughed at her friend's antics, exactly as intended. Genny was good for her soul, no doubt about it. They had been best friends since the summer of eighth grade, when Madison moved to Juliet to live with her grandmother. Through college, numerous moves and marriage, they were still inseparable twenty-five years later.

"Actually, being a personal shopper might be fun," Madison mused. "I like spending other people's money."

"Yes, but I always envisioned it as being a bit more glitzy. I thought when you were a personal shopper you got to buy things like fur coats and plush furnishings and Oriental rugs. So far you've been stuck buying hearing aid supplies and bladder control pads."

Madison's eyes twinkled with mirth. "But they were the new and improved version, I'll have you know. And Miss Sybille was thrilled with my selection."

"You might even say she was so excited she peed her pants!" Genny quipped.

The women dissolved into laughter, until the phone rang and interrupted them. Madison got up to answer the old-fashioned rotary dial wall phone in her grandmother's kitchen as Genny poured more coffee.

"Miz Reynolds?" a deep voice said through the receiver. "This is Cutter Montgomery. I was just calling to make sure you were doing all right, ma'am. I know you had a pretty rough morning."

"Cutter, how nice of you to call! That was very thoughtful. And yes, I'm doing as well as can be expected, I suppose."

"I thought you handled yourself like a real pro, Miz Reynolds."

"Mrs. Reynolds makes me sound so old. Call me Madison."

She could hear the smile on the other end of the line. "Would you settle for Miss Maddy?" he compromised.

The name sounded so delicious coming from his lips, she could not help but return the smile. "Miss Maddy will be fine."

"You take care now, Miss Maddy. Let me know if you need anything."

"Thank you, Cutter, I'll keep that in mind. Bye now." She was still smiling as she hung up the phone and faced her friend. "He is the nicest young man. If he was ten years younger, he would be perfect for Bethani."

"Forget Bethani. If I was twenty years younger, he would be perfect for me!" Genny grinned. "That boy is nine kinds of good-looking."

"If you were twenty years younger, you would be jail-bait. Go for ten."

Genesis waved her hand in dismissal. "I'd still be too old for him. He's only like twenty-five or something."

"So? Some guys like older women."

"And some women like older men," she countered. "Don't think you're getting out of telling me about your reunion with Brash deCordova." Her charming dimples flashed before the coffee mug hid them.

"Reunion?" Madison scoffed. "It's not like I ever had a relationship with him to begin with. Back in high school, he barely knew I was alive."

"We were but lowly freshmen, after all."

Madison settled at the table once more, feeling the effects of the strenuous morning. "I may not be able to walk in the morning," she moaned. "So what's his story, anyway?"

"Whose? Cutter's or Brash's?"

Madison shrugged. "Both, I guess. I've been away too long. I haven't kept up with all the local gossip and comings and goings."

"I was gone as long as you were, you know."

"But you came back six months before me," Madison reminded her smartly. *And thank goodness you're here*, she thought. She wasn't sure she could face her old hometown without her best friend by her side.

She had to admit, she had questioned the wisdom of Genny's decision to move back at first. What did a tiny town like Naomi have to offer her wandering and creative friend? But she said she was tired of drifting and was ready to come home. She had her mind set on opening her own business. When Madison's own world crumbled just five months later and Genny begged her to join her in the sister cities, Madison had not hesitated. She could not imagine being here now without dear Genesis.

Pulling herself from her musings, Madison added, "Besides, you get all the good gossip at the café. You're already up to speed on both towns."

Technically two distinct entities, complete with a long history of rivalry, a railroad track divided the towns of Naomi and Juliet. Gossip flowed freely over the boundary lines.

Genny nodded. "It's even better than being a hairdresser. I have as many male customers as I do female, so I get both sides of the story."

"So? What's their stories? Start with Cutter."

"From what I can tell, he is the local heart-throb for girls and women of all ages. I swear I saw your great Aunt Lerlene blush the other day when he opened the door for her. And you should hear the way even the junior high girls giggle when he comes into the café! He just has a way of wrapping the opposite sex around his little finger. I think it's those chameleon eyes. He has hazel eyes, just like yours, that change with whatever color he's wearing."

"Sounds to me like you might just be one of those women he has twisted around his finger," Madison teased.

Again her friend gave a dismissive wave. She never missed a beat as she continued with her story. "He's a looker, I'll give you that, but I don't believe in robbing the cradle. He's a welder by trade, hence the welding rig he drives around with 24/7. I think he might be Fire Chief or something. Seems like he's always wearing that radio and rushing off in the middle of a meal to go to a fire or a wreck. Always comes back to pay, though, so that says something about his character. He seems to be a very nice young man, always polite and respectful and always saying 'yes ma'am' and 'no ma'am'."

"Does he have a girlfriend?"

"Callie Beth Irwin likes to think so, but I don't think Cutter got the memo."

"And Brash?" She hoped her voice sounded more conversational than curious. "Why didn't I ever see him around town the times I came back to visit?"

"Well, you remember he got that scholarship to play football."

"Of course. Next to Tug Montgomery and his Heisman trophy, Brash is the biggest thing that ever happened to The Sisters."

Genny nodded. "So he tried out for the pros and got drafted by one of those teams up North. Minnesota or Milwaukee or somewhere like that," she said breezily.

"I thought Michigan."

"Okay, whatever. Somewhere cold. Anyway, he said he missed the warm weather. And then his girlfriend came up pregnant, so he came back to Texas and got married. By that time, you and I had already moved away. He got a job coaching at Texas A&M and commuted back and forth for a while. Then he got a job at Baylor and even moved to Waco for a few years, before he came back here to join the Police Department."

"From coaching to police chief?" Madison asked incredulously. "Calling football plays hardly qualifies him for chasing down criminals!"

"Ah, you forget, this is Friday-night-lights territory, where football reigns supreme. Being hometown football hero/turned college/turned pro/turned coach makes him royalty. He can be anything he wants."

"Gee, I feel safer already," Madison said sardonically.

"Hey, you jest, but from what I understand, no one wants to disappoint the mighty Brash deCordova, so for the most part, folks obey the law and toe the line." Genesis's dimples made another appearance. "To be honest," she grinned, "it makes town a little boring."

"Well, today's event should stir a little excitement. They can debate whether Ronny Gleason died of a heart attack or sheer exhaustion. I never knew the chicken business was so hard."

"Or maybe we could get lucky and it could be a murder."

"Lucky?" Madison stared at her friend in something akin to horror. "Have you lost your mind? You honestly wish there was a murderer running around The Sisters?"

"Well, only for a day or two. I'm sure Brash would rush in to save the day and protect us from all evil."

"I guess he could use his super-human football charm or something," Madison muttered.

"No doubt. But at least it would be a little excitement."

"Well, I, for one, have had all the excitement I can handle for a while. Finding a dead body should use up my quota for at least five years." She made her prediction as she stood and pushed her chair beneath the kitchen table. "Excuse me for a minute. I have to go re-wash my clothes. Again."

After Genesis left, Madison kept herself busy by sweeping and mopping the kitchen linoleum. She finished just as the front door opened, announcing the kids' noisy arrival home from school.

She bit her lower lip, wondering if her children had heard the news. If not, should she tell them? They were bound to find out eventually but they were both so sensitive.

"Hey, Mom!" Blake called out. "You home?"

"In the kitchen! But enter with care, the floor is wet!"

The floor was the least of their concerns as the teenagers crowded through the doorway, seeing who could push through the portal first. Blake, being taller and bigger than his sister, won. He elbowed her as he nodded toward their mother and smugly grinned. "See? I knew the rumors in Study Hall weren't true."

"What-What rumors?" Madison asked with dread.

"We heard you were having a steamy affair with some chicken grower, killed him this morning in a fit of rage, and got arrested for murder." Blake, sensitive soul that he was, plucked an apple from the fruit bowl and chomped into it noisily.

"What!"

"Oh, don't worry, we didn't believe that one," Bethani assured her mother breezily. She brushed a kiss across Madison's cheek on the way to the refrigerator.

"*That* one? There were more?"

Bethani turned around to favor her mother with an exasperated expression. Rolling her eyes to the ceiling, she said, "This is Juliet, the most boring town in the state of Texas. Of course there were more rumors. It is, after all, the favorite pastime of rednecks near and far."

Madison wrinkled her nose at her daughter's snide comment. "Careful, there," she warned. "Your voice is dripping with disdain. You don't want it getting all over your snack."

The teen rolled her eyes once more, pulling out the makings of a sandwich while her brother retrieved the bread from the cupboard. The teen's pretty face settled into a somber expression as she opened the lunchmeat. Madison did not miss the note of worry in her daughter's voice as she asked, "Was the other rumor true? Was he really burned beyond recognition?"

"Burned? What are you talking about, honey?"

"We heard you found that man you were working for. He had fallen into the incinerator and was burned so badly the police couldn't recognize him."

"Oh, my word!" This time, Madison rolled her eyes. "No, sweetie, that is not at all true. Mr. Gleason did not burn up in his incinerator."

"But you did find him, right?" Blake asked, his own expression suddenly serious. "That's what all the kids at school are saying."

"Yes, honey, I did find him."

"So we heard a couple of other versions, too. One was that he died from some crazy chicken virus." Fully recovered from his brief bout of worry, Blake was grinning once again as he layered three slices of ham onto his sandwich. "I, personally, preferred the version where you single-handedly saved an entire house full of chickens from noxious gas fumes. But alas," he bemoaned, putting his hand to his forehead with great flair, "you were unable to save the man himself, just his flock."

In spite of herself, Madison giggled at her son's dramatics. She quickly bit back her smile and chastised the teen. "Blake, a man did die today. It's no laughing matter. And don't forget to try out for the school's drama club, by the way."

"Sorry, going to be too busy playing baseball. Guess who made Varsity?"

"You made the team?" Madison squealed in delight. "That's fantastic, honey! Congratulations!" She grabbed her son and hugged him with enthusiasm.

"Chill, Mom," he laughed, caught somewhere between being embarrassed and being proud. You never quite outgrew the need to please your parents, after all. "It's just high school, not the majors."

"Cotton Kings today, Texas Rangers tomorrow," Madison predicted.

"You know," his sister drawled, gearing up for some drama of her own, "he'd get better exposure if he played for a bigger school. You know, like one that actually showed up on the map. Maybe we should move back to Dallas. For his future baseball career and all."

"You are so thoughtful, Beth. Always thinking of others, never yourself." Madison patted her daughter's blond head with a heavy hand as the girl sat down at the table.

"Ouch, Mom," she complained, but did not give up her efforts. "Hey, I'm willing to sacrifice for my brother. If we need to move back home for Blake, I'm in."

"We've barely had time to get settled here. We are not moving back to Dallas anytime soon," Madison declared as she made glasses of sweet tea for the three of them.

As she brought the offering to the table and took a seat beside Bethani, her daughter looked at her in concern. "Mom," the teen said with a frown, "your hand is trembling. Are you all right? What really happened today?"

4

News of Ronny Gleason's untimely death spread quickly throughout the small towns of Naomi and Juliet. Rumors were not contained to the high school. Like with most stories, tidbits of information were left out or exaggerated with each re-telling, until the news being shared bore little resemblance to the actual facts.

By the end of the day, the police station was inundated with callers concerned about the avian flu epidemic that was sweeping through their community. The Tuesday/Thursday Clinic was swamped with patients complaining of symptoms, even though it was a Wednesday and there was no doctor on duty. Trong Ngo, the Chiropractor and Acupuncturist who shared the space on Mondays and Fridays, was called in to field questions and ease the fears of panicked residents. The waiting room became so crowded that old Doc Menger, the semi-retired dentist who used the space on Wednesdays, canceled his last appointments of the day and sneaked out the back door. Worried parents called school board members at home, the pharmacy was overrun by people asking for an antidote, and Wednesday night services were canceled at two of the five area churches.

Exhausted and tired of fielding ridiculous concerns about a non-existent epidemic, Brash had reached his limit. He was flipping off the lights in his office and calling it a day when he caught sight of the station's latest arrivals. With a muttered curse beneath his breath, he backed his way into his office once more, turning on lights as he went. Ronny's parents would expect to talk to him.

"Mr. and Mrs. Gleason," he greeted them solemnly, extending his hand when Vina showed them into his office. "I can't tell you how sorry I am about your son."

While Mrs. Gleason sobbed quietly into a tissue, Fred Gleason puffed out his chest. "What we want to know is, what are you going to do about it?"

"I beg your pardon?"

"You heard me. What are you going to do about our boy?"

Brash rubbed a hand across his bleary eyes, considering the ridiculousness of the man's question. First of all, their 'boy' was at least fifty years old, if not older. Second, Ronny was dead: there wasn't one thing he could do about that. But these people were grieving their son's death, and even on his worst day, sleep or no sleep, Brash was not so insensitive that he would point out either fact.

Careful to keep the irritation out of his voice, Brash pulled out a chair for the weeping mother and offered her a seat. Settling a lean hip onto the edge of his desk, he motioned for her husband to take the other chair. "Have a seat, Mr. Gleason, and explain how I can help you."

"You can arrest the person who killed our boy!"

Brash sat up straighter, his shoulders stiffening. "Killed?"

"Of course 'killed'!" Fred Gleason bellowed. "Our son was as healthy as a horse! Hardly a sick day in his life. There's no other explanation for him to suddenly die, just like that!"

For the first time, Helen Gleason spoke up. "I've heard the rumors. Avian bird flu, they're saying. But Ronny kept those houses as clean as a whistle. His chickens do not have bird flu!" she insisted emphatically.

"I tend to agree with you, ma'am. At this point, there is absolutely no reason to suspect that his flock has a contagious disease, although I have requested Barbour Foods to take preliminary precautions and test for any airborne illnesses. As for accusations of murder, there is also no reason to suspect foul play at this point. Do you have information that I don't have, Mr. Gleason?"

"I not only have information, I have a suspect! More than a suspect. I know exactly who murdered my son!" the older man boasted. He jabbed his finger into Brash's jean-clad knee as he spoke.

Fred Gleason was not so distraught as to miss the dangerous glint that appeared in the Chief's eyes. Brash leveled his pointed gaze first at his own leg, then at the other man. Fred jerked his hand back, but he jutted his chin out in determination. "It's them dad-blamed new Ngyens!" he blurted out.

Annoyance flashed across the policeman's face. He had little patience for racism and prejudice. "Would that be a particular member of the family, or was it a group effort?" he asked sardonically.

"Now look here, deCordova! This is no joking matter! Our boy has been killed, and I'm telling you, I know who done it!"

Brash sighed heavily, regretting his smart comeback. "I do apologize, Mr. Gleason," he said with utmost sincerity. "My comment was uncalled for. But the fact is, I do need you to be more specific. I suppose you are referring to the Nguyen family who has recently moved into the area, and not the Wynn family who helped settle the town of Juliet?"

"Of course I mean them foreigners!" Fred Gleason bellowed.

Brash held his temper in check, no small feat when he was operating on zero hours of sleep. "Is there a particular reason you suspect one or more members of the Vietnamese community? To my knowledge, they are a hard-working and law-abiding society."

"They're hard-working, I'll give them that. But they make no secret of the fact they want to own half the countryside, 'specially all the chicken houses they can get their hands on! The chicken farmers around here have enough grief from their neighbors and so-called friends, without having to worry 'bout being run-out by them foreigners!"

"Again I ask you, did any one particular member of the Nguyen family ever threaten or harass your son that you are aware of?"

"I'm not only aware of it, I was witness to the fact! That Don Nguyen, he threatened my son right in front of me, he did!" Fred Gleason jumped to his feet and thumped himself on the chest with a meaty fist.

Brash narrowed his eyes. "How exactly did he threaten him, Mr. Gleason? Do you recall what was said?"

"Demanded my boy sell him the chicken houses. Claimed he stole them out from under him when he bought them five years ago. Said he should be the rightful owner and he'd make him sorry if he didn't sell."

"And when was this?"

"Year or two ago."

Brash tried not to audibly sigh. His bed was definitely calling his name. "Mr. Gleason, a harmless threat made two years ago hardly suggests a reason for murder. As I said, I'm terribly sorry for your loss, but I see no reason to suspect-"

Fred Gleason interrupted the Chief mid-sentence. "There's been plenty of strange goings-on at Ronny's farm lately. As recent as last week, someone was over there, prowling around."

"He didn't file a complaint," Brash pointed out.

"Wouldn't do no good," the distraught father countered. "He reported it plenty of times in the past. You, yourself, came out there last New Year's Eve, when the lights on his gate were shot out."

"Yes, that's true. But we saw no other signs of foul play. Even Ronny agreed it was probably just a bunch of kids, riding around shooting."

"That ain't all," Fred insisted. "There were plenty of other times. Ronny called in complaints a half a dozen times or more, but no one ever did anything, so he finally quit calling. Don't mean things didn't still happen."

"What kind of things, Mr. Gleason?" Brash asked patiently.

"Fans turned off. Lights left on or off. Dead snake draped across a control panel. Small items moved or missing."

"All of those things could be attributed to a half dozen legitimate reasons. Motors tripping out, human error, practical joke, someone borrowing something and forgetting to tell him. That still doesn't point a finger at Don Ngyen. And at this point, Mr. Gleason, I have no reason to suspect foul play of any sort. It's possible your son died of a heart attack."

"No." Mrs. Gleason spoke up, her voice clear and filled with absolution. "Ronny had a complete physical, not more than six weeks ago. His life insurance policy was up for renewal and they wanted him to be seen by a cardiologist. I know for a fact that he got a clean bill of health. No heart problems whatsoever." She looked Brash in the eye and agreed with her husband's claim. "Our son was killed, Chief deCordova."

"I will note your concerns with the coroner. But unless your daughter-in-law requests an autopsy or unless I have substantial reason to suspect foul play, I imagine your son's death could very well be ruled as a natural cause."

"What kind of lawman are you? You'll be letting the new Ngyens get away with murder!"

"Ma'am, even if strange things have been happening on the farm, do you have any reason to believe Don Ngyen is behind any of them?"

"He was seen out on 452, not three nights ago!" Fred charged.

"It is a County Road, Mr. Gleason, and open to the public."

Ronny Gleason's grieving father ignored the calm reasoning. "He's been bragging around town, saying he would be coming into some money real soon. Heard he ran up quite a tab at the feed store."

"That's between him and Jimbo Hadley, and no indication of murder." Sensing the futileness of the conversation, Brash stood. "Again, I am terribly sorry for your loss, Mr. and Mrs. Gleason. If you think of something else you would like to add to the discussion, or of some specific incident you recall, please do not hesitate to call our office." He moved toward the door, reaching for the handle.

"He got in a fist-fight with Ronny last week and threatened to kill our son! Is that specific enough for you?" Fred demanded.

Helen Gleason gasped aloud at her husband's outburst. "What? When did this happen?"

Fred looked uncomfortable as he tugged on his shirt collar in an effort to loosen it. His face was red and blotchy, and his gaze flitted around the room, avoiding eye contact with his wife.

"Mr. Gleason, I'd like to know the answer to that, as well," Brash said, abandoning the door handle in favor of his desk chair. He reached for a note pad as Fred Gleason pushed out a noisy sigh and finally met his wife's gaze.

"Last Friday night. The two of them got into a scuffle out at Bernie Havlicek's place."

Mrs. Gleason was clearly dismayed. "He was drinking again, wasn't he? After he promised not to touch another drop, he was drinking again!"

"Now, Mother, you don't know that."

"Yes, I do. Why else would he be out there? Bernie Havlicek is nothing but a no-good drunk!" Her voice rose with hysteria before breaking into a sob. "He promised me!" she cried forlornly into her tissue.

As Fred tried to console his wife, Brash had more questions. "Tell me about the fight, Mr. Gleason, and exactly what kind of threat was made."

"Well, at first they were just eying one another, none too friendly-like."

"*You* were there?" Helen gasped in shock.

Fred squirmed and dropped his hand from her shoulder. Facing the police chief, he all but ignored his wife. "Something was said, and the next thing I know, Ronny had shoved Ngyen. That man might be small, but he's strong. He shoved back, and had Ronny pinned up to the wall. He was shouting something in that foreign language he speaks. Every once in a while he would throw in a few English words. But I definitely heard the words 'I kill you', loud and clear. You can ask anyone there."

"And I will," Brash promised in a stern voice. "Just who all was there that night, Mr. Gleason?" For quite some time, there had been rumors of cockfighting and illegal betting taking place at Havlicek's home at the edge of Naomi, but pinning them down had proved difficult. Maybe this was the break they were waiting for.

"Uh, I-I don't rightly recall," Fred Gleason sputtered. His eyes took on a trapped expression.

"Then I have no way of substantiating your story."

"Well, I might remember one or two of the fellows there," he said reluctantly.

Brash wrote down the half dozen or so names he came up with before asking, "Do you go there often, Mr. Gleason?"

Again, the older man avoided eye contact with his wife. "Once or twice a month, maybe a little more." His tone lost all of his bravado of earlier.

"Frederick Albert Gleason, you have some explaining to do!"

Brash quickly broke into the domestic argument about to take place. "I'd like to know more about the threat, Mr. Gleason. What happened next?"

"Nothing, really. Somebody pulled Ngyen away, and I told Ronny it was time for us to leave."

"You *took* him there? You were encouraging our son to drink?" his wife shrieked. "You know good and well he has a weakness for spirits! How could you, Frederick Gleason!"

"Now, Mother, it was just a few of us fellas, getting together to blow off a little steam. He never got good and drunk or nothing. And I always drove, just in case."

As Helen Gleason broke into a tirade, Brash rubbed a hand over his face. He finally interrupted the woman with a sharp command. "That's enough!"

The couple looked at him in surprise, as if they had forgotten he was there. Brash knew the exact moment when it dawned upon each of the grieving parents why he was, in fact, present. Helen Gleason broke into tears while her blustering husband crumpled with grief.

"Thank you for coming in this evening," Brash said, forcing his voice to remain calm and soothing. He was not without compassion, after all, even if he was without patience. "I will look into your accusations and have a word with Don Ngyen. I think at this point, it would be best if you went home and took a few moments to collect yourself. I know this is a very difficult time for you both."

"I-I'm sorry, Chief deCordova. I don't know what came over me," Helen said, dabbing at her eyes.

"I do, ma'am," he said gently, coming around his desk to offer her an arm in getting up. "Grief is a powerful emotion. It can make us all say and do things completely out of character."

"I hope you never have to go through what we have today," she sobbed. "Losing a child is- is –" She broke off, crying too profusely to complete her thought.

Brash patted the elderly woman on the back, his own throat choking on emotion. All he could think of was his own precious daughter, and how he would never recover if something should happen to her.

5

The two towns comprising The Sisters community had a storied past.

At the turn of the twentieth century, Bertram Randolph was one of the wealthiest men in the entire Brazos valley. As the undisputed Cotton King in all of central Texas, he owned thousands of acres of prime farmland in River County. His plantation played such a vital role in the industry that the Trinity and Brazos Railway —soon known as the Boll Weevil— laid a set of track running strategically alongside his cotton gin.

During the heyday of cotton, the train made multiple daily stops at the Randolph depot. The frequent stops were necessary during ginning season to transport the crop to market; other times, the stops were necessary to fit the whim of Randolph's two daughters.

Naomi and Juliet Randolph were the epitome of the spoiled Southern belle. When Bertram's wife died at an early age and left him with two young girls to raise, he did the only thing he knew to do: he indulged them. No matter the whim, no matter the cost, the cotton baron gave his beloved daughters anything they wanted.

The one thing he could not provide for them, however, was camaraderie. Even as toddlers, the two girls were bitter rivals, constantly vying for their father's undivided attention. As the years progressed, so did their sense of competition. Their attempts to monopolize the people in their lives —their father, their nanny, the cook, the maid, the family pet, the other children who lived on the plantation— grew to such proportions that the only solution seemed not to be to share, but to divide. By their teen years, they even lived in separate wings of the house, and each had her own cook and her own maid.

The sisters often took the train into the nearby towns that bordered the plantation. During their shopping excursions, they invariably caused a scene in town. The accusations flew back and forth: the seamstress was catering to Juliet; the hat-maker chose the more exquisite material for Naomi; the restaurant was not large enough for both of them; Juliet's special order of books arrived, so why was Naomi's delayed? The squabbles escalated until finally Bertram Randolph had enough.

His solution was to give each daughter her own town. By now, the cotton industry had reached its peak and was beginning to decline. Some of his planting fields were already abandoned in favor of raising cattle, so he sectioned off a large plat of land on either side of the railroad to give to his daughters. A common area, however, would remain between them. As the gin was still an important part of the community at large, it became part of the shared property, along with the deep water well and the depot. The plantation had a school for the children whose parents lived and worked on the farm, and that, too, was designated as common ground.

Bertram built each daughter her own house, mirror images of one another on either side of the track. He also helped them get their towns started. For every proprietor willing to open an establishment in the new settlements, he offered a free lot on which to build their home.

First, however, they had to meet the approval of the town's namesake. Each woman had the final authority on which businesses and which people moved into their towns. And so the towns became as different and as opinionated as the women they were named after.

Juliet, who revered all things prim and proper, designed her town to be pleasing to the eye. Flowerbeds lined her side of the train track. City blocks were laid with meticulous care, with six of them deemed commercial property. Houses, particularly those along the main avenues of the town, required white paint, black shudders, and well-kept lawns; commercial buildings had specific height and color requirements, especially those facing the railroad. With the popularity of automobiles coming into vogue, neat parking spaces were designated around each commercial block; no parking was allowed on the brick-paved streets. And even though some types of businesses were absolutely essential to a town and could be delegated to the back streets, many establishments did not meet the standards required in Juliet, Texas.

Naomi's free spirit reflected in the town on the northern side of the track. There were two long, distinct commercial blocks running horizontal with the railroad, but no buildings faced the iron horses. Like its founder, the town was built to snub convention and propriety; instead of posturing for the railway, the businesses presented their backs to the line. The two strings of buildings opened toward each other, with parking spaces lining both. When new businesses came to town, they squeezed in at random, giving the streets odd angles and curves and unbalanced city blocks. The unconventional businesses shunned in Juliet were welcomed in Naomi. The same could be said for many of the residents. Naomi, Texas was soon known as either a gathering place for outcasts or a gathering place for entrepreneurs, depending entirely upon who judged it.

As the years passed and the cotton industry further declined, Bertram Randolph realized his plantation would fall to neglect if he did not find a suitable heir to take over his farming operation. Neither daughter was interested in the land, so he gave the bulk of the farm to his oldest and most trusted employee, Andrew deCordova. The deCordovas had been a part of the plantation for as long as anyone could remember, living and working alongside the Randolphs from the very beginning. It seemed only fitting that the fertile fields be left to someone who loved the soil as much as Bertram did.

With the massive plantation now divided into three entities and with their father's health quickly declining, it was the perfect time for the sisters to make peace.

But the arrival of a private physician, hired to care for Bertram in his last days, made reconciliation between the sisters forever impossible. Both women promptly fell in love with Darwin Blakely, but the handsome young doctor could not choose between them.

In the end, just before he was killed in a freak accident, the doctor gave them both a part of himself. To Juliet, he gave his name; to Naomi, he gave a daughter. Thus the circle of competition and bitterness continued, as did the legacy of the towns.

Juliet remained a town about appearances. Newcomers to the area who desired social standing, prestige, and an air of refinement settled within the perimeters of the town to the south. Through the years, property values in Juliet escalated and helped to control "undesirable" citizens. Cotton was the only big industry welcomed there. Until her death in 1984, Juliet Randolph Blakely remained in firm control of her town, personally screening each business and home that came into her town. With no children of her own, she left her estate to her cook's daughter. Bertha Hamilton Cessna, known to most of the town as Miss Bert, became heiress to the town of Juliet.

Across the tracks, Naomi remained a town known for its unconventional ways. Lower property values —and according to some, lower standards— brought in more industry for the northern town. It was not uncommon for someone to open a business in Naomi, but choose to live in the more prestigious sister city. When Naomi Randolph died in 1986, she was trying to convince a popular fast-food chain to open in her town, a first for their rural area.

By the time the twenty-first century arrived, both towns had grown and prospered, but old prejudices remained. The common area still existed between them, as outlined in each town's charter. The old cotton gin was now home to The Sisters Volunteer Fire Department. Just across the tracks, and easily accessible by a footbridge, the old Depot housed The Sisters Police Department and tiny jail. The shared deep water well sported a modern day tower, and the school had long since grown and moved out across the new highway, to property donated by the deCordova Ranch. The new highway ran perpendicular to the cities, crossing over the railroad by way of a tall overpass. Ramps exited off into each town, offering an alternate route across the tracks when a train was coming and, most importantly, connected the sister cities to a world beyond their petty rivalry.

Up and down the highway, billboards touted the beauty and friendly hometown appeal of The Sisters. They were home to a Heisman trophy winner. They had the State Championship basketball team. They had low property taxes and high test scores. According to the signs out on the highway, they had it all.

Below the overpass, however, buried within the boundaries of the city limits and within the confines of small minds, old rivalries and old loyalties still ran deep.

6

Following through with his promise to the Gleasons, Brash drove out to the Ngyen farm. The Vietnamese family had moved to the area five or six years before, when they purchased Louie Keeling's chicken farm. The old Keeling place bordered Ronny Gleason's and technically fell outside the jurisdiction of the city police; Brash, however, was also a Special Investigator for the River County Sheriff.

Brash took the white-rock road past the row of six strategically placed metal barns. He was vaguely aware of the Barbour Foods guidelines: each of the five-hundred foot structures ran in a straight line of east to west, placed in sets of two, and had to be at least a hundred and fifty feet away from neighboring property. The distance was much further for inhabitable buildings. On your own property, however, you could live as close as you liked to the outer perimeters of the active pad-site. Given the dust and traffic from all the eighteen wheelers and other necessary farm trucks that constantly circled the pads, and particularly given the smell emanating from the houses, Brash could not imagine why anyone would want to live anywhere near the farm.

Yet here he was, pulling up to the Ngyen home, not fifty yards away from the last chicken house.

He sat in the patrol car for a moment, studying the neat brick house before him. In the handful of years the Vietnamese family had lived there, they had made more improvements to the house than Louie Keeling had in thirty. He noted new shutters, new paint, new porch, new yard. Not a thing out of place.

He stepped from the car into a flurry of yipping and circling dogs. There had to be at least a half dozen or more, in all colors, shapes and sizes. They all seemed friendly enough, demanding attention more than concern. As Brash spoke to the animals in a quiet and soothing voice, Lucy Ngyen stepped from the house.

"Hush, now!" she called to the dogs in a heavily accented voice. Wringing her hands on the apron tied to her narrow waist, she stepped onto the porch with a cautious smile. "I help you, sir?"

"Morning, ma'am." Brash touched the brim of his cowboy hat as he crossed the space between them in a few long strides. "I'm looking for your son Don. Is he home, ma'am?"

A worried expression marred the smooth olive skin of her face. Her eyes darted around nervously, but after a noticeable pause, she nodded. "Yes, sir. Come in, sir."

Brash noticed the pile of shoes at the doorway and his hostess' bare feet. He wondered if it was a personal preference or an age-old custom, but good manners demanded he honor the habit. He put a hand against the doorframe to steady himself as he started to push off a boot.

"You no have to do," Lucy Ngyen was quick to say. "It our custom, not yours."

Relieved to keep his shoes intact, he nodded with gratitude as he stepped inside the home. "I mean no disrespect, ma'am, but I do believe I'll keep them on."

His hostess flashed a bright smile. "All good!" she assured him.

When she did not offer him a seat, Brash finally repeated his request. "I'd like to speak to your son, Mrs. Ngyen. You said he was home?"

The worry was back on her face, but she obliged. "Donny!" she called over her shoulder. "You have company!"

Brash heard movement from a room down the hall, then the shuffle of stocking feet on the old vinyl tiled floor. He noted that although the flooring was old and scuffed, there was not a speck of dust in sight. He lifted his gaze just as the twenty-something-year-old stepped into the room. Brash saw the surprise register on the young man's face, followed closely by the look of pure panic. Before Brash could say a word, the young man bolted.

In a flash, Don Ngyen darted past the peace officer and out the front door. Brash's reflexes were just a few seconds off. The younger man escaped his reaching grasp by mere inches. As Brash whirled and took chase, Lucy Ngyen began yelling in her native language, presumably telling her son to stop. Brash thought he heard the English word, but it was difficult to tell amid the excited bark of so many dogs.

After just a few steps, the dogs sensed their master was in distress, and suddenly the friendly pack was no longer so friendly. Forced to stop in his tracks, Brash put a hand on his holstered gun and practically growled himself. "Mrs. Ngyen, call off your dogs or I'll be forced to shoot! And get your son back here!"

Despite Lucy Ngyen's best efforts to stop him, her son kept running. Two of the dogs followed close on his heels as he raced toward the chicken houses, but the rest of the pack quietened as Lucy came into the yard and demanded their obedience. Brash wasted no time in jumping into the patrol car and peeling out of the driveway. He might be in excellent physical condition, but the other man was fifteen years younger and had a good head start.

The dogs started yelping again as they chased him out of the driveway. He kept his eyes on Don's retreating form as he pushed the petal to the floor. A bump and a high-pitched squeal told him one of the dogs had gotten too close to the tires; a glance into the rear-view mirror assured him no dog moving that fast could be seriously injured. It raced back to the house with its tail tucked between its legs, yelping the whole way.

Brash gave the pesky canine no further thought as he deliberately drove to the far right of his target. Bouncing across uneven terrain, through shallow ditches and scattered grass, the patrol car spun onto the white-rock pad just before Don Ngyen reached it in his bare feet. Sandwiching his car between the fleeing man and the end doors of the chicken house, Brash cut off his means of escape.

Before the younger man could change momentum and turn another direction, Brash was out of the car and demanding that he stop. "That's enough, Ngyen! Stop, now!"

There was such authority in the officer's deep bellow that the younger man did exactly as told. Without further incident, Don Ngyen's race from the law was over.

"What is wrong with you, Ngyen? Why did you run from me? All I want to do is ask you a few questions."

"I-I worried," the man said between gulps of air.

"What are you worried about, son?" The police chief's voice took on an affable tone. He could have been any good ole' boy from the South, not a law officer facing a fleeing person of interest.

"Police come here. I worry."

"There's nothing to be worried about, Don. I'm just making a few rounds, talking to folks." He sounded casual, but his eyes were alert as he remarked almost conversationally, "I suppose you know your neighbor Ronny Gleason was found dead yesterday."

He gave an animated nod. "Bad news, for sure."

"You know Ronny very well?"

A look of wariness came into the younger man's dark eyes. This time his nod was less spirited. "Pretty good. Neighbors. Both grow chickens. We talk sometime."

"I heard you and your father were buying Ronny's farm." It was a bold lie, but worth a try.

"No sell. We try, but no sell to us."

"Hmm, guess it was just a rumor. When was the last time you talked to Ronny?"

It was obvious that the chicken grower did not want to answer the question. He shifted his feet and refused to meet the officer's eyes. Even after clearing his throat, his voice still held the trace of nerves. He did, however, finally admit the truth. "Friday night."

"Oh? Was that on one of your farms?"

"No. At party."

Brash made no comment, just continued to watch the younger man.

In less than two minutes, Don Ngyen caved. "At Bernie Havlicek's." He offered the information without being asked. Another few seconds of the Chief's continued silence, and he blurted out more. "We do nothing wrong. Drink some. Play cards. Blow steam."

"Watch a little cockfighting, too, huh?" Brash's easy smile held a hint of good-natured conspiracy as he nudged the younger man's arm with his elbow. "I hear Pedro Gonzales grows some fine prize fighters."

Ngyen's chest swelled with swagger. "Not prize. Ours first prize."

"Oh, you and your dad raise fighting chickens, too, do you?" The surprise in Brash's voice was real. Until now, he had no idea. He tried to keep it low key as he ambled on, "I thought Barbour Foods didn't let you keep chickens of your own."

Realizing his error, the Vietnamese stuttered with an explanation. "I-uh-... we -uh-"

"Hey, I won't tell," Brash assured him. He settled back casually onto the hood of his patrol car, intentionally making his level of eyesight lower than that of the shorter and younger man. Trying to keep his voice friendly and his threat minimal, he clicked his tongue along the side of his mouth. "I don't want you getting into trouble with your contract and all. 'Course, I hate to see you in trouble with the law, either. You do know game roosters are illegal, don't you?"

Just because Don Ngyen did not speak good English did not mean he was ignorant. He lifted his chin slightly, asserting his confidence on the matter. "The roosters no illegal. Cockfights illegal."

"That's true," Brash allowed. "But why raise fighters if you're not going to fight them?"

Ngyen shrugged. "Some people fight dogs. We raise dogs, no fight them."

"But we're not talking about dogs, are we, Don?" His voice came out low and calm, but there was no denying its underlying authority.

The younger man dropped his eyes. "No, sir," he mumbled.

Letting the issue slide for now, Brash broached the topic he had come to discuss. "I heard you and Ronny got into it that night."

"Got into it?" With just three uttered words, Don Ngyen's accent got thicker and his IQ dropped lower.

The look the policeman gave him said he was not fooled by the act. Still, he rephrased the statement. "I heard the two of you got into an argument."

"Not so much argument."

"I heard you shoved him up against the wall. Heard there was shouting involved."

"He call me cheat. No one call me cheat!"

Brash peered at him from beneath the brim of his hat. "And exactly what would you be cheating at, Mr. Ngyen?"

Again, the man realized his folly too late. As he sputtered around, trying to come up with an explanation, Brash waved off the effort. "Son, running cockfights is the least of your worries right now. Not when witnesses say you threatened Ronny Gleason, and his parents are insisting that their son was murdered."

"Murdered? I hear he shock to death."

His expression of surprise gave way to confusion when Brash gave a humorless smirk and muttered, "Electrocuted?

That's a new one on me. At least we have a little variety going on."

Swallowing a gulp of courage, Don Ngyen squared his shoulders and finally looked the lawman in the eye. "I have trouble?"

Brash pushed himself off the edge of the car, towering over the younger man by nearly a foot. The look in his eye was enough to make any man cower. "Not at this time, but don't leave town. I may have more questions for you. And next time I won't be so favorable to a foot chase."

"I not run again," he promised, properly chastised. Brash had to admire his gumption when he lifted his chin and insisted, "I do nothing wrong."

7

"Girl, I've got suitcases that are smaller than the bags beneath your eyes!" Bertha Cessna proclaimed as she poured one of her juice concoctions into a glass. Shoving it toward her granddaughter, she ordered, "Here, drink this. It should perk you up some."

Madison eyed the drink with trepidation. "Uhm, what's in it?"

"Mostly fruits," the older woman shrugged.

"But not entirely," Madison muttered, taking a cautious sip. It was better than most of the drinks her grandmother created, so she braved a bigger swallow. "Not bad."

Granny Bert poured herself a glass and took a large gulp. Leaning back against the counter with a satisfied smile, she nodded, "Yep, a little castor oil is good for you."

"Granny!" Madison protested, sputtering around the sip she was in the process of swallowing. "I have to go to work today! Why didn't you tell me you put that in there?"

"Oh, pooh. You only had half a glass. And you'll be home before it starts to work." She added two tiny words behind the rim of her glass. "I hope."

Madison gave her grandmother a stern look and pushed the drink away.

"Seriously, girl, you look rough." Bertha Cessna picked up on her earlier compliment. "I take it you still can't sleep?"

Shaking her head, Madison said wearily, "It's been two days, but every time I close my eyes, I see his face. And his eyes…"

"Thought one was pecked clean out."

"That's the one I keep seeing." Madison shuddered involuntarily.

"I heard Fred and Helen are still stirring up a stink about it being fowl play." The old woman laughed at her own wit. "Fowl play, get it?"

"How could I not?" Madison murmured dryly. "You're cackling like an old hen."

"Good one, girl!" Not the least bit insulted, Miss Bert beamed as she bumped her with a bony elbow.

"But you're right, according to Ramona, his parents are still insisting he was killed."

"What does the plastic widow have to say about it?"

Madison gave her grandmother a reproachful look for the derogatory remark, but answered her question. "She says he had been complaining of heartburn lately and thinks it was a heart attack. She's upset because the coroner still has not released the body and she can't plan the funeral."

"Probably interferes with some plastic surgery she has scheduled," Miss Bert harrumphed. She drained her glass before continuing. "Did you know her nose used to have a large

Roman hump to it? Just like her Pappy's. She went away on a so-called cruise a couple of years ago, and next thing you know, she has a cute little snub nose. Completely changed her looks."

"I'm sure."

"She's had so many tucks and nips and snips, I'm worried the poor thing may come unsewn one day and puff up like a giant balloon! Course, she won't float away, not with those honkers to weight her down."

"Granny!" This time, Madison chided her grandmother with dismay.

"We all know they ain't real, girl. At her age and that size, gravity should have those jugs dragging the ground."

Madison refused to smile, no matter the visual image that popped into her head. "The things you say."

"Now who's clucking like a chicken?"

"You know, I feel really sorry for Ronny Gleason. It's bad enough that the man died and had his body pecked to pieces by his own chickens. Now he's the butt of a hundred bad jokes. Doesn't anyone around here have any compassion?"

"Of course we do," her grandmother insisted. "It's just that we all appreciate an *egg*-cellent joke now and then."

"You are incorrigible. I sometimes wonder about my decision to bring my impressionable teenage children here to live."

"Oh, pooh. They're right about the same age you were when you came, and look how well you turned out. I've raised four boys and half the town, and not a bad seed in the bunch," Miss Bert boasted, patting her granddaughter smartly on the hand. "Although I did wonder for a while about your dad, but eventually, even he turned out all right. Who'd ever thought my most rebellious boy would turn out to be a missionary? Goes to prove, you're never too old to make improvements."

"That's true." Madison had come to live with her grandmother during one of her father's more rebellious periods. Instead of settling down and making a solid career for himself, Charlie Cessna insisted on forging his own path. As his daughter was entering high school, the racecar circuit had been his preferred mode of defiance, complete with its short run of fame, fortune, and frivolous party life. The ultimate groupie, her mother followed him through every destructive phase of his life and was now adjusting quite well to his newest career choice. For over five years, her parents had been living in the wilds of Africa and appeared to be having the time of their lives.

"Your kids have good heads on their shoulders, no matter what their daddy might have filled their minds with. You don't have to worry about me being a bad influence. They'll turn out just fine."

Madison propped her hand into her chin and let out a forlorn sigh, ignoring the slight against Grayson. "I wish I had your confidence. I know these last couple of months have been tough on them, losing their father right before the holidays, then having to move away from their home and friends. I think Blake will be fine and roll with the flow, but I worry about Beth. She's clearly unhappy here."

"She'd be unhappy back in Dallas, too. Give her time, she'll come around."

"I know, but the sooner I get back on my feet and can move back to Dallas, the better I think she'll be. I just wish she could find a friend, the same way I did. Genesis was an absolute Godsend, and at least half the reason I came out as sane and normal as I did. I don't know what I would have done without her, especially these last two months."

"So why are you in such a hurry to leave her? All you can talk about is when you can move back to the city."

"My life is there, Granny."

"Do you have a house to go back to?" the older woman asked pointedly.

"No." She was forced to sell it and had been fortunate, at that; the bank could have easily taken it from her, given that Gray was three months behind on the mortgage.

"Do you have a job to go back to?"

"Nnooo." She had been Gray's receptionist. When he died, so did the business. Or what little was left of it.

"Do you have a man to go back to?"

"Of course not!"

"Do you have friends to go back to? True friends?"

"I-I'd like to think so." By now, Madison was squirming uncomfortably in her seat.

"The kind of friends who tell you when something is going on you should know about? The kind that come to your aid when you need them the most? How many of those friends do you have to go back to?"

Madison bit on her lower lip. "Apparently none," she murmured.

"Aw, honey, I'm not trying to hurt your feelings. I'm just pointing out that maybe your life wasn't so great in the city, after all. Maybe it's time to build a new life for yourself, among people who have the same values that you have."

"Maybe." She offered a noncommittal agreement. "At any rate, I won't be leaving anytime soon. That would take money, which I do not have. And speaking of money, I need to go make some." She stood up, just as her stomach gave a loud rumble and a cramp hit her. "Granny! How much castor oil did you put in that drink, anyway?"

The older woman scrunched her face in thought. "Well, that's a good question. I couldn't remember if I had already put it in or not, but I knew a little extra wouldn't hurt. Then the phone rang. By the time I got through listening to Sybille's long list of ailments and her theory on Ronny Gleason's death — she thinks he was murdered, by the way— I couldn't recall if I had put it in once, twice, or none at all, so I just added a small splash, just in case."

"From the feel of my stomach, I would say you put in it all three times. I swear, Granny Bert, you are going to be the death of me yet!" The last of her sentence floated over her shoulder, as Madison made a dash down the hall.

After a late start to the morning, Madison made her rounds at the Gleason farm and dutifully performed the tasks Ronny Gleason had hired her for. Three days into the job, she found a routine that seemed to work but did little in making the duties more pleasant. Some things, like decaying chickens and wet litter, had no pleasant spin.

Once home, Madison showered and dressed for her Friday afternoon pharmacy run for Miss Sybille. After all, she couldn't leave her grandmother's best friend without a full medicine cabinet and plenty of bladder control pads for the weekend. She slipped into a pair of charcoal gray slacks, strapped a trendy belt over the gray and red hounds tooth blouse, and stepped into her favorite black boots. It was her go-to outfit when she wanted to feel good about herself, even though she had been going to the ensemble for about four years now.

She ran a brush through her below-the-shoulder dark hair, thinking it might be time to update her wardrobe. Her closet over-flowed with well-made, classic pieces that stood the test of time; new accessories were usually all it took to update her look. She took the same approach with her hairstyle. Like the rest of her, the dark brown strands were long and straight, but the cut offered such versatility. Depending on the situation, she could wear it in a strict bun, a loose chignon, a simple braid, loose and free, or countless simple variations. Today she left it flowing free, as she grabbed a black sweater from the hall closet. Despite being late January, it was a sunny sixty-two degrees outside but she took the sweater with her just in case.

As she stepped across the threshold, she all but collided with the large hand that was poised to knock on the very door she opened. She squealed with surprise and drew back, just as Brash deCordova looked up and saw her there.

"That was close!" she laughed, reaching for her forehead in relief.

The chief of police merely stared at her, obviously at a loss for words. She found his stunned expression amusing, thinking she had truly caught him unawares. But when his eyes trailed over her for the third time, lingering a bit longer with each sweep, she realized there was more to his shock than being startled by her unexpected presence. He was just as startled by her appearance.

A warm flush of satisfaction swept over Madison as she recalled his silent but effective insult from three days ago. *Score one for me.*

It took a moment, but he finally found his voice. "You were on your way out?" he asked, nodding to the purse slung across her shoulder.

"Yes, but I've got a few minutes. Come on in." She backed her way through the portal and made room for his large frame to pass. She had a vague memory of another doorway he once crowded through, and how she would hang in the hallway, waiting for even the briefest glimpse of him. Funny, but even though his cologne was more sophisticated these days, the natural essence of the man was still the same. She inhaled an appreciative whiff as he stepped into her grandmother's living room. "Have a seat." She waved at the cozy sofa and matching wingchairs.

"Are you sure you have a minute? I don't want to make you late."

Madison glanced at the watch on her wrist. "I have to pick up the kids from school at three, so that gives me a good forty-five minutes to spare. I can run my errands afterward." She shrugged casually as she shut the door behind him.

"I think I heard somewhere that you have twins? How old are they?"

"Fifteen. They're freshmen this year, just like I was when I first moved here."

"Yeah, I think I was a senior that year."

Be still, my heart! Brash deCordova *had* been aware she existed, after all! Madison followed him into the room and perched on the edge of the sofa as he sank into one of the chairs. In spite of herself, she felt a tiny sense of awe that the great and mighty Brash deCordova was sitting in her living room. Well, technically, it was her grandmother's living room, but the sentiment was the same.

"What can I do for you, Chief deCordova?"

He flashed her a smile that, once upon a time, had her swooning near his feet. "You could start by calling me Brash."

Without a trace of swooning in her voice, she smoothly amended her question. "Okay, Brash, what can I do for you?"

"I have a few more questions about when you found Ronny Gleason." He reached for the notebook in his pocket, but not before he saw the slight shiver working its way through her shoulders.

"What would you like to know?"

"How far would you say his body was from the nearest motor?"

"Motor?"

"That round thing about yay-big at the end of every feed line," he said, indicating the size with his hands.

"I know where the motor is," she fairly snapped. "I have to kick it every time I pass by, to make certain the call-pans are working. That's what determines how much feed runs along the entire line."

"Sorry, I forgot you were an old pro at this already."

"I'm just a quick study," she countered.

He allowed her to gloat for a few moments before he asked again, "So how far away would you say he was?"

"Not far. Maybe a few feet. But you saw him the exact same place I did."

"Just confirming the distance," he said, jotting down something in his notebook. "Do you happen to recall if the feed lines were running?"

"I-I suppose they were," she said with a thoughtful frown. "If not, there would have been an alarm. He put me on the call rotation for the week and I didn't get an alarm that day, so apparently the lines were working."

"Call rotation?"

"Whenever there is an alarm, the computers call every five minutes until someone manually re-sets it. It dials the numbers automatically. If the first person doesn't answer, it goes to the next one, then the next. It keeps cycling until it resets or gets fixed."

"What kind of alarms?"

"All sorts, but the only ones I've gotten so far are augers, or feed lines, and low temperature alarms. I got two in the night last night, and had to go out to the farm to check on things."

"You weren't frightened, going out to the farm in the middle of the night?"

A sheepish smile twisted her face. "I made Blake go with me," she admitted reluctantly. At his quizzical look, she explained, "My son."

"Blake." He tried the name out, knowing it sounded familiar. A light of recognition dawned upon his face. "Aw, Blake, the new boy in school. And the most handsome boy to grace the face of the earth, to hear my daughter tell it."

"Well, naturally I think so," Madison smiled proudly.

"He must take after his mother."

His compliment made her ridiculously happy. *A hangover from my own teenage years,* she assured herself, as she brushed the fuzzy feelings aside. "Why do you ask?"

"I was wondering if the motor had tripped out. Were all the lights and fans working in the houses?"

"Yes. I remember that the Montgomery boy turned up the lights to full intensity, so I know they were working. And if the fans weren't working correctly, I'm sure there would have been an alarm. Even though there are propane heaters to keep the houses warm, the fans cycle on and off to keep air moving."

"Pretty amazing how all that works, huh?"

"You can't even imagine. They have the timers down to a science. Even the lights go on and off at specific times, determining when and how much the chickens eat and drink. It's really sort of sad how they manipulate the poor birds into thinking it's either night or day, depending if they want them to eat or sleep."

"Guess being in a house like that, they don't get much natural daylight."

"Just what comes in around the fans in the back-end of the houses. They are huge fans, though, so it's more light than you would think."

Again, Brash deCordova flashed her a smile. "You really do sound like you know a lot about your assignment. I must say, I'm impressed with your thoroughness."

She needed the money too badly not to be thorough, but she did not mention that fact. Instead, she said, "Believe me, I know more about chickens than I ever wanted to." This time, she did not try to suppress the shiver of revulsion dancing down her spine.

"Still eating the meat?"

"It's still up for debate. Just in case, we've had beef the last couple of nights. Tonight's menu calls for pork chops."

"Smart woman," the lawman chuckled.

Finding his compliments much too pleasing, Madison sat up straighter on the couch and deliberately changed the subject. "Do you mind if I ask why you're asking about motors and electricity and exactly where I found the body? I have a feeling you already knew all this, even before you asked."

"Just double checking facts before I make an arrest."

"Arrest?" The word came out on a gasp. "You mean, he was … killed? It wasn't a heart attack?"

"According to information just released from the ME, Ronny Gleason died from electrocution."

Madison's brow puckered in thought. "But that doesn't necessarily mean murder, does it?"

"No. But I would think voltage high enough to kill a man would be enough to short-circuit a fuse. You just confirmed that all the electrical components in House 4 were working properly after you found his body."

"So you're thinking someone killed him and then moved his body," she surmised. She missed the light of appreciation in his brown eyes at her sharp assessment. Her mind was jumping ahead. "Wouldn't he have been burned if he were electrocuted?"

"Not necessarily. But you tell me… when you discovered him, how much of his skin was still intact?"

She thought of the skin that had slipped from his face, revealing the muscle and bone below. Between the heat and the chickens, his skin was too deteriorated to know what kind of condition it was in. The bloody stubs at the ends of his shirtsleeves gave no indication as to whether or not his hands were burnt. And the mess that had been his throat and chest…

"So you have a suspect?" Thinking that a murderer lurked among them was almost favorable to thinking about the body she had discovered.

"Yes."

"Who is it?" she asked breathlessly.

"I'm not at liberty to disclose that information."

He sounded so formal, but they both knew that within ten minutes of the arrest, perhaps less, half the community would know the person's identity. It was how things worked in a small town. Having two small towns side-by-side merely multiplied the result.

"I guess we'll all know soon enough," she murmured aloud.

"No doubt." His smile was rueful as he closed the small notebook and slipped it back into his pocket. He ignored the pop in his knee as he got to his feet. "I appreciate your help and I hope I didn't detain you too long."

"No, no, I'm fine," she said, waving aside his concern as she, too, stood. At five feet, seven inches, sans heels, it was nice to be able to look up to a man, even when wearing boots. Gray always insisted she wear flats. Which was the very reason she had gone and bought these boots two years ago, she remembered mischievously, as she balanced on their three-inch heels. "I still have plenty of time."

"So how's your business going, by the way? What's the name of it again?"

"In a Pinch. And it's going quite well." Okay, so it wasn't too big of a lie, not really.

"That might be interesting work. At least you don't get burned out, doing the same thing day in and day out. Do you have a specialty, or do you do just about anything?"

"Just about anything. Anything legal, of course."

"Of course."

Madison glanced down at her watch as she opened the door. "I might be able to still make the pharmacy. I'll follow you out," she decided aloud.

"Do you have a business card? I could post it down at the station. Never know who might see it and give you a call."

"Sure. I have some in here somewhere." She dug around in her bag until she found the small bundle held together with a rubber band. "Here, take the whole stack. I have plenty more."

"Oh, well, okay." He took the offering with the slightest of frowns.

Without conscious thought, he walked her to her SUV. As she clicked the remote to unlock the door, he opened it and waited for her to get inside.

"Thanks again for your help, Maddy," he said as she tucked her long legs inside the vehicle.

"No problem, Chief. See you around." She wiggled her fingers in parting.

"Yeah," he said, shutting the door between them. "See you around."

8

Madison wanted nothing more than to stay in bed the next morning and enjoy a lazy Saturday of leisure. The twins did not have school and even Granny Bert 'slept in' on Saturdays, often as late as seven o'clock. Nothing demanded Madison's attention today. Nothing but one hundred and fifty thousand chickens, give or take a thousand or two. Her aching body insisted she had carried off at least that many dead over the past four days.

Forcing herself out of bed and into the tattered set of clothes she washed each night, Madison slipped down the hall toward the kitchen and downed a hasty breakfast. If she hurried through the houses, she would be through before noon; in other words, before the kids got up.

Just after eleven, Madison finished the last house, dumped the dead birds into the incinerator, and fired up the large contraption to burn its load. She was dirty and tired and smelled to high Heaven, and she was in no mood to deal with Ramona Gleason.

Yet there she was, waiting for Madison at her SUV as she drove up in the farm's golf cart.

"Hello, Mrs. Gleason." She tried to keep her voice pleasant as she turned off the motor and tucked the key into the glove compartment. Not a very original hiding spot, but the place Ronny told her he kept it.

"Mrs. Reynolds." There was a little frost in the other woman's tone as she looked over Madison's filthy and bedraggled appearance. Ramona was dressed in tight jeans, high-heeled shoes, and a blouse cut too low to be considered suitable for anywhere other than a nightclub. The weather had turned colder today, so she wore a short leather jacket that did little to cover her Mexico-origin bosom.

Madison felt the need to make small talk; anything to draw attention away from the sweat-drenched circles of her t-shirt. "How are you today?"

"Much better, now that the police have solved my husband's death. I would have sworn he had a heart attack, but apparently that Vietnamese next door killed him," she sniffed.

"Yes, I was surprised to hear they arrested Don Ngyen," Madison murmured.

"Why ever would you be surprised? That man made no secret of wanting our farm. He kept demanding that we sell, but Ronny wouldn't hear of it."

"So why would he kill your husband? He can hardly buy the farm if he's in prison," Madison rationalized.

"I suppose he thought he wouldn't get caught. What does it matter? They've arrested him and will release the body within a few days, which means we can finally have the funeral and be done with it."

Hardly the words of a grieving widow, Madison cringed inwardly.

"Which brings me to why I am here," Ramona said, breaking into Madison's thoughts. "I want to extend our contract."

The surprise showed on Madison's face. Before the other woman could continue, Madison held up her hand. "I have something to say, and I want to make it clear that I have no intentions of taking advantage of you. I have no idea what you're about to propose, but I must tell you, this job is far more strenuous and stressful than I originally thought. Your husband and I agreed to my standard rate per hour, but if I were to continue here, it would have to be at a two dollar an hour increase."

"Fine." Ramona Gleason never batted a false eyelash at her demands.

"Really? I mean, that's good. So what did you have in mind?"

"We sell this flock in ten days. I would like for you to finish the time out."

Madison did some quick calculating in her head. That would be a nice boost to her bank account! But would another ten days of this filthy drudgery be worth it? She glanced down at her ragged attire, able to smell herself despite the stiff breeze.

"From what I understand, things get harder toward the end of the flock." Madison knew that the growers kept the birds for roughly sixty-three days, at which time Barbour Foods sent trucks to pick up the flock. She remembered Ronny mentioned the extra work that went into selling; picking up the divider fences, emptying out the feed pans, raising the water lines at sell time so the forklifts could get inside the houses. Barbour Foods supplied the crews to catch and load the chickens into portable cages to be shipped off for slaughter, but the grower had numerous things to do as the days dwindled down.

"Fine," Ramona said, crossing her arms beneath her ample bosom. "Five dollars more an hour for the next seven days. I'll arrange for Barbour to take care of the last few days and selling. I'll have the Service Tech out here Monday morning to give you extra instructions."

Giddiness made Madison light-headed. Dollar signs danced before her eyes as she extended her hand. "Deal. I'll bring a new contract by in the morning, with the same payment arrangements; half up front, half when the job is completed."

Ramona Gleason gave a distasteful sniff but accepted her handshake. "Don't come before ten. I like to sleep in on Sundays."

Madison's step was energized as she hurried to her vehicle. She was careful to sit only on the towel she had draped over the driver's seat; no need in contaminating her car more than absolutely necessary. As she drove back to Juliet and her grandmother's house, she calculated the money once again, even pulling out her cell phone and double-checking her math on the calculator.

Her figures had been right, she noted with a satisfied smile. Those extra seven days would make another car payment; one month in advance, no less, offering some wiggle room in her over-tight budget. She gave a light-hearted shimmy in the seat, until a somber thought brought her upright.

When had her life changed so drastically that she got this excited about a few extra hundred dollars? Not so very long ago, she would have given little thought to spending that much or more on something for the house: a new accent rug for the guest bedroom, new drapes for the dining room, a piece of art for the entryway. Or perhaps she would have spent the day at the mall, picking out new outfits for the kids, maybe slipping in a new piece of costume jewelry for herself. Madison had never been overly extravagant, particularly on herself, and she knew how to shop for bargains, but she enjoyed buying nice things for her family and her home.

A new worry hit her. Was it her fault Gray left her destitute? Had she unknowingly spent more than they could afford? The bathroom re-model last year had been expensive; had that been the straw that broke the camel's back?

No, of course not, she told herself. *This is not your fault. This is all on Gray.*

These days, it was all too easy to wallow in self-pity as she second-guessed herself and the part she played in the downward spiral of her life. Depending on her level of wallowing, she alternately blamed herself/ blamed Gray/ blamed the economy/ blamed the world in general.

Before she could work herself up and begin laying the blame where it truly belonged, Madison's cell phone rang. A glance at the screen showed an unknown number. It might be another bill collector. Then again, it might be another client.

It was that last hope that made Madison pick up the phone. "In a Pinch Temp Services, Madison speaking. How may we help you today?" She gave a perky toss of her head, knowing the attitude would translate in her voice.

"Mrs. Reynolds?" a woman said in a thickly accented voice.

Warning bells went off in Madison's head. Another bill collector, from one of those companies who outsourced their accounts receivable. She was probably calling from the other side of the globe. Madison's voice lost its enthusiasm. "Yes, this is Madison Reynolds." *No, I don't have any money to give you. Yes, I realize this will look bad on my credit.*

The conversation playing in her head almost drowned out the other woman's halting English. Madison barely heard what she said, except for one very important word: hire.

"Wait. I'm sorry, what did you just say?"

"I need hire you. You take jobs, yes?"

"Yes, I do. What sort of job can I do for you, ma'am?" *Please, no more bladder control pads or pampered little poodles. And no chickens. Definitely no chickens.*

"I need you get my son out of jail."

Madison's foot faltered on the brake pedal. She was stopped at the railroad crossing that physically separated the town of Naomi from the town of Juliet; old grudges and rivalry separated the towns on a completely different level. A train lumbered its way through their sleepy little end of the Brazos valley, clanging and clicking and chugging its way southward. Perhaps the noise had distorted the woman's words. "Ex- Excuse me? What did you say?"

"My son in jail. I hire you to get him out."

"Who did you say you were again?"

"Lucy Ngyen. My son get arrested last night, but he good boy. Should not be in jail."

"Mrs. Ngyen, I'm afraid you've confused me with someone else. You need to speak with a lawyer, or perhaps to a private investigator. I take on small odd jobs, filling in when people don't have enough employees or when they just need a day or so's work done."

"I know what you do," the other woman said. There was an undeniable air of dignity beneath the broken English. "You take jobs. I need job done. I need hire you."

"But I don't do the sort of job you need doing, Mrs. Ngyen. I have no legal expertise."

"No need legal. Need smart. You smart?"

"I-I'd like to think so."

"You know New Beginnings Café?"

"Yes, of course." It belonged to her best friend, after all.

"You meet there in thirty minute? We talk."

"Mrs. Ngyen, I really don't think-"

"I pay you one thousand dollar."

Madison's foot slipped from the brake completely. The car rolled forward as she stomped around on the floor, too flustered to immediately find the pedal. The nose of her SUV lightly bumped the retractable railroad barricade. As she jerked to a hard stop, she asked the woman to repeat her offer. Surely she had misunderstood!

"One thousand. One thousand dollar."

Madison wavered with indecision. What could she do to help this woman? Her son was in jail. Presumably this was Don Ngyen's mother, the same Don Ngyen who was accused of murder. How could she possibly help?

How could you spend an extra thousand dollars? A little voice spoke in her head. *You could pay your car insurance. The cell phone bills. There might even be enough left over to get Bethani those shoes she's been wanting. The ones you couldn't afford at Christmas. And with Blake playing baseball, there's bound to be new expenses...*

"Missus? You there?"
"Yes. Yes, I'm here."
"You meet me, yes?"
It was crazy. It was useless.
It was a thousand dollars.
"Yes, Mrs. Ngyen, I will meet you."

※

The Saturday lunch crowd was a bit unpredictable at New Beginnings Café and Bakery. During the week, Genesis did a brisk and steady business, but every Saturday was different. Depending on what was happening in town on that particular day —a ballgame, yard sale, funeral, family reunion, bad weather— the café might be packed or it might be dead.

Today was one of those in-between days, when customers trickled in one table at a time. It was almost noon, and only a handful of diners were seated at the tables scattered throughout the historic building; two more sat at the long counter that edged the bakery. A group of seven had already eaten and gone, and of course, there would be stragglers throughout the day, coming in for a late bite of lunch. The café closed at four on Saturdays and remained dark on Sunday, but would re-open bright and early on Monday morning.

Genesis moved among the tables, carrying a pitcher of sweet tea to refill empty glasses. Technically, it was the waitress's job, but she enjoyed visiting with her customers and adding a personal touch to their dining experience.

"Good morning, Cutter," she greeted the young man who sat in a booth near the windows. No matter what day of the week, Cutter Montgomery was her most faithful customer. She supposed it was because he lived alone and did not like to cook. Then again, maybe it was because of her waitress, Shilo Dawne Nedbalek.

The dark-haired beauty made no secret of the fact that she had a crush on the firefighter. Of course, most of the females in town felt the same way, so he hardly had to seek out companionship. Genesis could not determine if he liked the waitress or not; half the time he flirted with her, the other half he argued with her.

"Morning, Miss Genny," he said, smiling warmly at her. He had an engaging smile, the kind that involved his entire face, not just his lips.

"Has Shilo Dawne been over to take your order?" His tea glass was already half empty and there was no menu in sight, but that was hardly unusual. He normally ordered the special of the day, no matter what was on it. Not for the first time, Genesis thought of the lucky woman who would one day be his wife; it appeared the man ate just about anything.

"She was here."

"Uh-oh, I hear that tone in your voice. What happened this time?"

"I do not know what is with that girl! I said one little thing about her hair being down, and she went off on some tangent! I was actually about to tell her how pretty she looked with those dark curls hanging free, when she went into a rage about how I wasn't the health inspector and there was nothing wrong with her hair down, as long as she wasn't the one cooking. That girl is too high strung, if you ask me."

"You'll have to excuse her. College classes start back up next week and she's trying to juggle her work schedule with her class schedule. She's just a little stressed right now."

"You need to give her lessons on how to be calm, cool, and collected, like you always are." He used his hand to gesture a smooth, even line.

"Aw, you think I'm cool and collected?" Genesis grinned, the very thought causing her dimples to appear. Those were not the words most people used to describe her energy level.

"I think you're just about perfect, Miss Genny."

"Cutter Montgomery, if I was ten years younger, I swear I'd give these girls around here a run for their money!"

The handsome volunteer fireman frowned. "You make yourself sound old. I don't know and I'm not asking, but you don't look a day over thirty."

"And you're the smoothest liar I ever did know!" Genny burst out with laughter.

"Besides, you know what they say. You're as old as you feel."

"Oh, great, I just aged a dozen years. I've been on my feet all day, making cupcakes for Christina Roma's birthday party. I'm feeling pretty old at the moment."

The young man offered a serious expression. "Hey, if you need someone to taste test for you, I'm available. Wouldn't want to serve all those little kids bad cupcakes or anything. Especially since the town is just getting over the avian flu scare and all."

"Thanks for the offer, I'll keep that in mind," Genny grinned. Her smile dropped away as she said, "Wasn't that ridiculous, the way everyone jumped to conclusions like that?"

"Hey, it's The Sisters. What can I say? Not a lot happens around here, so sometimes people have to spice things up a little. Create excitement where it's not happening."

"I heard all sorts of crazy rumors." Genesis ticked them off with her fingers. "He died of the bird flu, he died of strychnine poisoning from the chicken feed, he died of a heart attack, he died of gas fumes, he died of electrocution, he died of mysterious causes that –and I quote- 'will set this community on its heels when the truth is finally revealed'. Oh, and of course, there's the theory that he died of an overdose of Viagra. I, personally, am leaning toward that one." Her blue eyes twinkled with merriment.

"With that wife of his, I wouldn't be surprised," Cutter grunted. "Did you know that woman propositioned me, the very same day we found her husband dead? She asked me to come up to the house and see what was wrong with one of her electrical plugs. Said she had seen some sparks coming out of it one day and now it wasn't working, so she was afraid it might be a fire hazard. Turned out it was just a thrown breaker, but you should have seen the outfit she changed into! She plastered herself to me and cried on my shoulder for half an hour, then told me how lonely she was going to be in her big ole' bed, all alone."

"Poor Cutter," Genny cooed, "you shouldn't be so irresistible!"

He looked embarrassed, even though a pleased smile tickled his mouth. The smile turned downward when Shilo Dawne flounced back into the room, headed straight for his table.

She was wearing one of her typical outfits, a vintage-style handkerchief blouse over wide bell-bottom jeans. Looking at her now, it was no wonder people swore the girl was re-incarnated, having lived her first life as a hippie in the nineteen seventies. She was into all things natural, loved animals, babies, and flowers, and had at least three peace symbols tattooed onto her petite body. As she stormed her way toward the booth, green eyes flashing, a dark curl slipped from the crocheted headband she wore. Meant to be worn at the forehead, the colorful band was now twisted like a figure eight, interwoven among the dark locks piled high upon her head.

"There! Is this better, Mr. Montgomery?" she asked frostily.

He looked baffled by her demeanor, bringing a chuckle from Genesis and at least one other diner. "Uh, yeah, great," he offered lamely.

"That's all you have to say?" the girl demanded, hands upon her tiny waist. "You complain about my hair being down, so I go to the trouble of putting three yards of curls up on top of my head, and all you have to say is 'uh, yeah, great'?" She mimicked him in an unflattering tone. "You men are so exasperating!"

"Shilo, honey, Cutter wasn't complaining about your hair," Genesis broke in softly, touching the girl's arm. "He was telling me how pretty he thought your hair looked down. You misunderstood him."

The girl's face crumbled in chagrin. Then a bright smile lit her face, transforming her into a rare beauty.

Why, then, did Cutter look so aggravated? Genny wondered. She was just trying to help. In spite of his joking ways and the women who fell at his feet, she sensed that the young man was a bit bashful, and not quite as sure of himself as he portrayed. Genesis was fond of Shilo Dawne and Cutter seemed pretty special, himself, so why not do her part in getting the two of them together? It seemed perfectly logical to her.

"Well, I see Mr. Pruett is back," Genesis said when an older man shuffled into the diner. She wiggled her fingers in greeting. "I want to go ask him about his niece in California, the one who's a writer for all those television shows."

Cutter frowned in disapproval. "You know that old coot is loony as a bed bug. Don't be falling for everything he tells you, Miss Genny."

The café proprietor shrugged. "Even if his stories aren't true, they are certainly entertaining. Shilo Dawne, I'll take him his menu, then you can get his order, all right, honey?" It was Genny's subtle way of reminding her employee there were more customers than just the handsome man she hovered over.

"Yes, Miss Genny." The girl's voice was subdued this time.

Cutter flashed a conspiratorial grin at Genesis. "Well, what do you know? There's hope for her yet."

Genny just laughed and moved away from the table, nodding a smiled greeting to the Vietnamese woman seated at the back booth. If rumors were right, her son had been arrested last night. Genny's heart went out to the mother.

"What was that all about?" Shilo Dawne asked, cutting her eyes at Cutter. "What do you mean, hope for me?"

"I just think you could learn a lesson or two from Miss Genny."

"How so? I don't want to be a waitress forever. I have dreams. Big dreams."

"You could learn a lot from your employer, Shilo Dawne. Miss Genesis is about the classiest, most interesting woman I've ever known."

Even though the girl truly liked and admired her boss, she was too stubborn to admit it right now. Instead, she rolled her eyes and muttered, "Then what in the world is she doing back here in Naomi, the un-classiest town in the state of Texas?"

Watching the blond haired woman move among her patrons, full hips swaying and dimples flashing, Cutter's reply was simple. Genesis Baker had taken the tired old building and breathed new life into it, offering townspeople not only a good meal, but also a good place to gather. The décor, like the remodeled structure itself, was a mix of old and new, blending the best of both into a warm, friendly atmosphere. Even the menu was a blend of old tried-and-true favorites like hamburgers and chicken fried steaks, interspersed with trendier options such as Greek salad, grilled salmon, and spinach soufflé. But the best part of the entire café was the little corner where her special desserts were on display. The woman worked absolute magic with flour and sugar.

Looking back at Shilo Dawne, Cutter nodded with certainty.

"Seems to me she's making it a better place."

Genesis waved when she saw her best friend come into the café. Madison's flushed face and slightly damp hair suggested she just came from the shower.

"Be right there!" Genesis called over her shoulder, still engaged in a conversation with Tom Pruett. Madison waved her away, motioning her intentions to sit at a booth. In surprise, Genesis watched her friend take the seat opposite Lucy Ngyen at the back of the building.

Wondering what that was about, she only half listened as the old man continued to speak. "Yes, my daughter works with all the top producers and movie stars in Hollywood."

"I was thinking you told me that was your niece, not your daughter. And I thought she worked on sitcoms," Genesis interjected. She was still watching her friend and an envelope the other woman was shoving into her hand.

"Yes, yes, sitcoms, movies, documentaries, you name it, my girl does it. In fact, she's working on a documentary about my life right now. They plan to start filming by spring."

This got Genny's attention. "Your life?" she asked, turning back to the gray haired man.

"You may not have heard this yet, but I've had a pretty interesting past," the old man bragged. "After my stint in the Army, I was the conductor of an orchestra up in Dallas for several years."

"You were?" Genny asked, duly impressed. But her attention still lingered at the back booth.

"And not just any orchestra. An all-female orchestra. Every Saturday night, we played in ballrooms and auditoriums all across the city. People would come from far and wide to hear the sixteen-piece orchestra comprised solely of women. And not just any women. Each and every one of them were beautiful. It was a requirement for the job."

"Oh, really?" Genny craned her neck to see what was in the envelope Madison was opening.

"Oh, yes," Mr. Pruett nodded. "If the documentary goes well, they are considering a full-feature film, starring none other than Brandon Ricardo."

Genesis did her best to hide the amusement on her face. Sexy Nicaraguan bandleader Brandon Ricardo, playing the part of Tom Pruett? The thought was so preposterous she could hardly keep a straight face.

"Mr. Pruett, I think I see them motioning at me from the kitchen. I'll let you enjoy the rest of your meal in peace. Bye, now."

She hurried from the table before she burst out laughing, taking the roundabout path to the kitchen. The route took her past the amused I-told-you-so expression of Cutter Montgomery and the back booth where her friend sat.

"Can we get you ladies anything?" she asked, artfully interrupting their conversation with a warm smile.

"Coffee, please," Lucy Ngyen nodded, but the movement was jerky.

"Same for me," Madison said.

"Okay, sorry to interrupt. I'll be right back with that coffee."

꧁

Madison waited for her friend to leave before she turned back to the other woman. "Mrs. Ngyen, I'm still not sure what you think I can do for you."

"It all there," the woman insisted, pointing to the bulging envelope. "One thousand. You count it."

"No, no, it's not that. I believe you." She glanced at the envelope that clearly contained a few hundred-dollar bills, along with several fives, tens, and twenties. "But I'm not sure I can take your money, Mrs. Ngyen, because I'm not sure I can help you."

"You ask questions. No one talk to me, but you ask questions. People tell you things."

"No one is going to come out and tell me they killed Ronny Gleason."

"But maybe tell you who has cow with him."

Madison was clearly confused. "Cow?" she questioned. "Oh, you mean beef! Who has a beef with him!" She tried not to laugh, but a smile played around her lips.

"Yes, yes, who has cow with him. Who not like him. My Don not the only one."

"Are you saying your son didn't like Mr. Gleason?"

"They friendly, but not really, you know? We ask to buy Mr. Gleason farm, he say no. Not sell to squint eyes. Not very nice man."

Madison could well imagine her late client using a derogatory term such as 'squint eyes', but it took a lot of gall to say it to a Vietnamese's face. If he was that out-spoken and rude, he might very well have had some enemies.

"Do you know who else had a beef with Mr. Gleason?" she asked, leaning in with renewed interest.

"My number one son's wife work in nail salon. She hear things. Many people not like Ronny Gleason. She tell you." The older woman tapped the table for emphasis as their coffee arrived.

Madison avoided her friend's questioning gaze and kept her attention on Lucy Ngyen as Genesis moved away. "Mrs. Ngyen, even if I ask questions, and even if I find some answers, there's no guarantee that it will be enough to have your son released from jail."

"You keep money," Mrs. Ngyen assured her. "I give you more if my son set free."

"It's not a matter of the money," Madison protested.

"Missus, do you have a son?"

"Yes, and a daughter, too."

"How you feel if someone take your son away and lock him up? Say he do this bad, bad thing? What would you do?"

"Anything to clear his name. Whatever it took."

Lucy Ngyen nodded. "My Don a good man. Good son. He not do this. I do whatever I can to prove it. One thousand not enough? Then two. Three, even."

Madison covered the older woman's hand with her own. "No, Mrs. Ngyen, I don't want any more money. This is more than enough for what little I can do to help you. I just want you to understand that I may not be able to do a thing. I may not be able to help you."

"But you try?"

Her dark eyes were so hopeful, full of desperation but lit, too, with the glimmer of faith; faith in Madison. Not knowing what she was getting herself into, just knowing she had to help, Madison blew out a deep breath.

"Yes, Mrs. Ngyen. From one mother to another, yes, I will try."

9

One of Granny Bert's favorite sayings was that there was no time like the present. Taking the advice to heart, Madison decided to visit the nail salon that same afternoon. The sooner she could start asking questions, the less guilty she would feel about taking Lucy Ngyen's money. Madison was not a private investigator, after all, and knew there was little she could do to absolve Don Ngyen. But both mothers were desperate: Lucy to clear her son's name, and Madison to pay her bills. And so she had accepted the money, and she would do what she could to earn it.

And if sitting through a pedicure with her daughter, compliments of Lucy Ngyen, was what it took, then so be it. The mischievous thought flitted through Madison's mind as her feet soaked in the basin at Talk of the Town. Half hair salon, half nail salon, the establishment was the only place in Naomi to be pampered.

Oddly enough, Don Ngyen's sister-in-law Katie and Ronny Gleason's sister-in-law Deanna both worked at the salon.

Madison watched for interaction between the two, but she noted that the women were careful to avoid one another.

Madison struck up a conversation with Katie as the technician worked magic on her feet. Lulled into peaceful relaxation by the massaging chair and the warm footbath, Madison did not trust her memory to make sense of what she learned. Pretending to be texting, she took notes on her phone.

Ramona Gleason, she learned, came to the salon every Tuesday afternoon. Even though her sister-in-law was often within hearing distance, it never stopped Ramona from complaining about Ronny's tendency to drink/ Ronny's fondness for gambling/ Ronny's lack of sex drive/ Ronny's snoring/ Ronny's over-bearing parents. Poor Ronny seldom did anything right in the eyes of his wife. Other men, however, deserved her highest praise. She thought Brash deCordova was the sexiest thing to put on a uniform since Eric Estrada in the 1980's drama "CHiPs"/ young Cutter Montgomery ran a close second/ she loved to watch Noble Baines bowl from behind/ Jimbo Hadley at the feed store was the sweetest man she had ever known/ Reverend Greer at the Cowboy Church was so sexy she had to quit attending services for fear of sending herself straight to hell with her unclean thoughts/ did anyone know the name of that good looking man fixing fence for Howard Evans? He could mend her fence any day.

Ramona came every week, rain or shine, whether she needed a service or not. If she did not get a pedicure, she had her nails done. If not her nails, she got a bikini wax. If not a wax treatment, she had her hair trimmed and bleached. She had not missed a single Tuesday in over three years.

Madison also learned that Ronny had problems with a few people in town. An argument over a missed payment caused the farmer to drop his insurance policy with Marion Keeling's agency and take his business to the neighboring town of Juliet. After a drunken brawl inside the bowling alley, he was no longer welcome at the local establishment. A similar incident had him banned from high school football games a few years back. And when Katie left the room for a few minutes, the guest beside her murmured something about trouble with the Ngyens over roosters. Madison noted her comment, even though it baffled her.

Katie Ngyen talked some about her brother-in-law, telling Madison that the twenty-eight-year-old was the only one in their family to attend college. He had a degree in business and every spring prepared income tax returns for most of the people within the Vietnamese community. The rest of the time, he worked in the chicken houses with his father, but his dream was to one day have his own farm. Ronny Gleason promised to sell him his business, but each time Don approached him, the price had gone up. More than once, the men had argued over negotiations, but Katie insisted her brother-in-law was not a violent man. And even if he lost his temper, she said, he would never be capable of murder.

The visit to the salon did not provide Madison with a wealth of information, but it was a start. Most importantly, it gave her some quality time with her daughter. Bethani played on her cell phone while Maddy gathered information, but there was still ample opportunity for them to visit. The teen shared all the high school gossip and informed her mother of the newest break-ups/ hook ups. In the world of teenagers, Madison knew that relationship statuses changed weekly, sometimes even daily, so it paid to stay informed.

"Mom, how long are we going to be stuck here?" Bethani asked once they were back in the car and headed home.

"You mean at the railroad crossing?"

"No, Mom, I mean this boring town. Correction. These boring towns." She put emphasis on the plural distinction. "Even together, they hardly make a blimp on the radar."

"I wish you would try to like it here, honey. It's not really so bad, is it?" Madison looked over at her daughter with a hopeful expression, practically willing her to agree.

"Well, let me see," the teen said, using her fingers to keep track of her assessment. Her newly polished toenails were on full display in the front windshield, feet shoved atop the dash while they waited for the train to pass. "There is no mall here. No decent stores to even shop in. Just a couple of antique shops, an old lady dress shop, and a thrift store. And what the heck is a Five and Dime?" She continued on, not waiting for an answer. "There's not a single place here to buy an i-Phone. There are zero places for entertainment, other than the bowling alley. The sidewalks roll up promptly at eight p.m. There is no choir at school. There-"

"Hang on, let me have a chance for rebuttal. There is a perfectly nice mall in College Station, less than an hour from here. Even back home, traffic made it at least half that to the nearest mall. And there are several stores here, just not many that sell the kind of clothes and shoes you like to wear. A Five and Dime is like a dollar store before inflation, although believe me, Uncle Jubal does not sell a single thing in that store for a dime. You have an Android, so you don't need an i-Phone store. There is also a rodeo arena for entertainment and a sporting goods store with an indoor gun range. And since when were you interested in being in the choir?"

The teen shrugged, reluctant to back down so easily. "It's always nice to have options. The school also does not have a tennis court, a swimming pool, or a Debate Club."

"You don't play tennis, your old school did not have a pool, and you should check into starting a Debate Club, as you would be excellent at arguing. But, did you know, that The Sisters Fighting Cotton Kings hold claim to one Heisman trophy winner, two professional football players, and a three-time state championship ladies basketball team?"

Clearly unimpressed, the teen rolled her eyes. "How could I not? There are huge signs all over campus, repeating the claims with pathetic regularity. There's even a bronze statue of that Heisman trophy guy."

"Tug Montgomery," her mother confirmed with a nod.

"Hey, there's a really hot guy who drives around with a weird looking machine and a dog in the back of his flatbed truck. His name is Montgomery. Any relation?"

The crossing arms were going up, allowing access across the railroad tracks once again. Madison put the SUV back into gear and proceeded into the town of Juliet. "His son, Cutter."

"That's another thing," the girl complained. "What's with all the hokey names around here? Cutter. Billy Bob. Bubba Ray. Earl Ray. Two of my friends have grandmas or great grandmas named Dolly Mac and Lerlene. Seriously, Lerlene?"

"Hey, that's your great, great aunt. Who's the friend?"

"Sara Hamilton. And I use the term 'friend' loosely. She's a girl in my Algebra class."

Madison did a quick genealogy review in her head. "I think she's my second cousin Darrel's daughter. So is she nice?"

"She's okay, I guess."

"You could invite her over sometime."

"Yeah, and there's another thing. I live with my great grandmother. The house always smells like BenGay. And I share a bedroom with my mother. Not exactly a fun sleep-over destination."

"You gotta admit, though, Granny Bert is pretty cool," Madison said with a smile.

"Okay, I'll give you that. But still..." The teen pulled her feet from the dash and took on a sullen expression.

"Aw, honey, I know the last couple of months have been rough for you."

"You think? I've lost my entire world, Mom! My father, my home, my friends. You have no idea what it's like!"

"Yeah, honey, I kinda do," Madison chided softly. "That was my home, too, you know. My friends. And my husband."

Bethani twisted enough in the seatbelt to glare at her mother. "Would that be the husband you refused to sleep with for the last two years?" she sneered. "You had separate bedrooms, Mom. And don't give me that about his snoring. Don't you think we could hear the two of you arguing? Don't you think we could hear you yelling at him all the time? You stopped loving him, Mom, a long time before he died!"

The accusation hung heavy in the air. With a sharp intake of breath, Madison absorbed the verbal blow as her daughter whirled around and stared stonily out the window.

When she had her emotions under control, Madison spoke up, but her voice was low and raw. "Beth, I know you don't understand."

"Then make me, Mom!" the teen begged. When she looked at her mother, her blue eyes were swimming with tears.

"I can't, honey. Because I'm not sure I even understand it myself. Things . . . happen in a marriage. Things change."

"So you're saying all that stuff of about love and forever is just a load of crap?"

"No." A frown marred her forehead. "No," she said more forcefully, needing desperately to believe it herself. "Oh, honey, it's complicated."

"It's complicated, I'm too young to understand, you're old and wise and know what's best, so I should just suck it up and be happy to be here, right? I should forget about my old life in the city and," sarcasm gave way to a thick country drawl, "dig my roots down deep in this here good ole' Brazos valley soil, maybe even let it squish between my toes for good measure, embrace these country bumpkins and backwoods hillbillies, and give a deep 'yee-haw!', is that what you're saying?"

"Bethani Genesis Reynolds, I am ashamed of you! You are a snob!"

"And you are a hypocrite!" the teen challenged. "I've heard you make fun of this town before, Mom. You've told us plenty of stories about your uncle who got stuck in an armadillo hole when he was a baby, about how you kids used to climb the water tower for fun on a Saturday night, how a cow wandered into the church at somebody's wedding and ate half the flowers. That time Granny Bert sent you a newspaper because of some article in it, you laughed for days over some of these things they considered 'news' in this town. You said someone ought to pipe in sunshine and introduce them to the twenty-first century. You said there were too many cousins marrying cousins around here and that they needed some fresh blood. Yet suddenly you decide to sell our house in Dallas, move back here with your eighty-year-old grandmother, take a job where you come home reeking worse than death itself, and, on top of it all, you expect us to magically think you've drug us off to some cool, exotic place and be happy about it. Not happening, Mom!"

Madison made no comment as she turned onto Third Street and found herself behind a small procession marching down the road. She knew it was too much to hope that her irate daughter would miss the amusing sight, since it would only cement her perception of the town. Jimbo Hadley and his family were enjoying a nice afternoon stroll around the neighborhood. Billie Kate pulled a child's red wagon behind her, complete with an infant car seat held in place with bungee straps and duct tape. Their youngest child was perched inside while the other five children walked, each holding a leash in their hands. A menagerie danced at the ends of the ropes: a playful kitten, a fluffy black and white dog, a neatly trimmed goat, a sleek black steer, and a pot-bellied pig. Jimbo led the procession, riding a Shetland pony with an attitude. The man's long legs draped hilariously low on either side of the pony's rounded belly, and each time they passed a shrub or a trash can or a car parked along the curb, the pony brushed close, trying to rid itself of its rider.

Bethani turned to her mother with a triumphant smile, her blue eyes twinkling maliciously. "I rest my case."

"There is a perfectly good explanation for the goat and the steer. They are obviously show animals for the Livestock Show, and they're teaching them to follow a lead rope." Madison felt the need to defend the scene before them. "Plus, it's good exercise."

"Do you happen to know the kids' names?" Her gloating tone suggested she did.

"No."

"I do. I go to school with the older two. That's Buddy Ray and Jimmie Kate. There were hundreds of kids at my school back home. Not a single one of the girls was named Jimmie Kate."

"That's because she was named after both parents, Jim — Jimbo— and Billie Kate."

"Oh, well, if the hillbilly names are a family tradition, that makes all the difference," Bethani said with heavy sarcasm.

Madison ignored her daughter as she carefully maneuvered around the boy leading the show steer. The youth gave a friendly wave as Madison drove in the middle of the street to avoid them.

A touch of alarm made Bethani's next words sharp. "Mom! Why is that woman running out of her house, holding a broom like a weapon?"

Sure enough, a short, stocky woman came flying down her walkway, brandishing a broom as she yelled for the family to get off her sidewalk. The only one actually on the sidewalk — which technically belonged to the city, not the woman— was the youngest girl, a cute little redhead with pigtails and a prancing kitten.

At the woman's angry outburst, the child snatched up her kitten and jumped off the sidewalk, into the direct path of her brother and his steer. The startled animal bucked and ran, dragging the youth with it until the teenager could get it back under control. In the meantime, the goat jerked free of Jimmie Kate's hold, and the temperamental pony bolted. Both made a direct flight across the neatly trimmed and manicured lawn of the woman with the broom, trampling flowerbeds and shrubberies as they went.

Madison had to split her attention between the road and the bucking steer, but a glance in the rear view mirror confirmed that the goat had finally stopped. A particularly lush row of winter snapdragons captured its attention, even as the pony made a beeline toward the lone statue in the yard. Heedless of the man upon its back, the woman with the broom tried to whack the animal across the rump, missed, and sent the stone statue toppling.

As Madison made a right at the end of the block, Bethani turned completely around in her seat, trying to see what would happen next.

"Oh my gosh, this is hilarious!" the teen howled. She was laughing so hard that tears streamed down her face. "Go back, Mom, go back! I've got to see this!"

"I will not go back," Madison huffed, even though she secretly yearned to know how the broom lady would respond to killing her own statue.

"That- That- That is the funniest thing I have ever seen!"

"I'm glad you found it amusing."

"Maybe-Maybe I was wrong," the teen hooted, clutching her stomach because she laughed so hard. "Maybe this hick town is more – more amusing than I thought! M-Maybe rodeos are more f-f-fun than I thought!"

Madison claimed victory where she could find it, pathetic though it was. "See? You just have to keep an open mind and give the towns a chance."

"Just –Just wait until I post the video!"

"You filmed that?" Madison asked incredulously.

"Of-Of course! And I bet it will go viral by midnight!"

After the house was quiet for the night, Madison bundled up in a sweater and went out to the front porch. She lit the chiminea and sipped on a cup of coffee while she waited for the warmth to reach her.

The argument with Bethani may have ended in laughter, but her daughter's accusations still stung.

She had to admit, everything the teen accused her of was true. She *had* slept in a separate room from her husband. She *had* stopped loving him. She *had* made fun of her hometown and many of its residents. She *had* drug her children back here to the rural community and thrust them into the middle of small town life, expecting them to adjust. But she had no choice. Gray had seen to that.

But Bethani adored her late father, and Madison would not be the one to destroy the girl's idealistic image of him. Even when the accusations hurt, Madison would shoulder the blame of their broken marriage. No need to take everything from her children, not when they had lost so much already. Let them keep their pride and their memories, even if they portrayed the lie of a noble father.

"Thought I heard you out here." Miss Bert slipped up behind her, wearing a quilt around her shoulders and holding an extra cover out for Madison.

"Thanks." She tucked the colorful material around her legs before saying, "I didn't mean to bother you. I thought you were asleep. I told Blake to keep his music low if he wasn't going to bed yet."

"Nah. I saw his light go out ten minutes ago. I think he's already asleep."

"Bethani pretended to be, but I'm pretty sure she's still sulking. We had a big fight earlier, before the Hadley rodeo incident."

"Heard that Myrna Lewis called the police and filed trespassing charges." Granny Bert propped the front door open with her foot, reached inside to pull something out, then let it shut softly behind her. As she took the chair beside her granddaughter, she presented a glass of wine for them both. "I think tonight calls for something stronger than decaffeinated coffee."

"Mm, perfect." Madison reached for the red liquid and inhaled its sweet perfume before taking a sip. "So who is this Myrna Lewis? I don't remember her."

"Oh, she's a newcomer. Only been here about ten or so years. Her husband took over the insurance company when Ollie Muehler embezzled all that money and ran off with the preacher's wife. Dean Lewis is a quiet, mild mannered man. What he ever did to deserve that wife of his, I will never know!"

"She did seem a little high-strung," Madison agreed, thinking of the way she rushed from the house, wielding her broom.

"Claims to be some sort of horticulturist. Acts like that yard of hers is her child. Won't let anyone step on the sidewalk, much less her grass. I would love to have seen her face when that pony took off across it! And when that goat started munching on those flowers! Thought I needed some of Sybille's pads there for a minute!" Her grandmother started laughing again, but not nearly as loudly as she had the first half dozen or so times she watched the video.

"It was funny, not that I would ever admit it to Beth." Madison took another sip of wine, welcoming the warm sting that slid down her throat.

After a moment of silence, Granny Bert spoke. "No, girl, you didn't do wrong by bringing them here."

"Are my thoughts so obvious?"

"Loud and clear, just like that worried frown on your face. And you're going to nibble your top lip plumb off if you aren't careful."

Madison relayed the argument to her grandmother, then made an admission. "She's right, too, you know. I uprooted them without even talking to them about it."

"Would you have told them the truth about their father?"

"Of course not."

"Then don't feel guilty about making the only choice you had."

"I called her a snob," Madison admitted after a moment.

"Could be a case of the pot calling the kettle black."

"What-What do you mean?"

"Seems to me you have a pretty poor impression of this town, as well. Maybe if you were to give it a chance and have a different attitude, your children would, too."

Madison took the words under advisement. "Maybe," she agreed softly. "But it's hard to be too enthusiastic, when I spend the day covered in chicken poop."

"Chicken farming is good, honest work. It may be smelly and dirty, but it's paying your bills right now, at least until something better comes along."

"I didn't get a chance to tell you last night, but I have a new client. Lucy Ngyen hired me to dig around and see if I can find some sort of evidence that can clear her son's name."

"She thinks you're a P.I. or something?"

"I explained to her that I'm not, but she's desperate."

"I never believed her son killed Ronny Gleason to begin with."

"Why is that?"

"Why would he kill him? No reason. He wanted to buy the Gleason farm but Ronny kept jerking him around. That man could be a real horse's patooty at times." She took a long draw of wine while Madison listened with interest. "And Ronny was one of his best customers. You don't kill your money source, not when he's worth more to you alive than dead."

"Wait a minute. What kind of customer?"

"Cockfighting. The Ngyens raise fighting roosters, and Ronny Gleason was their best customer. If he wasn't buying the roosters and fighting them himself, he was placing bets on them. Don Ngyen is too sharp a cookie to take out his money man."

"How do you even *know* all this?" Madison asked in amazement.

"I keep my eyes and ears open, girl. You'd be surprised at some of the things I know about people in this town. Go ahead. Just ask me. I can tell you something about almost everyone or everything in this town."

"I heard Ronny Gleason was banned from high school football games for a while."

"Not just football, but basketball, baseball, the whole shootin' match. Showed up drunk one too many times, running his mouth. Threw a punch at the high school Ag teacher and got banned for two years. Next question."

"Who is the Ag teacher?"

"At the time it was Eddie Menger."

Madison looked confused. "Wait a second, that's the name of the Service Tech for Barbour Foods. I'm meeting with him on Monday morning."

"Yep. He punched Ronny back and lost his job over it. Since he already had a degree in Animal Science, he was a shoo-in for the job with Barbour. Next question."

"Who is Reverend Greer?"

"One of God's masterpieces," Granny Bert replied with a pleased smile. "You know the Hamilton and Cessna families have been going to the First Baptist church since it opened its doors way back when, even having our own benches and all. But I swear, for two whole months I was a steady member of the Cowboys for Christ Church. Reverend Greer knows how to stir a congregation and get the old heart a pumping and the praise going up to God, without even uttering a word. All he has to do is strut out there in his tight jeans and his white cowboy shirt, and every female in the place is struck by the Holy Spirit."

"Granny! You're talking about a man of the cloth!" Madison chided.

"I'm talking about how well that man fills out the cloth, child. And his face ain't half bad, either."

Because she did not know what else to say, Madison repeated her lame protest. "Granny!"

"You visit that church tomorrow, and you'll see exactly what I'm talking about."

"I heard Ramona Gleason went there for a while."

"She did, until the good Reverend finally had to ask her to either wear different clothes or to stop coming altogether. That's half the allure of the Cowboy Church, that you can wear your work-clothes and jeans to service and fit right in, but Ramona took it too far. She showed up in skin-tight skirts and tops that could double as a postage stamp, and for church services, no less!"

"What did Ronny Gleason think of his wife, dressing and acting like a hussy?"

"Do you recall what Ronny looked like?"

Madison tried to remember him when his skin was intact and he still had both eyes. "He was rather homely, as I recall."

"Homely?" her grandmother snorted. "I don't mean to speak ill of the dead, but that man was so ugly, when he was little his parents had to tie a pork chop around his neck to get the dog to play with him! So when a man who looks like Ronny Gleason can have a woman who looks like Ramona on his arm, he don't care much about anything else. Besides, he was the one paying for all the plastic surgery and the skimpy little outfits. He always seemed as pleased as punch to be her husband."

"So can you think of anyone else who might have wanted Ronny Gleason dead? One of Ramona's jealous lovers, maybe?"

"That's the thing. Even though that woman likes to display the goods, I hear she keeps them under glass. Never heard of anyone she actually cheated with, not when it came down to it."

"Was there anyone around town who didn't like Ronny?"

"Ronny Gleason was a gambling man. When he was rolling high, he was free with his money. But when he was low, he owed money to half the people in town. About a year ago, there was talk that he was in deep to a bookie out in Vegas. There were rumors of a mob connection, but you know how that can be. Still, there were plenty of people who were fed up with having him stiff them on loans."

"Like who?"

"Merle Bishop, for one. He runs the tractor dealership and let Ronny buy a half a million dollars' worth of fancy equipment for the chicken houses. Had to hire a lawyer before he ever got his money back. Rudy Dewberry wasn't so lucky. He closed his tire shop after Ronny got to him for thousands of dollars in rubber. Finally opened back up, but doesn't keep much in stock. Mostly you have to order what you want and wait a couple of days before they come in. And speaking of tires," the older woman said thoughtfully, "I need to get a spare for the motor home. I've got a road trip planned for next month, you know."

"Oh? Where to?"

"Galveston. A group of us goes every year, to break the monotony of winter. You might want to come along."

Madison laughed. "Thanks, but I doubt I'm up to a camping trip with you and your friends."

"Afraid you can't keep up with us, huh?" the eighty-year-old beamed.

"Exactly!"

10

Madison's day was brighter already. After making a deposit at the bank, she paid all her bills, tucked away a fifty for safe keeping, and made plans to take the kids into College Station later in the week for new shoes, all before driving out to the Gleason farm to start her work week.

She refused to let the dread well within her. The closer she came to the farm, the worse the feeling got.

Okay, so she hated her job. This job, anyway. She made the admission to herself with a deep sigh of resignation. That deposited check was her commitment to another full week of this torture, before the first seven days were even through.

The thought of the money was the only thing that kept Madison going. In the few days she had been there, the chickens had noticeably grown. Not only were the dead birds heavier and harder to haul out now, but even walking through the houses had become a chore. The bigger the birds, the denser the sea of feathers she had to wade through. Mostly she drug her feet among them, shuffling birds out of her way rather than taking actual steps.

She had to admit, however, that walking the equivalent of over two miles each day was good exercise, and her body was getting well-toned from bending over so many times and carrying out the heavy buckets of dead chickens. Hardly glamorous, but a workout was a workout. And this one paid the bills.

And despite the noisy cluck of the chickens and the disgusting smell, the time spent walking back and forth down the long houses was excellent down time, when she could put her body on autopilot and give her mind free range.

This morning, her thoughts were all over the place. Another quick mental review of her bank account kept the paranoia at bay; at least for another month, she was in good shape. Which left her free to worry about Bethani's attitude and reflect proudly on Blake's placement on the Varsity Baseball team. *Go Cotton Kings.* Another plus about this current job was that it took only a few hours each day to do, other than those occasional pesky alarms. Blake's first game was coming up in a week and there was no reason she would not be able to attend. If she walked houses first thing in the morning, she had the afternoons free to run errands, pick up the kids from school, go to games, clean house, and, if she was lucky, squeeze in another job or two. Since Mrs. Thompson was back in town and Mr. Huddleston was through with physical therapy, it left only the pharmacy runs for Miss Sybille and her 'investigative' work for Lucy Ngyen.

Her thoughts turned to Don Ngyen, locked up in the local jail. The Sisters actually had their own small jail and holding cell, housed in the old train depot that now served as the police station. No doubt Don would be transferred to the River County facility sometime today, but he had spent the weekend in town where his friends and family could easily visit.

Had the Vietnamese man actually killed Ronny Gleason? Madison wondered. It seemed unlikely, given the lack of motive. What purpose would Ronny's death serve the man? He could hardly buy and run this farm from prison.

She shuffled through the other options in her mind. If Ronny Gleason had a gambling problem, there could be plenty of people with a grudge against him. It sounded like he already had a problem with numerous creditors and a bookie out in Vegas; did he owe any of them enough to pay with his life? Maybe she could work it into the conversation the next time she spoke with Ramona Gleason.

And while considering suspects… There was something about Ramona Gleason that bothered Madison. It was more than all the fake body parts; something else about the woman rang untrue. Despite her touching scene on Brash's shoulder that first day, the widow hardly seemed distraught over her husband's death. Even if she was in a loveless marriage, shouldn't there have been some signs of sorrow?

Madison knew all about facing the death of the man you had married but grown apart from. Even though she no longer loved Gray, she was shattered by his death, and not just for her children's sake. His death meant there was no opportunity to fix past mistakes, no chance to make that last argument, no hope for closure on a marriage gone terribly wrong. Ramona Gleason did not display any of the same regrets.

Could it be that the police had arrested the wrong person?

With four houses completed, Madison only had two left for the day. As she pulled the golf cart down the road running between the last set of houses, she saw the Barbour Foods pickup truck waiting for her.

She saw the way Eddie Menger's gaze swept over her and the faint light of amusement that came into his eyes. Well, at least she was able to provide a few laughs for the man. Somewhere along that last house, thinking about Gray and Ramona, some of her good mood had evaporated. She pushed a handful of hair from her sweaty brow, not caring about the grime she left behind. Let him find that amusing, as well.

"Mrs. Reynolds, I see you're still with us," he said affably. "Good for you."

His comment seemed sincere enough, so Madison made an effort. "Good morning, Mr. Menger."

"Call me Eddie. So how are things going?"

"I think all right." Her tone was cautiously optimistic as she arched her aching back and stretched her neck. "I think I'm doing all the things I'm supposed to do."

"It looks like it," the service technician agreed. "The birds look healthy, and they are definitely growing. I wouldn't be surprised if this farm didn't win the week, as usual."

"Win the what?"

Realizing she did not understand the jargon, he laughed at his own folly. "Barbour incorporates competition in their pay-scale. Growers are guaranteed a base pay per pound, but they have the opportunity to make a bonus if they place well in competition."

"Wait. No one told me I had to do a competition!" she cried in dismay.

"No, no, relax, you don't have to do a thing. It's really just a matter of feed conversion, which is calculated among the farms selling that week. The grower that has the biggest chickens but uses the least amount of feed is considered the week's winner. He gets the biggest bonus, with the rest of it divvied out among the other top growers."

"What about the poor guys that aren't on top?"

"You said it yourself. They come out poor," Eddie Menger grinned.

Madison did not find the arrangement amusing. To her, it seemed grossly unfair, given that all the growers put in the same amount of time and effort.

"I hope I haven't hurt his chances of winning," she worried with a frown. She wanted no future in the chicken business, but she took pride in her work while she was here. Her frown curled with confusion. "His? Hers, I guess it would be. Or would it belong to whoever she sells the farm to?"

"Who said Mrs. Gleason was selling the farm?"

"She did."

The man scowled. "That's news to me."

"Surely you can't blame her. She knows even less about the chicken business than I do!" Oddly enough, she found herself defending the other woman. *We widows have to stick together, after all.*

"At any rate, the chickens look fine," Eddie said. "Ronny has always placed well in the past, and this flock shouldn't be any different. Just make sure they don't run out of feed and that you raise the waters lines a little every few days. You want your chickens to stretch their necks out to drink from the nipples on the line, not have to turn their head and have water run down their necks."

"Do you have the Ngyen farm, too?"

"Sure do. They always place well, too." A bit of swagger slid into his voice. "That's why I always do well among the Service Techs and get a little bonus of my own."

"I hear the Ngyens have wanted to buy this place for years."

He looked miffed that she was unimpressed with his status. "Yeah, well, that's what I've heard, too."

"So can I ask you something?"

"Sure, that's what I'm here for."

"Did Ronny Gleason raise fighting roosters of his own?"

"No ma'am," he said in a matter-of-fact manner. "Owning any feathered fowl is strictly forbidden by Barbour. The birds can carry disease from one flock to the other."

"But, I thought-" She stopped herself, not wanting to get the Ngyens into trouble. She had no stake in this matter. "So I understand you knew Mr. Gleason before you worked together."

He squinted his eyes just a bit, as if trying to decide what she was referring to. After a slight hesitation, he shrugged. "It's a small town. Everyone knows everyone."

Moving to safer ground, she changed the subject. "So this is a money making farm, you say?"

"Sure. Ronny always did better than most, but it's actually pretty hard not to make money in the chicken business. The growers have guaranteed sell through, after all. They know they'll have a buyer and a set price."

Madison looked over at the huge barn and thought of all the light bulbs inside, and all the fans. "But the electricity bill must be enormous. And the propane. Can they really make money doing this?"

"That's why it's important to keep a good relationship with your Service Tech, so you do well and get your bonus," Eddie Menger grinned.

Something glinted in his eyes, and Madison wondered if he was flirting with her. One glance down at her filthy clothes, and she decided she had been imagining it. "One other question," she said, changing the subject. "I got an alarm earlier that said low pressure. What does that mean?"

"It has to do with the static pressure inside the houses. A door might have been left open or a fan might not have come on. I'll double-check your programs and make sure everything's in working order. The low pressure aren't that concerning, but if you ever get a high pressure, get here as fast as you can. You can kill a whole house of birds that way."

Madison's eyes rounded. "What would I do in that case?"

"I'll show you on the computer, but the quick fix is to open a door to create airflow. Be careful, though, because the pressure will be so strong it will suck the doors closed and make them hard to open. In fact, you can create your own reverse tornado and suck the roof right into the house if you're not careful."

"You're kidding, right?"

"Not at all," the man assured her. "Come on, I'll show you what you would do in an emergency."

11

Police Chief deCordova was going nowhere fast with his murder investigation. Other than the argument and resulting threat made a few days before Ronny Gleason's death, he had no real reason to suspect Don Ngyen was guilty of murder. Even the grower's prior knowledge of death by electrocution could have been a fluke, and easily attributed to the various rumors connected to the case; alongside tales of the much-feared bird flu and being burned alive in the incinerator, electrocution was only one of the rumored means of death.

The Gleasons, however, were pleased to have someone in custody and were keeping up the pressure for Don Ngyen to stay behind bars. Brash knew that if the charges were dropped, and perhaps even if the Vietnamese made bail, there would be major trouble in Naomi.

Not at all certain they had the right man, the Chief was working other angles of the investigation, as well. The County Sheriff was more than happy to have him take Lead on the case, giving the Police Chief/Special Investigator full reign, particularly since it would fall primarily at the expense of The Sisters Police Department.

The trick, now, was to work the investigation into his already overloaded schedule. The incident with Myrna Lewis and Jimbo Hadley was an added complication he did not need. After the second time his officers were called to the scene for frivolous new 'evidence', Brash refused to send officers out. Now Myrna called the station at least twice a day, adding new complaints each time she found a crimped flower stem or broken blade of grass. She insisted the individual complaints be properly cataloged and recorded, waiting for the full list of offenses to be read back to her each time she called. The fifth and final time she called yesterday, Brash threatened to charge the woman with filing a false police report. It kept her at bay for now, but he had a feeling that he had not heard the last of Myrna Lewis on the subject.

Brash had a working list of people Ronny Gleason was known to associate with and/or owed money to. Despite being in the lucrative chicken industry, the deceased grower was a habitual gambler and, more often than not, experienced money problems.

Working his way down his list, one of Brash's first stops was at the tractor dealership to talk with Merle Bishop.

"Sure, Ronny was one of my best customers," the gray haired man confirmed. "Bought that fancy little Model 440SL. Sweet little number, low profile to fit inside the houses, but with plenty of horsepower to pull equipment and operate a front-end loader. Full cab, too, with heat and air and a jam up radio. Like I said, sweet."

"I bet it had a sweet price tag, too."

The dealer grinned. "Yeah, I reckon it did, especially after Ronny put all the accessories on it. Said he needed a tax write-off so he didn't have to pay Uncle Sam, so he got the whole works."

"What kind of payments did that have?"

"The way Ronny made them, not many. He got a little slack after the second payment. I kept sending him letters and went out to talk to him a time or two. I finally had to hire a lawyer to write a letter."

"Was he still paying on it?"

"No, about six months ago he waltzed in here with cash and paid it off. Cash, mind you! I was nervous as a freckle-faced boy on his first date, having that much money in the safe. Took it to the bank first thing the next morning, but not before I lost a full night's sleep."

"You know of anyone else he owed money to?" Brash asked. Thinking of a different angle, he added, "Or anyone else he paid off?"

"Paid his bill to Jolly Dewberry's boy. That's why he opened back up, but it's not quite full service now, mostly an order-as-needed type deal. I heard he paid cash for that new Tahoe his wife is drivin', paid up the propane bill he was always behind on, and took a couple of trips out to Vegas."

"Do you happen to know where he got all this money?"

The older man shook his head and laughed. "Didn't ask 'cause I didn't care. Got my money —in cash— and that was good enough for me."

The police chief heard a similar story from Rudy Dewberry, who ran a tire shop out of his father's old-school full service gas station. When Brash called the gas company in a nearby town, he heard the same thing; not only had Ronny paid his bill in full, he even pre-paid his future bill by several thousand dollars.

Just before noon, Brash stopped by the Keeling Insurance Agency. A few years back, Ronny had gone lax on making insurance payments and Marion had no choice but to drop his coverage. With no signs of lingering resentment, the man reported they had no further dealings after that, other than town functions and occasional bowling tournaments.

Across the street from the insurance company, there were two choices for lunch, one on either end of the block. Not feeling like Mexican food, Brash headed for New Beginnings Café. Besides having good food, it did not hurt that cute little Genny Baker ran the place.

The place was already packed, but Shilo Dawne Nedbalek caught his eye and motioned to an empty table tucked away in the far corner. He ordered the daily special without checking the board to see what was offered.

"You're just like Cutter Montgomery," she chuckled.

"Speak of the devil." At his comment, she whirled around with a big smile, encouraged when Cutter started her way. She missed the Chief's sweeping hand movement behind her, inviting the younger man to join him.

"Hey," Cutter said in greeting, but his eyes were on the policeman. "How's it going?"

"Can't complain. Have a seat."

Cutter took off his cowboy hat and turned it upside down on the table, next to the Chief's hat. Freed from their confines, his dark blond locks curled in charming disarray. Cutter settled in his chair before looking up at the waitress and offering a smile. "I'll have sweet tea and the lunch special, Shilo Dawne."

"And hello to you, too, Cutter Montgomery!" she huffed.

"Sorry. Hello, Shilo Dawne. I'll have sweet tea and the lunch special, please ma'am." He grinned in mischief. "Better?"

She snorted and flounced away, her hand-crocheted blouse billowing behind her.

"You know, Shilo Dawne's a nice gal and all, and a pretty good waitress, but *man* is she temperamental!" Cutter complained in her wake.

The Police Chief laughed at the other man's ignorance. "The girl obviously has the hots for you, and the first thing you think of when you see her is food. It's hard on her ego."

"Nah, Shilo Dawne's my kid sister's age. She used to come over to the house all the time."

"And I'll bet she always wanted to do whatever you were doing, right? I bet you couldn't turn around for bumping into her."

Cutter thought back to a dozen times, exactly as the Chief described. "Maybe," he conceded. He quickly changed the subject. "So how's the investigation coming along on Ronny Gleason's death?"

"The official term is 'stalled'. I can't find much to point toward Don Ngyen's guilt. Then again, I can't find much to point away from it, either."

"I sure never took Don Ngyen for the violent type."

"Tell me something, Montgomery. The chicken business is pretty lucrative, isn't it?"

"From what I understand, yes, particularly the broiler houses like Ronny had."

"So how does a man who makes that kind of money wind up owing half the people in town?"

"It may have something to do with the fact that they only get paid four times a year, when they sell a flock. Some people can't manage their money that well. But I heard he paid off most of his loans. I know I finally got paid."

"You, too? What did he owe you for?"

"He hired me to build those big iron entrances at both his house and his farm. I was halfway done with the fence along his driveway when I realized I wasn't getting paid. That was two years ago. Then back in August, he showed up one day and paid his bill in full, plus gave me enough to finish out the fence."

"I've been hearing that all day. Apparently, he came into some money about six months ago. Serious money."

Shilo Dawne appeared with their drinks, smiling sweetly. "Here you go, fellas. Your lunches will be right out."

Confused by her sudden change in demeanor, Cutter was suspicious. "You're not going to dump a bunch of salt in my plate, are you?"

"No, but I might dump that tea glass on your head!"

As she stomped away, Cutter looked helplessly at his laughing companion. "What'd I do wrong this time?"

"You don't know a lot about women, do you, son?" Brash asked with a mixture of sympathy and amusement.

"Apparently not." His frown was comical.

"Now that I think about it, why aren't you married?"

"Why aren't you?" Cutter shot back.

"Tried it once. Didn't work so well."

"Strange as it sounds, I'd actually like to be married," Cutter admitted. "Problem is, I've never found a woman I want to spend my life with."

"What about Shilo Dawne? Or Callie Beth Irwin? I thought you were seeing her."

"We've gone out a few times, but that's about it. All either one of them can talk about is getting out of this town and making something of themselves."

"Nothing wrong with ambition. Trying to make something of your life is actually a good attribute," the lawman reminded him.

Cutter took a big swig of his sweet tea, his head bobbing up and down. "I agree. I just don't think you have to leave The Sisters to do it. I plan on being somebody, right here in Naomi, Texas."

Brash had to admire the younger man's attitude, even if he wondered at his probable success. There weren't many career choices in the small community, and most of the younger generation moved away soon after high school. Like himself, a few of them returned to the bosom of their hometown a few years later, after discovering the big wide world could also be cold and uncaring. Of the ones who did stay behind, most were content in their mediocre jobs and predictable futures, but it was good to know that some, like Cutter, meant to have it all.

When their meals arrived, it was at the hand of the café's owner, not the disgruntled waitress. Shilo Dawne passed behind her boss, however, wearing a smug expression on her pretty face as she said, "Salt free, of course," before continuing on her way.

"I'm not sure why Shilo Dawne wanted me to deliver these, but here you go," Genesis said, expertly placing a heaping plate before each man.

"Are these your smothered pork chops?" Appreciation glowed in Cutter's eager eyes.

The blond woman laughed. "Don't you even read the menu board?"

"No need. Everything you make is delicious. Just look at this." He jabbed a finger at each dish as he spoke. "Pork chops, real mashed potatoes, butter beans, steamed broccoli, and corn bread. Heaven on a plate."

Again she laughed. "You said the same thing yesterday about corn chowder and jalapeno cornbread."

"And I'll say it again tomorrow about …"

"Bacon, broccoli and gruyere frittata with an avocado and grapefruit salad," she supplied.

"No idea what that is, but I know I'll like it," Cutter predicted.

"You eat just about anything, don't you?" Genny mused with a dimpled smile.

Brash was the one to answer. "The kid has an iron stomach," he muttered. Not that he was interested, but the woman had hardly glanced his way. She was too busy beaming down at the kid. Belatedly, Brash remembered how cocky and annoying the younger man could be.

Genesis arched a playful brow. "Careful there, Chief, that almost sounds like an insult to my cooking."

"Not at all. I agree with the kid. Never had anything here that I didn't like." His own eyes twinkled with amusement as he added, "Just remind me not to order the special tomorrow."

Like her best friend, Genesis had spent most of her freshman year daydreaming of having Brash deCordova flirt with her. Twenty years later, it was still an exhilarating thrill.

Not appreciating how the lawman kept referring to him as 'the kid', nor the way the older two now all but ignored him as they grinned foolishly at one another, Cutter felt the need to break into their little bubble. "Some folks are too set in their ways to try new things," he interjected. "My dad's the same way. By the way, he said to say hello, deCordova, and stop by some day so you two can reminisce about the good ole days."

Clearly aggravated by the younger man's fresh attitude, Brash had no opportunity to reply. Myrna Lewis rushed up to the table and demanded his full attention.

Some women were tall and slim and graceful, Brash ruminated, like Madison Cessna: Reynolds, he corrected himself. Others, like Genesis Baker, were made for hugging, soft and rounded in all the best places. Myrna Lewis was neither of these. She stood barely over five feet tall and there was nothing lean, nor soft, about her. Her body was a solid chunk with little-to-no shape. She did not have Maddy's long, graceful neck or Genny's full, alluring hips; her neck and her waist blended into her stocky build with little definition. Instead of a stylish haircut to offer some sense of femininity, Myrna Lewis wore her dark mop in a short, severe bob with blunt edges. To make matters worse, she had absolutely no sense of fashion.

She stood glaring at him now, hands in the general area of her hips, her gray sweat pants hanging like a flannel sheet down her body. Elastic at the ankles pinched them in with a balloon effect and showcased the bright red Crocs on her feet, complete with white socks. She wore a harsh yellow t-shirt that advertised her favorite weed killer. Strapped somewhere near her waist was her trademark fanny pack.

"Chief! Chief deCordova, I want you to look at this!" the woman demanded. She opened her hand and presented the frayed edges of what was once, he supposed, a flower.

"What is it?" he asked, just to be certain.

"Nothing, now! Before that four-legged beast bit into it, this was one of my prize cabbage roses." She stabbed a sausage-like finger at the remnants in her palm. "Look at this delicate edging of purple, bleeding to lavender. You don't get that sort of intense shading in ordinary cabbages. These beauties come from the Pipher Nursery in Rosenberg, which specializes in only the finest horticulture. And that goat ate them!"

"Yes, Mrs. Lewis, we have that in our files."

"Oh no, you don't! I just now discovered this destruction. I need you to add this to the long list of damage that Hadley family wreaked on my lawn! This is simply an outrage, that people like that are allowed to roam down the streets with their animals, trampling through people's yards at will!"

By now her outburst was drawing the attention of other diners. Brash tried to defuse the situation with a voice of reason. "Now, Mrs. Lewis –"

She cut the officer off without concern. "Don't use that patronizing tone with me! There should be an ordinance in town about animals roaming free! At least in Juliet, we have a higher standard of living than to allow four-legged beasts free rein."

"They had lead ropes, did they not, Mrs. Lewis?" Brash's calm voice now had a distinct edge to it.

"What good are lead ropes, if they drop them and let the animals roam wherever they might!" She avoided a direct answer with her accusation.

From behind them, a young voice spoke up. "That's not what happened."

All eyes turned to the teenager who stood from her seat and approached their table. A flush of embarrassment stained the girl's fair cheeks, but she lifted her chin and looked beyond the ranting woman and straight at the Chief of Police. "I saw what happened. They didn't just drop the lead ropes. The animals were spooked when this woman ran out of the house, waving a broom over her head and screaming at the little girl to get off her sidewalk."

There were snickers in the background and one burst of out-right laughter. Brash shot a menacing look out into the café, quietening the crowd with his thunderous scowl. He threw extra effort into his glare, trying to suppress his own inappropriate tickle of amusement. Whoever she was, the girl had spunk.

Again before Brash could speak, Myrna Lewis cut him off. With her best haughty stare, she looked the young girl over. Never mind that the youth was taller than she was; the boy looming behind her was easily five ten. "And just *who* are you?" she demanded. "And why should we believe a derelict youth? You should be in school, not butting your nose into adult conversations. Why are you even here?"

The girl's eyes were a cool, cutting blue. Instead of cowering to the woman's nasty rebuke, she stiffened her back and pulled herself to her full height, forcing the other woman to look up at her. "I'm not a derelict. I am an A Honor Roll student. Well, okay, A/B in Algebra, but A in everything else. And school got out early because of a teacher's conference. And our aunt owns this café. Well, okay, so she's not technically my aunt, but she's family."

While Brash made the connection that the blond fireball had to be Maddy's daughter —she had the same tall, willowy frame, the same admirable spunk— Myrna Lewis sneered at the girl. "So you claim to have been there. Or is that 'well, okay, not really, but almost'?" She used a silly little-girl voice to mimic the teen.

The teenager looked down at her in disdain, garnering the respect of most of the people present when she merely stated the obvious. "You are not a nice woman."

Judging from the look on her face, Brash assumed that Myrna puffed out her chest. The truth was it was difficult to tell, given her perpetually bloated silhouette. "How dare you!" she sputtered angrily.

With a disgusted sigh, Brash threw his napkin onto the table and stood up from the table. As he unfolded himself to his full height, he towered over the sputtering woman by almost a full twelve inches. "Ladies, why don't we have a seat and talk this over? I'm sure these good people would like to eat their meal in peace."

Not at all ashamed of eavesdropping, at least a dozen of the people scattered throughout the restaurant shook their heads in denial. From three tables away, Virgie Adams spoke for most of the patrons. "Actually, I'd like to hear what the young lady has to say."

"Yeah, speak up, would you? I can't hear you over here!" Henry Bealls said, cupping his ear over his hearing aid.

Beside him, his wife tapped his arm and admonished, "Oh, hush up, Daddy, you couldn't hear them if they were sitting at our own table!"

"Heard the little gal tell her she weren't a nice lady," he grumbled.

Ignoring the entire room, Brash circled around to put his back to them. It might not keep the nosy crowd from listening in, but it let them know what he thought about it. Taking the girl's arm, he gently led her to one of the empty chairs at their table. Cutter got up and went to stand beside Genesis, but neither offered to leave. They hovered nearby as the blond haired boy went to stand behind the girl who was obviously his sister.

When Brash held a chair out for Myrna, she shook her head and remained standing. He murmured, "Suit yourself", as he returned to his own seat. "Miss, I did not catch your name."

"Bethani. Bethani Reynolds."

"Maddy's daughter," he nodded. Glancing up at the boy, he added, "And son, I presume?"

Blake was confused as to why the policeman was calling his mother by the familiar nickname, but he nodded and politely offered his hand in a firm handshake. "Blake Reynolds."

Impressed by the youth's manners, Brash shook his hand before returning his attention to the girl. "So, Bethani, tell me where you were when this took place."

"Mom and I were on our way back from getting pedicures. We came up behind the Hadley family, walking their show animals and family pets down Third Street. We were trying to go around them when all of a sudden, this woman came racing down her walk, waving a broom and yelling. The little girl jumped off the sidewalk and starting crying, bumping into Buddy Ray. The show steer got spooked and almost ran in front of us. Jimmie Kate tried to hold on, but the goat jerked its rope out of her hand. She even has the rope-burn to prove it. And the pony just took off, even with her father on its back and trying to stop it."

As she told the story in full detail, it was easy for her listeners to imagine the scene in their heads. Genesis bit into her lip to keep from laughing, but Cutter was less successful. She ended up elbowing him and keeping the pressure of her arm into his side, until he was able to control himself. Many of the other patrons did not even try to hold in their laughter. One even called out, "You should see the video!"

"Video?" Brash asked in confusion. He turned to Myrna. "You have surveillance cameras in your yard?"

"No," the woman said thoughtfully, "but that's not a bad idea."

"Bethani, how did this little fiasco make it onto a video?"

For the first time, the girl looked unsure of herself. "I-I took it on my phone."

"And did what with it?" the officer prodded.

"Uhm, I –uh- I shared it with a few friends."

"We saw it on You-Tube!" someone offered from the crowd.

Myrna Lewis gasped. "You take that off! You can't do that, not without my permission! I'll sue you!" She turned to the policeman, jabbing his shoulder with her stubby finger. "Chief deCordova, arrest this girl! She has infringed on my civil rights! She has no call to be posting pictures of me on the internet without my consent!"

Brash clenched his jaw and stared straight ahead, deliberately not looking at the irate woman. His voice was a growl as he warned, "Mrs. Lewis, if you do not remove your finger this instant, I will make an arrest, all right, but it will be yours, for assaulting a police officer. Move. Your. Finger."

The woman snatched her hand away, visibly shaken by his threat.

Bethani sat at the table trembling, her big blue eyes swimming with tears and fright. Blake had his hand on her shoulder in stoic support, but his own Adam's apple worked up and down nervously.

"Bethani, maybe we should call your Mom to come down here. But don't worry, honey, no one is going to arrest you," Brash assured the frightened youth.

"Madison is on her way. I've already texted her," Genesis offered, holding up her cell phone.

"And I never said I was dropping the charges!" Myrna insisted, although her voice held less bravado than before.

"The girl is a minor. She will *not* be arrested," Brash reiterated firmly.

Myrna Lewis crossed her arms over her shapeless body and tapped a red-clad foot. "I'd like to see this video. That will prove, once and for all, that the barbaric goat ate my cabbage roses!" she said with a satisfied sniff.

"As I recall, Mr. Hadley admitted as much."

"He admitted to the snap dragons, not the cabbage."

"Snap dragons, cabbage roses, daisies, whatever. He admitted that his goat trampled your flower beds and ate your flowers."

"But these are my *prize* cabbage roses! That makes a considerable amount of difference in the cost of damages. That is why I insist that you inventory this latest evidence." She held out the tattered tidbit of the all-but-forgotten cabbage.

"Of course, I will also have to take into account the evidence that Miss Reynolds has." Fed up with the woman's incessant complaints about such trivial matters when he had a murder investigation to conduct, Brash crossed his arms across his wide chest and studied her thoughtfully. His steady gaze was stern enough to make her squirm.

"Ev-Evidence of what?"

"It sounds to me like you assaulted the Hadley family. A child, no less."

The bell above the café door jangled, announcing a new guest.

Without thought to her dirty, ragged clothes or the odor that clung to them, Madison rushed inside, worried because of the cryptic message on her phone.

Bethani needs you at café, ASAP.

She stepped into a café full of people, all staring at her. The entire place was so quiet they could hear the rustle of her clothes. And she could hear the tiny sniffs as those nearest her got a whiff of her foul smell and discreetly covered their noses. Madison would have apologized, but she caught sight of her children, at the back of the room with Brash deCordova. The Chief of Police. No longer worried about apologizing, Madison left a trail of tainted air as she hurried to the back.

"Bethani! Blake! What is wrong? Genny, I got your text. What is happening?" She shot the questions off in rapid-fire succession, not waiting for the answers. "Brash, what is this about?" she demanded of the officer, her hazel eyes dark with worry.

In spite of himself, Brash grinned. *This* was how a woman should look with her hands on her hips. There should be this distinct boundary between her slender waist and the curve of her hip. There should be this enticing rise and fall of her breasts as she labored to get a steady breath. There should be this fire flashing from her eyes, little sparks of blue and green that made a man think of kindling another kind of fire, another kind of flame. His eyes slid back to Myrna, who had propped her fists onto her sweatpants again, her dark eyes dulled with bitterness.

No comparison.

Biting back the smile, Brash rose and asked, "Mrs. Reynolds, would you like to have a seat? Mrs. Lewis, have the other chair." When Myrna started to protest, he changed her mind. "Now."

12

It did not take Madison long to discover that people treated her differently, once they knew of her work in the chicken houses. Even though she took long, hot showers and removed all trace of the chicken smell, she soon discovered there was a mental stigma associated with the chicken industry.

Those opposed to having poultry farms in the area were fighting the growth of more houses. With no thought to old friendships and community alliances, they fought the progress with heated words and any legal grounds they could think of. Never mind that this was a farming community and animals of any kind created their own particular odor. Never mind that the chicken industry breathed new life and new wealth into the rural area. Never mind that it increased the tax revenue and boosted sales in the local stores; it also dropped property values for the surrounding properties. Often driven out by the unpleasant smell, neighbors were forced to sell their homes —some of which were passed down through generations— only to find they could not get top dollar for their property. Even if their homes or ranches had been there first, the value decreased because of the proximity to the newly built chicken houses. For a small community still healing from old rivalries, this new strain of contention was an unneeded complication.

Nor had the ordeal with Myrna Lewis helped matters any. Although most of the people in the café had taken Bethani's side and applauded the girl for standing up to the local busybody, there were some who took one look —and one whiff— of Madison and decided that her daughter had not been properly raised. Based solely on Madison's temporary job in the chicken houses, they agreed with Myrna that the teenager's 'eye witness' testimony could not be trusted. And without Myrna's permission to be filmed, they felt the video should not be used, even in the court of public opinion. The fact that it aired on public media was not only downright disgraceful, it showed poor parenting and a lack of good judgment.

The upside was that Bethani was now heralded a hero at school, particularly among the kids involved with the livestock show. In an ironic twist of fate, the video she had taken to poke fun of the organization had somehow endeared her to the very people she mocked. It did not hurt that the cutest boy in school, Drew Baines, was president of the Future Farmers of America and personally thanked Bethani for defending their right to walk their animals on public streets. Even though Chief deCordova and her mother strongly 'suggested' she take the video down —meaning, of course, that she had to— the memory of it lingered in their minds, as well as on one or more hard-drives. And Bethani was invited to her very first party in Juliet, hosted by none other than Jimmie Kate Hadley.

With more time spent at the Gleason farm, Madison had less time to spend asking questions on Don Ngyen's behalf. She felt guilty for not doing more to earn the money Lucy Ngyen paid her, so she squeezed in questions every chance she got, even if they were few and far between.

She tried asking Eddie Menger more questions the next time she saw him, which was only a few days later. Since he knew the Vietnamese man, she thought he might have some insight to his personality and the likelihood that he had, indeed, committed the crime.

"Personally, he didn't seem the type, but the police have arrested him, so I guess that's that," the Service Tech said with indifference. "Now, about these last few days with the flock. There are a few special things you'll need to take care of."

"If 'special' translates to heavy, I'm not sure I can manage," Madison admitted.

"Is there someone who could help you with some of the heavy lifting? A man, maybe?"

"Well, Benny Ngyen offered, but I didn't feel right about it, since-"

"Benny Ngyen!" the man broke in, clearly aghast. "Why in the hell would he offer to help you? And you can bet Ronny's wife won't let him step foot on the place, since his son was the one who killed Ronny!"

"We don't know it was Don for sure," Madison countered. "And since I'm helping them, Mr. Ngyen offered to help me."

"Helping them? How?"

"Actually, they hired me to do some work for them."

"What kind of work?" Eddie Menger asked, his tone suspicious.

"I'm not sure I'm at liberty to say," Madison hedged. "My contracts with my clients are confidential."

"Fine. That's fine, whatever," he said, waving both hands in a signal of dismissal. "Just know that it is against Barbour policy for growers to have personal contact with one another, particularly to be visiting one another's farms. It could lead to cross-contamination."

Madison frowned, biting her lips in concern. "I-I wouldn't want to cause trouble for the Ngyens. Nor for Ramona, after all she's been through. But I'm not a grower. I'm contract labor."

"Doesn't matter. For the next seven days, you are acting on behalf of Ronny Gleason. You need to put off your job with the Ngyens until after we sell this flock."

"But by then it may be too late!" she cried in dismay. "I need to find the evidence now, while it's still fresh on people's mind!"

"Evidence?" he asked sharply. "What are you talking about?"

Realizing her slip, Madison made mental notes on why she was not qualified to be a private investigator and should not have taken the assignment to begin with. Then she thought of a thousand reasons why she had, all of them green.

"Tell me about these special tasks," she said, quickly changing the subject.

"I'll show you how to take down back fences in one house, but you'll have to do the others on your own." He made the offer grudgingly, even as he grumbled, "I'm already late for an appointment."

An hour and a half later, Madison struggled with the long fence panels in House 4. This house always gave her the heebie-jeebies, because this was where she had found the body. Try as she might, she still had trouble walking down that fateful path toward the fan ends. As she managed to wrangle the holding stake free and take the fence apart, she fought memories of the fence Cutter Montgomery erected around the prone form of the dead man. She shook off gruesome images in her mind as she hauled the fence to one side of the house, where it hung on pegs when not in use.

Madison was making her way back along the waterline, almost to The Spot, as she had come to think of it, when suddenly the house went dark. With not even the fans cycling to provide light through their spinning blades, the house was pitch black. When off, the fan covers folded inward to close, meaning there was now no natural light to guide Madison's path. She stumbled over a chicken, heard its angry cluck, and stopped in her tracks.

Logic told her not to panic. If it were a power failure, the back-up generators would kick in and keep everything in working order. And just because she was only feet away from where she found Ronny Gleason's' body six days ago, it did not mean his ghostly form would suddenly appear to traumatize her.

Logic, however, was not always her strong suit. Just before hysteria overtook her, the lights came back on. Madison practically ran to the back of the house and to the freedom just beyond the big end doors. That last fence panel could stay there until tomorrow; she was not going back in that house today.

With foul play suspected, an official autopsy was performed on Ronny Gleason's body. Unlike on television, the process was not immediate. Several days after Madison discovered his ravished form, officials released his body for burial.

Out of respect for her brief client, Madison went to the funeral. Her heart ached for his grieving parents, but Ramona's theatrical performance failed to move her. Perhaps it was the form-fitting black dress the woman chose for the service, or the way she clung to Reverend Greer afterward, but Madison thought the woman's tears were of the crocodile variety.

"So there were a lot of people at the service?" Genesis asked, pouring her friend a cup of coffee. The two women practically had New Beginnings to themselves, with most of the afternoon crowd still lingering at the graveside services. Madison had declined going to the final service, deciding the funeral had served in paying her respect.

"The church was packed. Standing room only."

"Everyone was probably hoping for an open casket, thinking they might get a glimpse of something gory."

"Unfortunately, I had more than a glimpse, and I am *still* seeing it in my sleep!" Madison shivered visibly. "And again yesterday, when the lights went out in House 4. It was all I could do not to get hysterical."

"Ever figure out what happened?"

"No, but I guess it worked itself out."

"Just six more days and you'll be done with this job."

"They cannot come soon enough."

"Oh, hey, I think I may have you another job lined up. I've been singing your praises to Dean Lewis. Has he called you yet?"

"Would that be Dean Lewis from the Dean Lewis Insurance Company, husband of Myrna Lewis? I doubt she would ever allow him to hire me!"

"One and the same, but there's an insurance convention coming up, and he doesn't have anyone to man the office for him. Myrna is going with him this year, because it coincides with some big garden show she likes to attend. We're thinking she'll want to go badly enough that she won't bother to ask who's watching the shop."

"We?"

Genesis grinned. "I've been pulling hard for you, girl. Trying to work all the angles. He should be calling you any day now."

"Hmm, well, we'll see," she said, her tone doubtful. "By the way, you should have seen the dress Ramona was wearing."

"Sinful?"

"More suitable for a nightclub than her husband's funeral. And you should have seen the way she was hanging all over the preacher."

"But isn't he yummy?" Genesis grinned, displaying her dimples.

"I can see why all the women are flocking to his church. He is definitely an advertisement for God's fine workmanship."

Giggling like two teenagers, the friends indulged in Genny-doodle cookies and a second cup of coffee.

"And speaking of fine workmanship... here comes Brash. Funeral must be over," Genesis said, nodding as the chief of police stepped from his car, dressed in dark pressed slacks and a long sleeve white shirt. He even wore a jacket and tie for the occasion. From inside the café, the friends watched with unabashed appreciation as he removed the jacket and tossed it back inside the cruiser. The movements pulled material taut against his best features.

"The man's still a looker," Genesis admitted with a wistful sigh. "Why is it that men age better than we women?"

"Beats me. It's really not fair, is it? Those little wrinkles at the corner of his eyes make him look dignified. So does the silver in his hair. His chin is as firm as ever. And, look, not a bit of flab on his abs or thighs. Or his butt."

"Believe me, sister, I'm looking," Genny murmured.

Together, they watched as the unsuspecting man slammed his car door and jogged up the two steps to the sidewalk. There was no jiggle of lax muscle or excess fat, just six feet of solid male.

Another melancholy sigh, this one from Madison. "You do realize we're drooling."

"I know. But let's enjoy the view, just for a moment longer."

"Only for old-time sakes, of course."

"Of course!" Genny flashed a grin.

The moment the door opened, the women became quite engrossed in their coffee cups.

"Are you open?" Brash asked cautiously, peering at the empty tables.

"Sure. Come on in." Genesis motioned for him to join them. With a flourishing hand movement, she indicated the seat opposite her on the other side of the booth.

With the slightest of frowns, Madison scooted over and made room on the bench seat for him.

"Maddy was just telling me about the funeral. She said it was standing room only," Genny said as he settled in beside her friend.

"Half of the people there probably never said more than two sentences to the man when he was alive, but they all wanted to hear what was said about him when he died," Brash agreed. "Most seemed disappointed that it was closed-casket."

"From what I understand, there wasn't much choice."

"None at all." Brash turned to Madison and acknowledged her for the first time. "Myrna Lewis giving you anymore trouble?"

"Not so far."

"Your daughter sure handled herself well that day. Put the busybody right in her place."

"I hope she wasn't too rude," Madison worried. Something in the twinkle of his brown eyes sparked her concern.

"No, she was firm but respectful. You've done a good job raising your kids, Maddy."

Relaxing, Madison smiled. "Thanks. I need to hear that every now and then, especially now that I'm a single mother. Who knew parenting could cause such massive insecurities?"

"It's too important of a job to screw up," Brash agreed.

"You just have the one daughter?"

"Yep. Megan. She's fifteen, going on twenty. Not sure I could handle more than one, to be honest," he chuckled.

"Imagine having two at that magical age," Madison said. "Although I must say, boys are much easier. Less drama. More food, but less drama."

"I remember that age. Never could get quite full back then."

"That sounds like Blake! Luckily for me, I have a best friend who happens to own a café." Madison looked over at Genesis and beamed.

"He's my official sampler. If Blake won't eat it, it's definitely not going on the menu," the café owner agreed.

Watching the interaction between the two friends, Brash grinned.

"What's the smile for?" Genesis asked, noting how his eyes bounced back and forth between the two of them.

"I was remembering why I never dated either one of you back in high school," he said, still grinning. "I never could decide between the two of you. Tall willowy brunette, or short little blond. While I was trying to choose, Tommy Evans and Matthew Aikman swooped in and claimed you for themselves." He seemed to have forgotten his own choice of girlfriends during that time, the beautiful and popular Shannon Wynn.

"You know what they say," Genesis said with a cheeky grin. "You snooze, you lose. And, of course, that's assuming either one of us would have gone out with you."

Oh, please! If as we would have ever said no! Madison could not help but roll her eyes at the ludicrous thought. Brash glanced her way, saw the futile expression, and gave a warm, pleased laugh.

"Assuming," he agreed modestly, but there was a smug ring to the word.

Madison quickly changed the subject, before she embarrassed herself further. "Anything new on the case?"

"Which one?" he asked wearily.

"How many do you have?"

"Too many. Besides the obvious one of Ronny Gleason's murder, there are a dozen or so small ones. Someone has been lurking around The Gold and Silver Exchange for the past week and set off the security alarm one night. There was a hit and run fender bender in Juliet last week, a DUI out on the highway this week, and a report of stolen hubcaps from a residence here in Naomi. There's an ongoing boundary dispute between Hank Adams and Allen Wynn, rumors of an illegal cockfighting ring, complaints about someone trespassing at the Ngyen chicken farm, and reports of a Peeking Tom over on Maple Street. And, of course, there are daily complaints from Myrna Lewis about additional damage from the Hadley adventures."

"Granny Bert told me about the cockfighting."

"Yeah? What did she say?"

"Uh, mostly that Ronny Gleason liked to bet on them." She refrained from mentioning Don Ngyen, not wanting to implicate the man or his family.

"He's not the only one. We know some of the parties involved, but I think it goes deeper than just a few local guys, getting together to place a few bets."

"Organized gambling?" Madison asked in surprise.

"It's a theory I'm looking into."

"Wow, here in The Sisters?" Genesis murmured.

"It's hard to pin down, because the exact location keeps changing. We know who some of the ones selling the roosters are, but they're not the ones making the real money." Brash looked down at Madison again. "What else did Miss Bert have to say about it? Being the firecracker that she is, I'm not surprised if she knows more than we do."

Madison tried to recall the exact conversation. "I think she said that sometimes Ronny ran the fights, other times he just bet on them."

Brash gave a self-deprecating grunt. "That's bad, when we have to get intel from an eighty-year-old grandmother."

"Better to have her working for you, than against you!" Madison jested.

"Ain't that the truth." Turning a hopeful gaze toward her friend, he asked, "What's a guy gotta do around here to get one of those Genny-doodle cookies?"

"Hang on, I'll see what I can do." She gave him a conspiratorial wink and said in a staged whisper, "I have connections."

As Genny disappeared to fetch more cookies and coffee, Brash kept up the conversation. "So how are things at the chicken houses?"

Instead of answering, she gave him her new mantra. "Six more days. Just six more days, and I'll never set foot in another chicken house."

"That bad, huh?"

Madison had to be honest. "It's hard, sweaty, stinky work. But to tell the absolute truth, it's really not as bad as you'd think. Still, I don't want to make it my life's profession."

"I hear ya."

"You said something about trespassers at the Ngyen Farm?"

"Yeah, probably just some pranksters, giving them a hard time about Don. But they said a few odd things have been happening around there this week." He noticed the frown that tugged on the corners of her mouth. "What?"

"I wasn't going to say anything. I thought it was just me. But I-I've noticed a couple of odd things this week, too."

"Such as?"

"Little things, but still…. One morning the keys to the golf cart were in a different place than I always put them. Another morning the light was on in a control room, even though I could have sworn I turned it off when I left. And the dimmer switches on the lights in House 4 were changed. Not to mention that the lights went out completely when I was in there yesterday."

He grimaced in sympathy. "House 4, huh?"

"Exactly. I do good to even go in that house, with the lights at full intensity."

"For what it's worth, I've been very impressed with how you've handled yourself, Maddy. Not many people could still hold it together after finding his body like that."

She knew she did not deserve the warm look of praise in his eyes; the truth was, it was desperation that kept her going, nothing more.

Something else pricked along Madison's conscience. This jab of guilt had nothing to do with misguided accolades of bravery. This jab was direct from her strict moral upbringing and Granny Bert's steady influence. Madison knew she had no business noticing how dark and warm Brash deCordova's eyes were, how the seat between them zinged with tiny ripples of electricity, how he seemed to lean in toward her as he delivered his compliment. She had no right to be attracted to him; not because she was newly widowed, but because he was a married man.

Genny could not have arrived at a better time. Smiling up at her friend, Madison shifted away ever so slightly and said in a bright voice, "Looks like your cookies are here!"

13

The telephone woke Madison from a dead sleep at three a.m. Groping around on her nightstand, she found her cell phone and checked the number. Gleason Poultry Farm. Surely, the chickens could do without food for a few hours.

She hit the *Accept* button and pressed *1* to listen to the automated message. She hoped her sleep-fogged mind would remember which house called when she woke up in three hours.

Instead of hearing the usual message of "auger overtime", she heard the dreaded words Eddie Menger warned her about. "Alert. House 3 has one alarm. Message one, high pressure."

Visions of killing an entire house of chickens swam in her head. Madison jerked upright, forgetting not to disturb Bethani. The teen mumbled a protest but turned over in their shared bed and went immediately back to sleep.

Remembering a horror story Eddie told her about a grower ignoring a high pressure alarm and killing twenty thousand birds, Madison did not take time to dress. It would take fifteen minutes to drive out to the farm as it was. Stuffing her feet into a pair of Bethani's cowboy boots —her daughter liked the style, not the life— and pulling a jacket over flannel sleep pants and a threadbare favorite tee, Madison bypassed her son's room as she rushed down the hall. Unless she waved food under his nose, it took far too long to rouse her son from sleep. She would have to make this trip solo.

She rushed out into the night and into the cold, wet patter of light rain. Ugh. *Of all nights for a high pressure alarm!*

Despite the slick roads and limited sight of view, she made it to the Gleason Farm in record time. There were no other cars on the roads slowing her down, and for once she did not worry about speed zones. This was a life or death situation, after all, even if it was not human lives at stake.

She reset the alarm and checked for its probable cause. Following the instructions Eddie had given her as best remembered, she wondered if she should call him. *No, you've got this,* she told herself, as she watched the numbers slowly back down on the computer screen. She waited five minutes to see if the alarm would cycle again, then gave it another ten minutes for good measure.

When she was finally satisfied that the chickens were not in danger, she crawled back into the dry, warm comfort of her car. It was not only cold and wet outside, it was pitch black. Cloud cover kept even the moon from illuminating the dark night around her.

She told herself there was nothing to be afraid of, but her foot was heavy on the gas pedal as she pulled out of the farm and onto the blacktopped county road. If she hurried, she could beat the 3:42 train that ran like clockwork between the cities and potentially separated her from her nice warm bed.

The rain was picking up, making the black road glisten beneath the beam of her car lights. She turned the wipers to a higher speed as she approached a hidden driveway on the left. *The county —or was it the city?— should do something about those overgrown bushes*, she thought. It created a blind spot.

From behind the tangle of evergreen, a truck suddenly darted out. Bright lights flashed on, shining directly into her face as the vehicle headed straight for her. Bracing for impact, Madison knew she was about to be T-boned by the old model truck. She jabbed her foot onto the gas anyway, praying it would be enough to spur her forward and out of its path.

It all happened in a split second. The SUV surged ahead with the influx of fuel. The rusty old truck —was it red, or was that just the glow of taillights?— missed her by inches, and sailed across the pavement and onto the soft dirt of the road's shoulder. Beneath her, the SUV's tires skipped across wet asphalt and began to hydroplane. All thoughts of stopping to help the other vehicle vanished as Madison fought to control her own. The last thing she could afford right now was a new car! Not even an insurance deductible was in her budget, and certainly not an increased policy payment.

As the random thoughts flitted through her mind, Madison regained control of her vehicle. Luckily, she was still headed in the right direction. With a glance into the rear view mirror and a muttered apology to the other driver for not going back to help, she gathered her senses about her and pushed gingerly on the gas pedal, propelling herself forward at a much slower pace.

No longer caring about being caught at the train, Madison continued into town at a moderate pace. The near miss caused her hands to tremble on the steering wheel. The crossing arms were coming down just as she pulled up to the crossing. Not willing to risk another close call by darting around the barricade, she chose to come to a complete stop and wait out the train. Cranking up the heater, she rested her head against the back of the seat and took deep, calming breaths.

When the truck rammed her from behind, she was totally unprepared for the blow. Her head snapped forward and she heard the screech of wood along the hood of her SUV as her vehicle scraped beneath it. Her foot slipped off the brake pedal, even while the force of the other vehicle pushed her closer to the moving train. Madison quickly found the pedal and stomped on it with all her might.

Relief washed through her when the SUV came to a skidding stop. She was sideways in the road and much too close to the train for comfort, but she was no longer moving. Had the other driver lost control on the wet streets and hit her by accident? And where was the other vehicle, anyway?

Madison glanced around to locate the other driver as she fished her cell phone from her jacket pocket. She had just dialed 9-1-1 and pushed "send" when she saw the truck again.

It was a familiar old red truck, now sporting obvious damage to its front fender. Incredulously, Madison watched as the truck backed up and started forward again, aiming directly for her. By the dim beam of the streetlights, she got a glimpse of the person in the driver's seat. All she could see was the evil and iconic "Scream" mask, glowing an eerie white in the dark, rainy night. Madison screamed as the truck made contact with her rear fender wheel.

She tried to push on the gas and move out of the way, but her tires locked up. Above the shriek of metal-on-metal and the steady clank of the train, Madison was still able to hear the 9-1-1 operator repeating her request. "Ma'am! What's your emergency, ma'am?"

"The Naomi side of the train tracks!" Madison screamed into the cab of her vehicle, unsure of where her phone had landed. "Hurry!"

Another hit from behind, and she was surged helplessly forward again. Madison felt for the door handle, wondering what option offered the best odds —staying in her car or jumping free— when she saw the caboose sail by, mere inches from her face. At least now, she only had the murderous driver to worry about. The thought should have been more comforting than it was.

Madison braced herself when she saw the pickup retreat once more. "Not again!" she wailed, preparing for impact. The rain was coming down harder, making it difficult to see the truck behind her, but she tracked its whereabouts by the glow of the head light. Apparently one light had been rendered useless in the crash, but the other was backing slowly away from her. Did she have time to work her seatbelt free and jump out of her SUV? Would she be more vulnerable on foot?

Deciding to risk it, Madison pushed against her door. Nothing happened. She frantically tried to get the door open, but the heavy portal refused to budge. Not even the electric windows worked. Preparing for another clash was her only choice. Squeezing her eyes shut, Madison crossed her arms in front of her face for protection.

Seconds ticked by and nothing happened. Was the truck trying to get a longer head start to build greater momentum and do more harm? Another few long seconds, and still nothing. Madison opened one eye and peeked into the rear view mirror. All she saw was rain. She twisted around in her seat and finally caught the glow of taillights, sailing off in the direction in which they came.

The police arrived from the other direction. The red and blue strobe lights were distorted through her windshield. Despite rivulets of rain and the spider web of cracks etched across her SUV's front window, she could make out the police cruiser, even before she heard the wail of their siren.

Madison groped around on the floorboard for her phone. "The police are here now," she breathed into it before shutting it off with a shaky finger. She stuffed the phone back into her pocket as she saw Brash running toward her.

He jerked on the door but found it jammed.

"It's stuck!" On either side of the glass, they both yelled the words at the same time.

"Are you okay?" he yelled. He stuck his face against the glass, looking into the vehicle to see for himself.

"Yes!" She nodded. "I'm okay! Go after them! They went that way!" She frantically pointed back toward Naomi.

"I'm going to get you out of here."

Brash tried all four doors, only to find that none of them worked. As he surmised that the electrical system was fried, the Fire Department arrived on scene. Cutter Montgomery jumped from the cab of his truck, already wielding an ax. Soon another truck with two occupants arrived, and with the help of the Jaws of Life, they peeled away layers of her vehicle door until she was free.

So much for going easy on my insurance, Madison thought, as Cutter and another man slid her from the wreckage of her SUV. She felt her pajama leg snag on a curled piece of metal and an immediate warm sensation against her skin, but a little blood was the least of her worries. She just wanted free of the ruined automobile.

"Are you sure you're all right?" Cutter asked as he handed her off to Brash.

"Y-Yes." Her lips were quivering from equal doses of fear, cold, and shock. Brash draped a rain slicker around her shoulders and offered the support of his arm at her waist. "Can you walk? We need to get you out of the rain."

With his help, she made it to the front seat of his cruiser. When he reassured her that the ambulance was on its way, she adamantly shook her head. "No. I don't need an ambulance. I'm fine."

"You need to be checked out, Maddy," he said in a gruff voice.

"I need to get warm. And dry."

The compromise was to have the ambulance meet them at the police station, which was across the tracks and visible from where they sat. The roof of the old depot featured a deep overhang, offering shelter from the pouring rain as the paramedics examined Madison. Other than a few scrapes and scratches, the worst being on her leg, the medics declared her remarkably lucky and accepted her refusal of transport to the nearest hospital. Helping her into the police station, they wrapped her in thermal blankets and left, instructing her to seek medical attention if she became disoriented or experienced blurred vision.

"I don't know what all the fuss is about," she complained when they had gone. "I kept telling them, I didn't hit my head. The worst cut came when they were pulling me out of the car."

"It never hurts to be vigilant. Here, hold this; it will warm your hands up. And drinking it will help, too." Brash put a steaming mug of coffee into her hands.

After a few cautious sips, Madison sighed and sank back against the cushions of the small couch where she sat. "I am going to be sore, that's for sure," she predicted.

"What were you doing out at this time in the morning? And in this rain? In your pajamas, no less!"

Later, Madison would be terribly embarrassed about the fact that she wore a thin, threadbare t-shirt. She would realize that when wet, the material became almost translucent, revealing the fact that she wore no bra. But at that moment, she was not concerned with her wardrobe. All she cared about was soaking up the glorious warmth of the blanket and the beverage.

She took another sip before answering, "There was a high pressure alarm at the farm."

"Why didn't you take your son with you?"

"No time. Plus I guess I was panicking a little, thinking about how I could kill all those chickens if I didn't hurry."

"So tell me what happened. Start from the beginning."

She had already told the story in fragments, most often in response to a question asked. This time she told it in full sequence, one cohesive story with as much detail as she could recall. Brash let her finish completely before he began asking questions.

"What kind of truck did you say it was?"

"It was old and rusty, with sort of a rounded hood. I'm pretty sure it was red."

"What model was it?"

"That's my son's department, not mine." She offered a wry smile, thinking of how Blake was already dreaming of the truck he would one day have. He was already saving his money, hoping to have enough cash to buy some mode of transportation by the time he got his driver's license in the fall.

"No idea whatsoever?" Brash prodded.

"It-It reminded me of that truck your cousin Billy Joe used to drive back in high school."

He nodded immediately. "'75 Ford."

She shrugged with indifference as he jotted down notes. He asked several more questions, until he asked the one she dreaded most. "Maddy, do you have any idea why someone would want to harm you? This was not a random act of carelessness. It can't even be blamed on wet roads, not when he backed up and rammed you a second time. Someone wanted to hurt you and hurt you bad. You say you have no idea *who* it was, but do you know *why*?"

She pursed her lips and blew out a long breath. After glancing into his eyes for only a moment, she avoided his gaze and admitted, "I may have some idea." He waited patiently for her to continue. "I have a new client. Lucy Ngyen hired me to try and exonerate her son for the murder of Ronny Gleason."

"What! You aren't a private investigator!" the chief of police exploded. "You have no business taking on a job like that!"

"I told Mrs. Ngyen I wasn't qualified, but she's desperate. She's afraid her son will go to prison."

"Not if he's innocent, he won't."

Madison gave her one of her famous motherly glares. "You know as well as I do, the prisons are full of wrongly accused suspects. The fact that he speaks poor English decreases his chance at getting a fair trial."

"Now wait just a minute! You don't know that!"

"It's nothing personal against you, Brash, or your profession. It's just a fact."

"And how exactly are you going to help Don Ngyen? What could you possibly discover that the police haven't already learned?"

Madison resented his superior attitude. With a haughty arch of one brow, she asked in a cool voice, "Did you know Ronny Gleason wasn't really going deep sea fishing this week? He had a flight booked for Vegas."

"How do you know that?" Brash demanded.

Satisfied she had taken him by surprise, Madison offered her own smug smile. "I have my sources. Did you also know he had been there five times last year?"

"That might explain how he payed off his debts," Brash muttered to himself. Aloud, he asked, "Did Ramona tell you all this?"

"No," Madison admitted. Her lips turned down with disapproval. "Actually, to be his wife, she didn't seem to know very much about her husband's comings and goings. Or his finances."

Could be a case of the pot calling the kettle black.

Granny Bert's words echoed in Madison's ear. She shook her head to dislodge the inopportune reminder.

"So how do you know all this, if his own wife doesn't?" Brash challenged.

She gave a nonchalant shrug. "I've made a few inquiries here and there."

Brash's face settled into hard lines. "Okay, this stops now. No more playing junior detective. This is what always happens; people watch those shows on TV and think they know enough to play detective. You are not qualified to be investigating this case, Madison."

"Why?" she shot back. "Because I am not some hot-shot football player? How exactly did being a football coach qualify you for the job of Chief of Police?"

"For your information, I minored in Criminal Justice. And I can assure you, I am a certified Law Enforcement Officer for the state of Texas. Leave the investigating to me, Maddy."

"But Lucy is desperate." *And so am I.*

This time his voice was slightly softer. "I understand that. And I'm still investigating the case, even though we have her son in custody."

"But I have to do my part, too. I've already taken the job." She made no mention of the money she had taken. And already spent.

"If it makes you feel better, you can tell Mrs. Nguyen I will check into the information you've gathered. So there. You've done your job, Maddy, now let me do mine." Beneath the steel of his words, Madison detected the distinct hum of patronizing.

He obviously expected her to follow his request, so he was not concerned when she made no reply. Later, Madison would remember how smug and superior he sounded. Later, she would realize she must be onto something, to make someone try to kill her. But right now, she was exhausted.

"Do you think you could give me a ride home? I'm guessing my SUV is out of commission for a while."

"Good thing you have an uncle who owns a used car lot."

"I do?" she asked in surprise.

"Sure. Cessna Motors, over on Third."

She arched a dark brow. "In Naomi, I'm sure. Used car lots are probably too junky for Juliet," Madison correctly guessed.

"What can I say?" Brash grinned. "Miss Juliet was a snob of the first order, but she knew how to keep a town all neat and pretty."

Later, too, it would occur to Madison that Brash's grin was as charming as ever, and still had the power to make her heart skip a beat. For now, she could only think of going home and getting out of her cold, wet clothes. When she tried to stand, her knees gave way.

Brash swooped in to catch her. "I'm calling the ambulance back," he said, his face sharp with concern.

"Don't you dare. Just get me home to bed."

His grin was slow and rakish. "Thought you'd never ask," he drawled slowly, his eyes glinting mischievously. When she blushed in spite of herself, he laughed aloud. "How about we swing by Ngo's Donut Shop? Mina Ngo should have her first batch of donuts just about ready."

"It is that late already?" she murmured, tossing a glance at the clock on the wall. Before too long, the kids would be waking for school and it would be time to go back to the chicken houses.

Depressed by the mere prospect, Madison's steps were sluggish as Brash ushered her out the door.

14

"I resent the fact that you did not call me this morning and tell me yourself about the wreck."

Genesis gave an exaggerated sniff as she poured a cup of coffee for her best friend.

"What was I supposed to do, call you at four in the morning?"

"Yes! I had to hear it from someone else."

"Who? Who already knows about it?"

"By now, half the town. At least Cutter Montgomery thought to call and tell me about it first thing this morning. Do you have any idea how badly I would have panicked if I had driven into town this morning and seen your car, all banged up and still sitting there beside the railroad track? I'm so glad he thought to call me!"

"He's a real champ," Madison muttered with sarcasm. "I'm sorry I didn't call you immediately. But that's why I stopped by here on the way to work, so you could see for yourself that I'm fine."

Genesis eyed her with critical assessment. "You have a bruise on your left arm, scratches on your right hand, and you were limping when you came in. You have dark circles under your eyes and you look like you're in pain."

"I am, but it has nothing to do with the wreck, or at least not much. It has more to do with carrying all those chickens. The limp could be from my aching back or the cut I got when the firefighters pulled me out. All the other scrapes and bruises and aches and pains could be from last night or the last two weeks, it's hard to tell. And with all I've been going through these last few months, the dark circles are nothing new. I'm usually wearing makeup when you see me."

"Still, you should have called me."

"Yes, Mother." Madison used a properly chastised voice, followed by a flashed smile.

"Smart alec," Genesis muttered. She transferred her gaze to the parking area beyond the plate glass windows. "Why is Granny Bert's motor home parked outside?"

"That's my current mode of transportation. She had an appointment in Bryan today and needed her car."

"So you're driving a brand new motor home to work at the chicken houses?"

Madison shrugged. "It's not like I can call a cab. She made me promise I would change out of my dirty clothes before I got back in it, though, and spray it with Lysol when I got home."

"What are you going to do about a car?" Genesis's tone reflected Madison's own worry.

"I don't know. Blake, dear sweet soul that he is, suggested I go ahead and buy his car now, and he will graciously loan it to me until he gets his driver's license."

"That's thoughtful of him."

"Bethani suggested we move back to Dallas immediately, where there will be taxis and public transit. Which she has never ridden in in her life, I might add."

"Sounds like they are both full of helpful suggestions."

"They're full of something," Madison agreed. "Granny says I'm welcome to the Buick whenever she's not using it, which translates to roughly never. She's always running the roads somewhere."

"It's good for her, though. It keeps her young."

"That's true. I doubt I'll be half as spry when I reach that age." Rotating her head on her shoulders and hearing joints pop, she added, "If I live that long."

"We might could work out a schedule with my car. If you could catch a ride to the café, you could use it during the day until I got off," Genesis offered.

"I couldn't ask you to do that."

"You're not asking. I'm offering."

"Thank you, Genny. And not just for the offer of your car. For everything. If it hadn't been for you, I would have never kept my sanity these last few months."

"You've been there for me during all my rough spots. The least I can do is be here for you."

"The scales have become grossly imbalanced these past two years."

"Gray's fault, not yours," her friend was quick to point out.

Silence settled between them, until Madison broke it with a mischievous grin. "So who was the good looking guy I saw in here the other day, the one in the suit and crazy tie?"

At mention of the tie, Genesis laughed. "That would be Professor James Callaway. He teaches dual-credit Business courses at the high school."

"I saw the two of you talking. He looked interested."

Again Genesis laughed, but a slight blush crept across her heart shaped face. "And just how could you tell this?"

"Oh, the way his eyes lit up when you laughed. The way he leaned across the table when you refilled his glass. The way he watched you walk away."

"Don't go reading something into it. I don't have time for romance in my life right now. I'm much too busy, getting this place off the ground."

"Looks like it's off to a great start, though," Madison said, glancing around. Most of the booths and tables were full with breakfast customers. A small line stood at the bakery counter.

"Oops, and it looks like Toni needs some help at the register." Genesis pushed herself to her feet. "Break's over. Duty calls."

Madison sighed. "Mine, too. But at least I'm now down to four days."

Brash would never admit it aloud, but Madison Reynolds might just be on to something.

Somehow, she had discovered pieces of information that he had not picked up on. He chided himself for not already checking out the dead man's claims of a fishing trip, but frankly, until now, he had no reason to doubt the story. What else was he missing?

It was rather obvious by now that Ronny Gleason had a gambling problem. Five trips to Vegas in a single year confirmed it. Why else would a man go so often? The buffets and floorshows weren't that good. Hell, it hadn't taken Frank

Thompson but two trips out there to convince the dancer known as Glitter to ditch the stage and return to Texas with him. And if the trips to Vegas and the telltale financial problems didn't prove his weakness for gambling, his involvement with cockfighting did.

Proving his involvement, however, was harder to do. No one would say a word about the gaming operation. Fred Gleason had given him a half dozen names of men who were at Bernie Havlicek's the night of the fight, but every one of them insisted they had done nothing more than drink and play cards. The fight, they said, was over which man raised better birds for Barbour Foods.

The fact that someone tried to harm Madison Reynolds proved that she was making someone very nervous with all her questions. Being new in town —or newly returned, he supposed was more accurate— it was unlikely she had any enemies. On the off chance some sort of trouble had followed her from Dallas, Brash put out a few feelers and asked Vina to do some digging into her past. Not expecting to find much, he concentrated on finding the red truck that had ran into her, but that too, was proving fruitless.

With few leads to go on, Brash reluctantly did what he should have done days ago. Like it or not, it was time to pay Ramona Gleason another visit.

༄

The woman seemed to have some sixth sense about any male getting within a hundred feet of her. Before Brash even stopped the cruiser in her driveway, she was standing in the front door, posing provocatively in a bathrobe.

"Why, Chief deCordova, to what do I owe this pleasure?" she asked in a sugary voice.

"I have a few questions I'd like to ask you, Mrs. Gleason." He used his most formal voice, hoping to set the tone for the professional visit.

"Of course, of course. Come right in," she encouraged. She leaned over to push the door open wider, stooping just enough to offer a deliberate glimpse down her robe. She was totally naked beneath the plush red cloth.

"Uh- uhm- we could – we could discuss this out here." Brash knew he was stammering like a randy teenager at his first peep show, but the woman's audacity took him completely by surprise.

"Why, I'm not even dressed!" Ramona slid a long leg out from beneath the robe, as if he might not have noticed until now. "And it's cold out there. Come on in, where we'll be nice and cozy."

Step into my parlor, said the spider to the fly. The old phrase played in Brash's mind as he cautiously walked through the door.

Ramona motioned for him to take a seat on the sofa, but he deliberately chose a chair. With an amused smirk, she seated herself directly across from him. The robe was tied only by a sash at the waist. She crossed her leg without worry of how far the material fell away.

The memory of another long leg, one marred by the angry curl of jagged metal, crossed Brash's mind. What would Ramona say if she knew he much preferred Maddy's flannel sleep pants and thin tee to her own seductive garb?

"Mrs. Gleason, I need to ask you some questions about your late husband."

The sigh that slipped out was just short of resigned. "Yes, very well. What would you like to know?"

"Why had Ronny hired someone to work in the houses for him?"

"He was going on another one of those silly fishing trip."

"He had gone before?"

"Yes, at least three or four times, just last year."

Brash took out his notepad and started jotting down notes. "Did you ever go along?"

She gave him an incredulous look. "Do you have any idea what the salt air does to skin as delicate as mine? Of course I didn't go."

"Do you know who he went with?"

Ramona waved five long nails in the air, painted almost the same shade as the robe that steadily slipped from her shoulder. "One of his friends. Paul or Pete or Pedro, something like that."

"Mrs. Gleason, would you mind if I took a look at Ronny's cell phone again?"

"You can take the thing with you, if you like. We'll get it later. It's in the bedroom."

Brash cleared his throat, as if willing the seductive tone out of her last words. He wasn't about to step foot in that woman's bedroom, not even for a signed confession from Ronny's real killer; that room was probably home to countless of scandalous confessions-needing-made.

"You know, one thing strikes me as odd. Most growers I know stay close to the farm at the end of the flock, saying too many things can go wrong. Didn't you find it odd that he was leaving for a week, just a couple of weeks before your sell date?"

"I don't keep up with all the little details of the chickens."

"Hmm. So what about Las Vegas? Did Ronny ever go out there?"

"We went last year, around our anniversary. We stayed in this fabulous suite, bigger than most houses in Naomi! There was even a baby grand piano and four fireplaces in it."

"That must have cost a pretty penny."

"Do you remember the piano scene from Pretty Woman?" Ramona asked out of nowhere. When the policeman answered in the affirmative, the bleached blond gave him a heavy-lidded look and purred throatily, "Ronny assured me it was worth every penny." As she re-crossed her legs, he knew for a fact that blond was not her natural hair color.

"So you're –uh- saying –uh- that Ronny only went to Vegas once last year?" It was difficult to concentrate, but Brash did the best he could.

"That's right."

"But he –uh- went fishing several times."

"That is correct," she cooed, taking victory in the tiny beads of sweat that dotted the Chief's forehead.

"I'd like to ask you some questions about your finances, Mrs. Gleason."

"Please, call me Ramona."

"Did you and your husband have any financial problems, ma'am?" It took him a while, but Brash got back to business. It helped that he kept his eyes firmly glued to his little notebook. "From what I understand, growers get paid four times a year, is that correct? That must be tough, making ends stretch that far."

"I wouldn't know. I have my own account and monthly budget. Ronny took care of all the bills and paperwork." From the sound of her voice, Brash guessed she was offering a brilliant smile, but he didn't dare look up. "I just spend the money."

"Would it be possible for me to take a look at his bank statements?"

"Why?" Her voice no longer sounded flirty. It sounded sharp.

"I heard Ronny didn't always pay his bills in a timely manner. I heard he was particularly lax on making payments on his tractor and several sets of new tires. But that last fall he suddenly paid off most of his debts."

"Again, I wouldn't know."

"That would be around the time you bought your new Tahoe. Do you happen to know if he financed your vehicle, or if he paid for it out right?"

"He wrote a check."

"So do you know how he suddenly came into so much money?"

"Not a clue." Her answers were short and acute.

"Did your husband have any life insurance policies that you know of?" This time, he looked up from his notebook.

Ramona Gleason sat up straighter on the sofa, for once not posing for the best angle. "Exactly what are you implying, Chief?"

"I'm not implying a thing. I'm asking if your husband had life insurance policies."

"Yes, of course he did. We both have policies. It was a requirement from our bank when we bought the farm, in fact."

It was time to do a little fishing. "I hear that a lot of the growers like to get together and attend cockfights. Do you know if Ronny ever went to any of them?"

171

The widow shrugged nonchalantly. "He was always disappearing to something. I don't know if it was cockfights or card games, but he was gone at least two or three nights a week."

"You never asked him?"

"We had an agreement. He didn't ask me where I went or how I spent my allowance, I didn't ask him where he went or how he spent the rest of the money."

"Do you remember ever hearing your husband mention the name Clyde Underwood?" Clyde was a small-time bookie, known for running bets in the area.

"Not that I recall."

"The Merriman brothers?" They played for slightly larger stakes.

"No."

"What about Tom Haskell?"

"There was a Tom or Tim that called here sometimes. As I recall, he was a rather rude man."

"I would imagine so." Tom Haskell was currently a resident at the Huntsville State Prison, yet he still managed to run a profitable gambling ring from behind bars. Brash had heard his name whispered in connection with cockfighting, but there was no real proof that he was involved. Of course, there was also no real proof of the cock-fighting ring itself. But if Brash was a betting man, he thought the odds were pointing in favor of its existence.

"Would you mind getting me that cell phone, Mrs. Gleason? Then I can be on my way and let you get back to doing whatever you were doing."

Ramona got slowly to her feet, bending just deep enough to give him another free shot. With swaying hips, she sauntered across the room. In spite of himself, Brash watched the fascinating swish of red plush fabric. When she reached the doorway, she stopped and turned back toward him. The robe had miraculously come untied, hanging open just enough for a full-body peek. "Like I said, it's in the bedroom."

The light that came into Brash's dark eyes was not the one she had expected. The harsh glint reflected in his voice as he said evenly, "I'll wait here while you get it, Mrs. Gleason." He deliberately looked back down at his notebook, but not before he saw the fury that hardened her face.

With a huff, she flounced around and stomped noisily down the hall. When she returned a few minutes later with the phone, her robe was cinched tightly around her waist.

"Thank you, Mrs. Gleason. We'll get this back to you as quickly as possible."

"I have no need for it."

Brash paused when he got to the front door. "I have just one more question for you. Do you know why anyone would want to kill Ronny?"

"I have no idea what went on inside that foreigner's head."

"I assume you mean Don Ngyen?"

"Of course. That's who killed him, wasn't it?"

"There was enough evidence for an arrest. But can you think of anyone else? Or what reason Mr. Ngyen might have had for wanting your husband dead?"

"The Ngyens wanted to buy our farm, even though we told them it wasn't for sale. Maybe it was retaliation. Maybe Don Ngyen was a sore loser."

"Maybe," the Chief agreed. But his tone said he was skeptical.

15

Dean Lewis finally called In a Pinch Temp Services for help. He confirmed that his wife knew nothing of the call, but that he was desperate; he needed someone to work in his insurance office for at least three days and there was no one else to ask.

Driving her grandmother's borrowed Buick, Madison stopped by the office the next afternoon and got a quick intro to the job. With contract and retainer check in hand, Madison sailed off to the school campus with lighter spirits. As she waited in line to pick up the twins, she made plans on how to best spend the money.

Nothing as fun as new clothes or something for the house, but it would cover the cell phones for another month. And there might even be enough to get her hair cut. Madison ran her fingers through the grown-out ends, trying to remember the last time she had it trimmed. Before Gray died, certainly. There had been no money for it since then, especially at her favorite Highland Park salon.

The front door of the car jerked open, interrupting Madison's pity party. "Hey, Mom, my friend Megan wants to know if I can come over and spend the night." Madison was as surprised by the term 'my friend' as she was by her daughter's sudden appearance.

"I don't think I've ever heard you mention a Megan," Madison said with a slight frown. "Who are her parents? Does she come from a good family?"

Right or wrong, in all small Southern towns a person was judged by his or her family. Coming from a 'good' family made all the difference, even if the person in question was, in fact, questionable.

Bethani rolled her eyes. "Megan deCordova. Her Dad's the Chief of Police. Surely that meets with even your standards."

Bethani wanted to spend the night with Brash's daughter? Even as she absorbed the unexpected news, Bethani was saying, "Here comes her Mom now. I told her you would want to talk to her before you would let me come."

"Wait Beth, I –"

Whatever protests she would have made were drowned by a sudden squeal. "Maddy! Maddy Cessna, is that really you?"

Madison swung around in the driver's seat and saw the woman and daughter duo approaching. The girl was a beauty, with long, straight locks the same dark russet shade as her father's. She was dressed in jeans, turquoise cowboy boots, and plenty of bling. A pair of trendy glasses perched on her upturned nose, a trait she obviously took from her mother.

Beside her, looking even more beautiful than Madison remembered, was Shannon Wynn.

Brash married Shannon? her mind screamed. When had that happened? She vaguely recalled Genny saying he had come home from the pros to marry his pregnant girlfriend. *Shannon Wynn got pregnant with Brash's baby?*

Apparently so, her mind reasoned, as her eyes bounced back and forth between the two. Except for the hair, the teenager had most of her mother's attributes, right down to the cute little nose. That nose had been just one of the many reasons Madison had never liked the black-haired beauty; everything about Shannon Wynn had been perfect. Perfect hair, perfect height, perfect nose, perfect smile. Beside her, Madison always felt like a gawky giant, all arms and legs and nose.

Even now, Madison glanced down at herself inside the car, thankful for the camouflage. There was nothing wrong with the dark slacks and sensible shoes she wore, nor with the simple long sleeved blue top. But the outfit could have as easily come from her grandmother's closet as it had hers.

Close to forty, Shannon deCordova looked as trendy and chic as the teenager beside her. Still slim but curvy, she wore a simple cranberry sweater over a pair of rhinestone-studded jeans that looked similar to her daughter's. Her boots were wool-lined leather and matched the sleeveless vest she wore. Both bore a designer label.

Perfect size, perfect look. Perfect daughter, perfect husband. Perfect life. Madison struggled not to roll her eyes. Perfect, perfect, perfect.

Reluctantly rolling down the window of the borrowed car —and realizing the long, over-sized vehicle did nothing to boost her ego— Madison managed to smile and sound at least somewhat enthusiastic.

"Shannon, hi!"

"I couldn't believe it when I heard you moved back here!" the black-haired woman said. A gust of wind whipped the dark locks across her face. As she used both hands to push the hair away, Madison noticed several rings flash in the sunlight. Though some of them were trendy pieces of costume jewelry, at least three had the sparkle of real diamonds. Without aid of a mirror, she expertly patted her hair back into place. Perfect once again. "I hear you're staying at Miss Bert's?"

"Well, yes, until we can get more settled."

"Oh, I think that's wonderful. At times like these, you need the love and support of your family and friends." Madison looked for sarcasm in the woman's words, but they seemed completely sincere. Shannon was still going on, not a touch of ridicule in her tone. "What's that silly saying about not being able to go home again? Whoever made that up must not have come from a real home to begin with. And Miss Bert is the perfect antidote to anything that ails you!"

"She is something, all right," Madison said with a smile.

"Brash told me you had an accident the other night. I hope you're all right?" Again, the concern in her voice sounded real.

"A little shook up, but I'm fine. Unfortunately, my car didn't survive. I just got word that the insurance company totaled it."

"That's terrible. But I hear that's sometimes for the best, when a settlement is concerned." She looked over at her daughter, who was waiting anxiously for the conversation to change. "This is my daughter Megan. She's invited Bethani to spend the night, and I just wanted to come over and make sure you were on board."

"Hi, Megan."

"Hello, Mrs. Reynolds. It's nice to finally meet you, after hearing about you all these years."

Madison shot a glance at Shannon, expecting to see worry on the other woman's face. No telling what stories she had told the girl, all of them painting Madison as the evil witch. She had been an outsider, after all, not transferring to The Sisters until her freshman year, but it was enough to qualify her for Valedictorian when they graduated. After a bitter fight over whether or not elective courses should count toward the grade point average —Madison took challenging courses like Advanced Trigonometry and Human Psychology, while Shannon took Photography and Drama— Shannon won the title by a small margin. Grades, however, had hardly been the only spot of contention between the two of them. Madison had to wonder how the other woman had portrayed their rivalry.

Instead of dread, Madison saw a smile spread over Shannon's face as her daughter continued. "I know all about the little circle of love floating around The Sisters High." She used a singsong voice to relay the tale. "Maddy Cessna had a mad crush on Brash deCordova. Brash deCordova had a mad crush on Shannon Wynn. But Shannon Wynn only had eyes for Matthew Aikman, who, alas, could see no one but Maddy Cessna. And so the circle went, round and round, until they all fell off."

The girl was so dramatic that Madison found herself laughing, right alongside Shannon. "I don't think I even remember your mom liking Matthew. But at least in the end, she got her man," she said.

"Yes I did," Shannon beamed boldly.

As ridiculous as it seemed, the knowledge somehow stung, even after all these years.

Ridiculous, because twenty years had passed and she had not seen any of the members of that circle since. By the time Brash went off to college and came home for occasional weekend and summer visits, she was dating Matthew. Then Matthew was graduating, and they discovered a long-distance relationship was just too difficult. A year later, she went off to college and met Grayson, and her life gravitated away from The Sisters. She kept up with a few of her old classmates, but Shannon Wynn was not one of them.

"So can I go, Mom? Please?" Bethani came around to stand by her newly made friend. Together, they made pathetic faces, complete with begging noises.

Madison laughed at their antics and gave in. She was thrilled that Bethani had made a friend, even if she was less enthusiastic about the girl's parents. "Oh, all right. But you'd better behave yourself and mind your manners."

"Of course! You're the best, Mom!" Bethani stooped down to brush a kiss on her mother's cheek. "We're going by Aunt Genny's for snacks, then we'll swing by and get my clothes."

"Are you sure this is okay with you?" Madison asked, glancing at Shannon.

"Of course. We'll be delighted to have her." Shannon's smile looked genuine enough, so Madison gave her blessing and bid them goodbye, just as her phone binged with a message from Blake.

Don't forget, practice this afternoon, then bowling with the guys. Be home by curfew. LYB.

A smile touched her lips. Even at fifteen, he never failed to include their family's trademark 'Love you bunches'. It was a phrase that Gray started when the twins were little. The sentiment was something the kids had never out-grown; too bad their father had.

With a sigh, Madison watched her daughter walk away with her new friend and her perfect mother. No doubt tomorrow Bethani would be singing the other woman's praises, relaying all the details of her perfect home and her perfect life.

"With Brash." Madison said the words aloud, just to remind herself that Brash deCordova was a married man. For good measure, she threw a little self-righteous anger into her voice. He had no business making her heart pitter-patter the way he did. He had actually flirted with her! Here he had the perfect wife waiting at home for him and a daughter as cute as a button, yet he had flirted with her. Her! With her mousy hair and her lanky form and her age-neutral wardrobe.

A glance into the mirror confirmed her worst accusations. Her hair looked rangier now, more grown-out than it had before her reunion with Shannon. After seeing her old rival, the reflection in her mirror was disheartening.

You have a little extra money, a playful voice whispered in her head. *And an afternoon without kids.*

Pulling out of the school parking lot, the Buick lumbered its way to Talk of the Town.

"I don't care," Madison told the beautician. "I want something new, something completely different."

"Do you want to keep the length?"

Gray always insisted she keep her hair at least shoulder length, preferably longer. "It doesn't matter," she said for the first time in eighteen years. "Surprise me."

With a gleeful smile that should have made her client nervous, the young stylist set to work. Madison saw lock after lock of dark hair fall to the floor, but she refused to feel panic. With all the other changes in her life, why not change her look, as well? At least this change was of her own making.

As Madison closed her eyes and drew in deep, relaxing breaths, bits and pieces of conversation floated her way. Her ears perked up, even as she pretended nonchalance.

"I'm telling you, that new Ngyen boy did it. My Harold saw the fight they had, just a few nights before. Said that new Ngyen kept yelling 'I kill you!'."

"But why would he want to kill poor Ronny?" asked Deanna Gleason as she styled the other woman's hair.

"Money, pure and simple. Ronny bought something from the new Ngyens and never paid them for it. Apparently he turned around and made a small fortune on whatever it was, and the new Ngyen boy wanted his share of the profit."

"What was it?" Deanna asked in hushed wonder.

Madison could not hear the woman's shrug, but she imagined it in her mind. "Beats me," the woman said.

"I know for a little while Ronny seemed to have money to spare. He bought Ramona that fancy SUV and sent her off for another one of her 'spa' treatments. But about a week before he died, he was out at the house asking Cal for a loan. We didn't have a penny to spare, not after new braces for little Calvin and all that new tack Trisha needed for Ranch Rodeo."

As the conversation drifted toward Deanna's daughter, Madison tuned out the conversation. She dared a peek into the mirror and gulped. There was much less hair than before.

"Don't worry, I'm not through yet," the stylist assured her. "You're going to look fabulous when I get done!"

"Fabulous may not be possible, but I'll settle for different."

"With your bone structure and long neck, this style is going to be perfect. Trust me."

A few more snips, and the stylist pulled out the blow dryer. As she worked with a round brush to style her hair, she gave Madison pointers on how to hold the brush and where to direct the blower's heat, but she turned Madison's back to the mirror as she finished. After stepping back and scrutinizing her work, the stylist made one more snip, trimmed the back of Madison's neck with a razor blade, and added a fine mist of hair spray. She had a triumphant smile on her face as she whirled the chair around and presented Madison with the image in the mirror.

The woman looking back at Madison was much too elegant to be her. The simple new bob hairstyle looked anything but simple. Short in the back and stacked to fall forward at a point just below her chin, the layers added softness to her angular face. Her neck looked long and elegant, her high cheekbones more finely chiseled. Her nose looked smaller and her eyes looked larger. Large and luminous. Without the split ends and sun damage, her hair looked darker and healthier.

Madison tugged on the pointed lock of hair at her chin, just to make certain it was her image she saw. "I-I can't believe it!" she breathed in awe. "I look so – so-" She broke off, at a loss for words.

The stylist was quick to offer a supply. "Gorgeous? Elegant? Sophisticated? You look all of that and more."

"D-Different. I look different."

"Don't you just love it?" the girl squealed happily.

Madison had to smile and be honest. "I do."

She left the stylist a generous tip. It would have been enough to treat herself to dinner out tonight, since she would be home alone. But she needed time to adjust to her new look, before she sported it in public.

And besides, the girl deserved the tip. She had worked magic, after all.

※

Madison came home to a quiet house. A note from Bethani said the teen had come and gone and was now off to her friend's house. Blake would be out until eleven, and there was no telling what time Granny Bert would be in. She was out with Miss Sybil and a couple of other friends, catching a movie and dinner in College Station. Which meant Madison had a nice, quiet evening of solitude.

She fixed herself a Lean Cuisine frozen dinner, the only way she could afford a chef-inspired meal these days. When she caught them on sale, it was cheaper to serve the frozen meals to her family than to buy ingredients for a full meal. Even serving Blake two portions, it only took a tossed salad and a loaf of crusty bread to turn the frozen entrees into an economical meal for four. If Granny insisted on one of her smoothies, the count was only three.

There was a nip in the air tonight, perfect for snuggling on the porch by the chiminea. Madison pulled a jacket on over her faithful tee shirt and flannel sleep pants, gathered a quilt and her e-reader, and went out to the porch with a bottle of wine. The light from her reader gave off just the right amount of light, without the harsh glare of the porch bulb.

She read a full chapter before she set the book aside and concentrated on her wine. Every so often, she would rake her fingers through the ends of her hair, unaccustomed to the short nap on her neck. Gray would hate this new style, making her love it all the more.

Thoughts of Gray made her heart ache. Only forty-one, he was taken far too early in life. His death left her with a hollow feeling inside. Though she no longer loved him as a wife should love her husband, some part of her still loved him. He was the father of her children, after all, and once upon a time their marriage had been good. When she pushed aside the anger and the betrayal, she still felt the heartache of his death.

The telephone rang, making her worry it might be an alarm. The last thing she wanted tonight was to go back out to the farm. But the caller I.D. showed an unknown caller. She picked up, hoping it was another job inquiry.

Silence greeted her on the other end of the line. When she repeated her greeting, a hoarse voice whispered, "Go home."

"I-I beg your pardon?"

"Go home. You don't belong here." With that, there was silence.

Frowning down at the phone in her hand, Madison tried to make sense of the call. Was it the same person who tried to run her off the road? But why? And who? Who wanted her to leave Juliet that badly?

Brash looked down at the file in his hand, debating what to do with it. The background check on Madison Cessna Reynolds had come back, making for some interesting reading.

He now had proof she was not some heart-broken widow, come home to heal her shattered heart. She had filed for divorce two years ago, then dropped the suit. Private sources confirmed the marriage had never been the same after that, merely a shell for the sake of the children. Grayson Reynolds owned his own investment company, but a series of problems —the sinking stock market, a series of bad investments, accusations of a Ponzi scheme— left the company in shambles, even before his death. After his death, Madison had all but lost what was left of their life in the city. She sold the house for a loss, managed to pay off debts with his paltry life insurance policy, and came home to Juliet, the only place she could afford. From what he could see, Madison Reynolds was broke.

Okay, so she was not a grieving widow. Propriety said he should still respect the traditional mourning period, if for no other reason than to keep tongues from wagging. The last thing Maddy needed was to have her name drug through the mud here in The Sisters. Looked like that had already happened in Dallas, he thought, judging from the other information he had discovered.

Pushing the file deep into the pile on his desk, Brash reached for the folder he kept on Ronny Gleason's death. All the details were there, but he felt like something was missing. What little information he had gathered pointed in the direction of Don Ngyen, but his gut told him the Vietnamese man was innocent.

Brash felt certain there was more to the gambling angle than what he knew. Rumor had it that organized crime was involved, but the ties were unclear. Some people insisted it was the Las Vegas mafia, one informant claimed it was Clyde Underwood trying to make a name for himself, still others insisted Tom Haskell was running the entire operation from the state pen. He was fairly certain Underwood would never resort to murder, but he could hardly say the same for the other two.

From what he understood, Ronny Gleason bought fighting roosters from both the Ngyens and Pedro Gonzales. It was unclear if he organized the cockfights himself or simply entered his roosters as contestants, but either way, he bet heavily on the outcome of each fight. On the Friday night before his death, he accused Don Ngyen of cheating, insisting the Vietnamese kept his best rooster for himself, to enter in the fight against Ronny's cocks.

Even though he wanted to think the young man was innocent, there was a lot of circumstantial evidence against him. If his part in the cockfighting ring was discovered, he would be in trouble with both the law and Barbour Foods. If Ronny Gleason threatened to reveal his involvement, the man might have felt murder was the only way to ensure his silence.

Rolling scenarios around in his head, Brash still could not make Don Ngyen fit the profile of a killer. He knew the County Sheriff was pushing to send the case to the DA; elections were coming up and he wanted the case settled and done. Which meant if he was going to come up with any other suspects, Brash had to do it soon.

He fingered the latest item added to the file, the photo of a burned out pick-up truck. No doubt it was the one that hit Maddy. He had it in the file because his gut told him that somehow the accident and Gleason's death were tied together. Somehow her innocent questions around town threatened someone enough to make them attempt murder, proving in his mind that the man sitting in the county jail was innocent.

Which left the murderer still running free, and with his sights set on Maddy.

Maddy, with her long hair and long lean body and long killer legs. The girl who once had a not-so-secret crush on him. The girl he wanted to date but never quite got around to asking out. The girl who later dated his friend. The girl who was no longer a girl, but a very beautiful, vulnerable woman. Maddy.

He thought about the day that he first saw her, when he thought the years had not been kind to her. What a fool he had been. Maddy was as beautiful and graceful as ever; more so, really. Her trim figure had matured, widening her hips just enough to make them irresistible. Some men preferred breasts, like the over-large pair Ramona Gleason flaunted in his face, but Brash had always been a sucker for full hips and rounded butts. Now that she had filled out a little, Maddy Cessna Reynolds was just about perfect.

Snapping the file shut, Brash grabbed his cowboy hat and headed for the door, before his mind could convince him it was a bad idea.

16

Madison tried to regain the feeling of serenity the call had interrupted. Even though the evening temperatures were dropping, the warmth from the chiminea and the wine kept her feeling toasty, inside and out. She wasn't going to cower beneath the threatening tone of the call, not when she wasn't ready to go in yet.

She saw the police cruiser pull up in front of the house. The overhead streetlights reflected in the colorful bar across its cab, casting a brief arc of red and blue as the car rolled to a stop alongside the curb. Maddy watched as Brash got out of the car, settled his cowboy hat atop his head, and ambled up to the porch. He had the swagger of a man sure of himself and his lot in life. Before she could stop herself, Madison admired that trait in him. Heavens knew she had no such assurance in her own life.

Brash bounded up the steps and stopped outside the front door. He did not see her there in the shadows. Madison watched as he positioned his hand to knock, then hesitated. After a long moment of silent debate, he pulled his big fist away. He turned to retrace his steps, his demeanor not quite so confident now.

The smoke from the chiminea wafted his way, hinting at her presence on the porch. He turned, and his eyes found hers in the darkness.

Something in Madison's mind warned this might not be the best idea. She was working on her second glass of wine, and she had never believed in the dainty portions they doled out at restaurants. And Brash had clearly come here for a reason, even if he had changed his mind before he knocked on her door.

"Hey," he said quietly.

"Hey."

He made no move to come toward her. She offered no invitation. After a terse moment of silence, she finally spoke. "You needed something, Chief?"

He seemed relieved to have a reason to be there. Her reference to his official title was the only catalyst he needed to wheel about and proceed into the shadows of the porch. By silent agreement, she moved the edge of the quilt and he took a seat beside her on the swing.

"I have news about the truck that rammed you the other night," he told her as he sat. He was grateful for the groan of metal chains and wooden slats, for it helped disguise the creak of popping joints.

"Oh?"

"We found a vehicle matching its description about fifteen miles out of town, out on County Road 497."

"Minus a license plate, I'm sure."

"And no VIN number. The cab had been set on fire, destroying any fingerprints or evidence we might could recover.

But there was front-end damage and silver paint along the bumper, the same color as your SUV."

"So now what?" Madison asked.

"The Sheriff's department is going around the general area, asking if anyone recognizes the vehicle. Maybe someone will come forward with information."

Madison tugged the quilt closer around her, suddenly chilled. "But it's doubtful."

"It's worth a try."

"I had a strange call just before you got here." She relayed the details to him.

Even though it was useless, he grabbed her phone and checked the caller identification. "And you're still sitting out here in the dark? You should be in there with your family."

"No one's home this evening."

"Then what are you doing out here all alone?" he chided.

The wine made her smile a bit more saucy than it should have been. "I'm not alone. You're here."

She saw him frown as he looked down at the phone and stubbornly punched redial. No one answered, just as they both expected. Madison finally took the phone from his hands and advised him to give up.

"Hey, your hair is different," he said, catching a better glimpse of it through the glow of her phone's screen.

"Yeah, I thought it was time to try something new." She ran timid fingers through the shortened length.

"It looks good." The phone's backlight timed out, enveloping them in darkness once again. Brash shifted on the swing, just enough to set its chains aflutter. The same flutter echoed in Madison's chest as he stretched his arm out along the seat behind her. "You look good, Maddy," he said, his voice as warm and inviting as the quilt that engulfed her.

"Thank you."

It was the stuff her high-school dreams were made of. Sitting alone in the dark with Brash deCordova, his arm practically around her, the spicy scent of his cologne filling her nose as the spicy pull of the man filled her senses.

He's married, a little voice whispered in her mind.

Madison tried to shift away, but for the life of her, she seemed to have melted, right there beside him on the porch swing.

His hand came out to toy with her hair. "I like it," he said. "You look stunning."

Stunning. Brash deCordova called her stunning. Madison knew she had no right to feel such pleasure at the compliments of a married man, but the words left her with a warm glow.

If she were being honest with herself, hadn't that been part of the reason she had gotten this impromptu haircut? Seeing Shannon again brought out all her old insecurities, the ones that somehow haunted every grown-up teenage girl to some degree. Madison told herself she was being ridiculous, that she was a mature woman, a widow and mother of two, with no time for the petty competition of her youth. And, really, what competition was there? Shannon had won. Shannon had married the man of Madison's foolish high school dreams.

Yet one glimpse of Shannon's perfect image and Madison knew she had to do something. The look in Brash's eyes that first day, when she had been covered in chicken poop and worse, still haunted her memory and made her ego smart. And if she were still being honest, it was the same way Gray's lack of interest these past two years still stung her pride. Gray quit complementing her long ago, perhaps when he quit noticing how she looked.

Her pleasure at Brash's words, she told herself, was less about vanity and more about validation.

So why, then, did her voice come out so husky when she whispered, "Thank you."

"Maddy." Brash breathed her name on an exhaled breath, as he moved closer in. His hand found the curve of her shoulder as he gently squeezed his fingers.

That second glass of wine was making her reflexes slow. Madison knew she should jerk away from his touch. And she would. Just as soon as she could make herself move.

Being kissed by Brash was something she dreamed of her entire freshman year. Even after he went away to college and she started dating Matthew, there was still a part of her that had a crush on the mighty football player. As the years passed, she had all but forgotten about the man, but it had only taken coming home to Juliet, sleeping in her old bed, seeing the same old familiar faces and places, to make her feel like that young girl again. Foolish dreams and all.

Madison moistened her lips nervously. This was the moment she had always dreamed of, the moment she still wanted to happen, even after all these years. All she had to do was lift her face. Lift her face and move in a fraction of an inch. Her dreams were within her reach.

But it could not happen. Would not happen. He was a married man.

"No, Brash," she mumbled. Gathering her wits about her at last, Madison pulled back and said more forcefully, "No! This is wrong!"

To his credit, he snapped his arm down to his side and his demeanor immediately changed. "I'm sorry, Maddy," he said with all sincerity. "I know your husband has only been gone for a few months. I meant no disrespect."

"This has nothing to do with me being newly widowed. I ran into Shannon today," Madison announced abruptly, watching how he reacted to the news. She expected chagrin, or at least surprise. His handsome face displayed neither. With a slight frown, she kept pushing, "Did you know my daughter is spending the night with your daughter?"

"Really? I've got the night shift, so I haven't talked to her today." Maddy was confused by the look of satisfaction that touched his face as he nodded with approval. "But that's good. I'm glad our girls like each other. And Bethani seems like a great kid." A smile slipped into his words. He leaned closer, bumping his arm gently against hers. "Just like her mother."

Madison jerked away. "Brash deCordova, how dare you!"

The lighting was dim, but she saw his brows draw together in confusion. "I don't understand. You said this wasn't about me rushing you."

"This isn't about *my* marital status, it's about yours!" she chastised him.

"Mine?"

"I can't believe you. I knew you were a 'player' in high school." She used her hands for air quotes. "But I would have hoped you had outgrown it, especially with your new position as Chief of Police. I would think you had developed some sense of propriety."

"What on earth are you talking about, Maddy?" he demanded, sounding as much irritated as he did confused.

"I am talking about your *wife*. How dare you sit here and try to kiss me, when my own daughter is at your house right this very minute, being entertained by your wife and daughter!"

"Who said I was trying to kiss you?" he snapped, stung by her very verbal rejection.

Madison knew it had been a while, but surely she hadn't misread the signs... touching her back, leaning toward her, getting that look in his eyes...

She shook away her own doubts and insecurities, focusing on her indignation. "Don't you have any shame?"

"What I don't have is a wife," he told her bluntly. "I don't know what kind of man you think I am, Maddy, but I am not a married one."

"But... But what about Shannon? And Megan?"

"Shannon is my ex-wife. We've been divorced since Megan was four."

"But...But..." She knew she was sputtering, but it was too much information to process. "But Megan said she knew all about me. She was talking about some circle... Shannon had a ring... and she said she got her man!"

"She did. Shannon and Matthew Aikman have been married for about eight years. They have a five-year-old son together."

"Shannon and... and Matthew?"

"Yeah, Shannon and Matthew. They're a great couple. They're perfect for one another."

"But he was one of your best friends."

"And he still is. I wouldn't want any other man helping to raise my daughter."

Still stunned, Madison murmured, "I-I don't know what to say."

"You could start with 'I'm sorry'." His face showed no sign on humor. He sounded genuinely offended as he muttered, "I can't believe you thought I would kiss you if I was a married man."

"I- I am sorry, Brash. Truly, I am. I just... you're living here again... and when I saw Shannon and your daughter, I just- I just assumed you were still married."

"We agreed to raise our daughter here, even if we weren't doing it as a married couple. I wanted to be near Megan, so I moved back the first chance I got. Now that we're not married, Shannon and I are really good friends and talk regularly."

"I guess that's how she knew about my wreck," Madison murmured.

"This is The Sisters. Everyone knows about your wreck."

Feeling like an idiot, Madison merely shook her head as she contemplated her own stupidity. Silence settled heavily between them.

"Well, I guess I'd better go," Brash said gruffly, starting to get up.

Madison put a hand on his arm to still him. "Don't go, Brash," she said softly. "I really am sorry."

"So am I." He stood and looked back down at her. "You don't think very highly of me, do you, Madison?" His voice sounded sad in the darkness.

"I don't think too highly of myself right now, either," she confessed. After all, she had wanted him to kiss her, even believing he was married.

"For what it's worth, I have changed, Madison. I'm not the arrogant jerk I was in high school."

Properly chastised by his rebuke, Madison made no comment as he walked toward the steps. She frowned at her own folly, rubbing the stubborn ache that lodged itself in her forehead.

"You should go in, Madison," he advised, turning back toward her. The easy camaraderie between them had vanished, right along with the old nickname he used to call her. His voice was stiff and formal now. "After that phone call, you shouldn't be out here alone."

Without being told again, Madison gathered her things. The pleasure had gone out of the evening anyway.

Like a true gentleman, he waited until she was inside. "Thank you for stopping by with the news," she said.

"The news?"

"Of the truck."

"Oh, yeah, sure." They both knew it had been a lame excuse to come see her. "Lock the door."

"I will. Goodnight, Brash."

"Goodnight, Madison."

She started to push the door shut, but stopped to say, "Brash? I really am sorry."

He nodded. "'Night, Maddy."

She closed the door with a smile. At least he had called her Maddy this time.

Madison went back to reading until Blake got home.

"Mom! What happened to your hair?" the teen asked the moment he stepped through the door.

She ran her hand over the short fringe along her neck. "I got it cut."

"It looks hot!" Blake grinned his approval. "Next thing I know, you'll be dating."

In spite of herself, thoughts of Brash floated through her mind. For her son's benefit, she laughed aloud and brushed the statement aside. "I don't see that happening any time in the next decade. There aren't a lot of single men running around the streets of Juliet. Or Naomi."

"There's more than you'd think. The assistant baseball coach is single. And so is my History teacher. Even Chief de-Cordova is single."

Now you tell me!

Blake dropped his ball bag in the chair and headed for the kitchen. As always, the teen was hungry. He emerged a few moments later, munching on an apple and holding a banana in his hand for reserve. "I could probably hook you up with Mr. Perez. He's pretty cool for an old dude."

"Carter Perez?"

"You know him?"

"That 'old guy' is two years older than me. And my cousin, by the way."

"You're shitting me."

"Blake Andrew Reynolds, you watch your mouth!"

"Sorry. But you're kidding, right?"

"No. He's like my third cousin or something. His grandfather was Granny Bert's oldest brother." She noticed the crest-fallen expression on her son's face. "What's wrong, babe?"

"I- uh- I've kind of been flirting with his daughter, Teryl. I had no idea she was kin to me."

"Well, she'd be like your fifth or sixth cousin. In a city it would never come up, but in Juliet, it might cause some gossip."

"I thought they always say hillbillies are inbred?"

Madison scrunched her nose at his comment. "Around here, everybody knows everybody else's entire family. You aren't simply Blake Reynolds. You're Blake Reynolds, Bertha Hamilton Cessna's great-grandson. And Teryl Perez is Clyde Hamilton's great-granddaughter. No matter how many 'greats' you throw in, people only hear the Hamilton connection."

"So that means I'm kin to the old dude that has the store?"

"Uncle Jubal Hamilton is Granny Bert's youngest brother."

"His grandson is on my baseball team. Which means his sister would be kin to me, too," Blake reasoned.

"That's the way it generally works," his mother said wryly.

"So their cousin Sara is kin to me, too."

"Uncle Jubal and Aunt Lerlene's granddaughter by their middle son," Madison confirmed.

"Tabitha Cessna?"

"Your . . . third cousin. Further complicated because her grandmother married Clyde Hamilton's son, so you're actually kin on both sides."

"You're killing me, Mom!" the teenager complained. "There's only so many girls in high school, you know. You just took out half my class."

"You're too young to be worrying about girls anyway. Concentrate on your baseball. And your studies."

"Yeah, but there's some big Valentine's Day Dance coming up, and all the kids are talking about it. I was thinking I'd ask Teryl, but I guess that idea is out the window," he said glumly.

"Sorry, kiddo. I can't help it if you come from a prolific family."

"I hear the Hamilton and Cessna families own like half of Juliet."

"Well, sort of," Madison admitted. "Miss Juliet, the town's namesake, didn't have any children of her own, so she sort of adopted Rose Hamilton's children. Rose was her cook at the big house."

"You mean that big old house on the corner, the one they say is haunted?"

"It's not haunted, just empty. And it actually belongs to Granny Bert now."

Blake looked around the craftsman style home. Though well maintained and large for its kind, the house was tiny compared to Miss Juliet's. "So why does she live here?"

"She says this is her home. She raised her four boys here and she and Grandpa were happy here."

"So why did that Juliet chic leave her house to Granny Bert?"

"Miss Juliet more or less named Granny Bert heiress of the town when she died."

"Granny Bert, an heiress?" Blake hooted.

"I know, it seems strange. The crazy thing is, Miss Juliet was all straight-laced and very prim and proper. Granny Bert is anything but. It always struck me odd that she left her legacy to someone so different than she was."

"Maybe she knew if the town was going to survive, it needed new leadership."

Madison beamed at her son's intuitive observation. "That's pretty insightful, Blake."

The fifteen-year-old tossed the apple core into the trashcan and started peeling the banana. His mind was already back on the dance. "What about Chasity McCauley? Is she kin to me?"

"Even closer than Teryl. Her mother Hallie is my first cousin."

"Oh, well, she's kind of stuck-up anyway. What about Addison Bishop, Harley Irwin or Danni Jo Combs?"

"I think you're good."

"Finally!" He threw up his arms in triumph. "Someone whose grandma isn't my grandma's fourth cousin!"

"It's not quite *that* bad," his mother chided with a frown.

"So one more thing, Mom. If I go to all the trouble of finding a girl who actually isn't related to me and I ask her to the dance, will we even still be here then? Or will we already be back in Dallas?"

Madison was slow in answering. She ran a nervous hand through her hair, momentarily sidetracked by the much shorter ends. "How do you feel about living here, Blake?" she asked instead.

"It's alright," the teen shrugged. "Back home, I'd never have a shot at playing varsity. Coach says I'll even get to start some games. The classes are about the same, maybe even a little tougher here. Aside from this new problem of being related to half the girls in town, I guess it's not so bad."

"I know I uprooted us and brought us here to live, promising we'd go back to Dallas as soon as possible. But the thing is, that might be a while," she admitted nervously. Better to break the news to Blake first, then his sister. "How would you feel about that?"

"Most of the kids here are pretty cool. And Granny Bert says she can get me a job this summer, so I can start saving up for my car."

"Then you'd be okay with staying here for at least a year or so, you think?" Heavens knew it would take that long, probably longer, to save enough money to even visit Dallas, much less move back there.

"I'll probably have a better chance of getting a baseball scholarship through a small school, anyway. Coach says I have real potential. And on the plus side, I just realize I must be kin to Principal Hamilton, too, which is always a handy little thing to mention when I get a tardy slip."

"Blake, not another one! Why are you always late to class?"

"It wasn't me, I swear. Granny Bert took us to school the other morning and we had to stop to talk to some lady walking her dogs. She had like four of those big poodles. She and Granny Bert got in a long discussion about how they neither one can sleep at night. The poodle lady said the chickens had kept her up, squawking all hours of the night."

"You must be talking about Glitter Thompson. Big, puffy pinkish-blond hair and lots of makeup?"

"That's her."

Madison puckered her lips. "But there aren't any chicken houses around her."

"That's what she said. But she said her neighbors must have gotten a few, because they carried on half the night and the rest of the neighbors were yelling, making a huge racket."

The Thompson lived at the edge of town near an abandoned farmhouse. It occurred to Madison that the empty yard out back would be the perfect place to hold an illegal cockfight.

"Blake Reynolds, I will say it again. You, my son, are a genius!"

17

"I still think we are insane," Genesis said as she pulled away from the curb.

"Granny Bert would want to know why I was borrowing her car, two minutes after she pulled in the drive. And if I know her, she drove home from Bryan without getting gas."

"You know she likes to buy local whenever she can."

"But I can't very well go on a stake-out and run out of gas, now can I?"

"Tell me again why I agreed to drive you out to the old Muehler place?"

"Besides the fact that you're my best friend and you still owe me for that time I drove you all the way to Fort Hood to see that Bobby guy before he shipped out, only to find three other girls there, doing the same thing?"

"Besides that."

"I'm trying to earn the money Lucy Ngyen paid me so I can keep it with a clear conscience. If I can prove there was someone else with enough probable cause to want Ronny

Gleason dead, they might just drop the charges against Don Ngyen. They are circumstantial, at best."

"So where do we come in? And why are we dressed all in black?" A flourishing hand movement indicated her own stylish black velour sweat suit.

"So no one will see us in the dark." Madison looked into the mirror and stuffed a few loose strands of hair beneath the black toboggan she wore. She was already wearing the hat when Genesis arrived, so her friend had not seen the new hairstyle yet. "I brought you a toboggan, too, to cover your blond hair."

"Are we doing anything illegal?" Genny asked suspiciously.

Madison appreciated the fact that Genny was automatically agreeing to help, even before hearing the details. No wonder the other woman was her best friend in the entire world.

"Of course not! We're simply going for a late night walk."

"In the dark. In the cold night air. Down a dark lonesome road." Genesis recapped the situation in a speculative tone. "Granny Bert might have believed your story, but only because she had one too many margaritas and had to let Miss Sybille drive home. Madison Josephine Reynolds, what are you up to?"

Her easy-going friend only called her by her full name when she was angry or suspicious. Biting her lip with worry, Madison finally confessed all. "I think I may know where they're holding the illegal cockfights. Glitter Thompson told Granny Bert the noise from all the roosters and neighbors was keeping her awake at night, but she doesn't have many neighbors, and the few she has don't keep chickens. I think they're using the old Muehler place that backs up to the Thompson's."

"They?"

"I don't know, that's what we need to find out. I need to find out who else has a cow —my word, now she has me saying it!— a *beef* with Ronny Gleason."

"Fine, so call Brash. There's no reason for us to go out there."

"I want to be sure, before I call in a tip. If I call through Crime-Stoppers, I'll earn a cash reward if it leads to an arrest."

"You sound like those commercials," Genesis complained. "So what are we going to do, drive up and shine a spotlight out there?"

"Of course not! That's what the dark clothes are for. We'll have to park out of sight, walk up to the farmhouse, and slip around back."

"Madison, this sounds like something we used to do in high school. This does not sound like something two grown women do."

Madison found herself giggling. "I know, right?"

"How much wine did you drink tonight? This doesn't sound at all like you. May I remind you that for the past twenty years, you've lived in the city, in a refined neighborhood with fancy houses and fancy neighbors? I bet you never spied on them in the dark like this."

"None of them were having illegal rooster fights in their backyards."

"I'm trying to establish myself as a reputable business owner, you know. What if we get caught?"

"We won't be attending the fight. No one will even know we're there." As they passed the Thompson house, Madison began looking for a place to park the car. "We can't just park out in the open. We need to find some trees or something to disguise it."

"You know what concerns me the most?" Genesis continued as if Madison had not spoken. "None of this sounds like you. To be honest, this sounds much more like something I would think up. You are always the reasonable, responsible one. You were on the PTA, for Heaven's sake, and all those committees in Dallas. What has happened to you? I think you've inhaled too much ammonia at the chicken houses. Yes, that must be it."

Madison heaved a deep sigh, struggling to find the words to describe her change of character. Even to her, it seemed bizarre. "I think it's living back with Granny Bert again, in my old house, my old room, my old bed. She still has up all my Homecoming mums and my posters of Tom Cruise and Billy Ray Cyrus from his 'Achy Breaky Heart' days. I think it's messing with my head. I feel like that same lost teenager again, trying to figure out where I belong in life."

Madison pointed to a stand of trees and bramble that lined a small section of fence on their left. The paved city street would give way to dirt in about ten yards. Genesis nodded and said, "I see it", without Madison having to say a word. She swung a wide right, whipped the car around, and pulled as far off the road as possible. The dark vehicle blended well with the dark shadows. Should they need to make a hasty getaway, the car was now pointed in the right direction.

As they sat in the darkness, Madison made a confession. "I made a fool of myself tonight." Genny waited patiently for her to continue. "What was the one thing I always dreamed of in high school? The one thing I wanted more than anything else?"

"To go to a Bryan Adams concert?"

"No, my wildest dream. The one that was almost too impossible to come true."

"To kiss Brash deCordova."

"I was this close." Madison held up her hand and demonstrated a sliver of an inch, by glow of the dashboard's light. "Pathetic as it sounds, tonight I realized there are some dreams you never quite outgrow. And I was this close to making my wildest dream come true."

"What happened?" Genny's tone was breathless.

"I called him a liar and a cheat. Maybe I didn't say liar, but it was implied."

"But... why?"

"I thought he was married, Genny. Bethani introduced me to Brash's daughter and her mother. I just assumed they were still married."

"Okay, logical mistake," Genesis said, trying to defuse her friend's guffaw. "That doesn't sound so bad."

"That wasn't the worst part. Not the really foolish, shameful part."

"I'm almost afraid to ask."

With a defeated exhale, Madison pulled the toboggan from her head.

"Your hair!" Genesis gasped. "You cut it all off." Genny's surprise quickly gave way to delight. "It looks fantastic! Wow, Maddy, you look fabulous."

"Really? You think so?" Madison raked through the mess with her fingers, knowing the cap had destroyed the stylist's hard work.

"I know so. You. Look. Amazing."

"Thanks, Gen," she smiled at her friend. "But don't you see? I did it for him. Secretly, even if I was hiding the truth from myself, I did it to catch the attention of a married man. I know it was wrong, but when I saw Shannon again, she looked so beautiful, so perfect. It felt like high school all over again. I felt like the same gawky giraffe next to the beautiful, exotic leopard. All I knew was I couldn't stand it any longer. I wanted to look different. Different enough that Brash would notice. I'm a horrible, horrible person, Genny." She dropped her face into her hands, fully ashamed of herself.

"You are no such thing. You didn't do anything wrong. And Brash is not a married man."

"But I didn't know that! I wanted him to kiss me," Madison admitted miserably, raising soulful hazel her eyes to her friend.

"Did he?" Genesis asked pointedly.

"No. I finally came to my senses and stopped him."

"So see, you didn't do anything wrong. Even if he really was married, you wouldn't have kissed him."

Madison leaned her head back against the neck rest. "I'm thirty-nine years old, Genny, and I'm living with my grandmother." The words were hard to say. "I've lost my husband, my home, my job, and now my car. I don't recognize my life anymore. And thanks to this new haircut, I don't even recognize my own reflection!" She made a sad attempt at laughter. "I don't know where it all went wrong, and I'm not sure I know how to make it right. Coming back may not have been the wisest thing to do."

There. She had said it. She had admitted it.

Genny's voice was soft and curious in the dark confines of the car. "And why do you think that?"

"I thought coming back would make things clearer for me. I thought I could come home, clear my head, lick my wounds, and then go back to my life in Dallas. But instead, I keep getting the past all mixed up with the present. It's been too easy to fall back into the old habits of things, the old spirit of life in Juliet. The old dreams. Dreams that include a man I hardly even thought about for the past twenty years. One step back into Granny Bert's house, and I'm a teenager all over again."

"Maybe it's because the first time you came to live with her, you were lost and going through a hard time, too. Your parents more or less gave you to her. It would be difficult at any age, but at fourteen it's horrible."

"But living here, with Granny, was the best thing that ever happened to me."

"So it's only natural that you want to come back here and recapture some of that magical healing," Genesis reasoned.

"But this time, instead of making things clearer, it's making me more confused. How could I allow myself to be intimidated by my high school nemesis like that, after just one ten-minute conversation? Have I not grown at all? It's not like she even threw the first barb."

"Now probably is not the best time to mention that Shannon is actually a very nice person, nothing like the monster we made her out to be in high school."

Madison nodded miserably. "To be honest, I kind of got that impression. Did I mention that Bethani is spending the night at her house tonight?"

"I know. They came by the café after school."

"Oh that's right. While I was at Talk of the Town, trying to impress the girl's father. I am officially pathetic."

"If you are going to keep talking about my best friend like this, I am going to get really mad."

"Your best friend is a hot mess right now."

"My best friend has gone through a lot recently. She just needs a little time to regroup and refocus. And for the record, I don't think reviving old dreams is such a bad thing."

"Don't be playing match-maker," Madison warned. "Despite my crazy lapse of good judgment today, I really am not interested in a relationship right now, with Brash or any other man."

"I didn't necessarily mean your dreams about Brash, although that is not such a bad thing, either. I meant of your dreams overall. You used to dream of staying in Juliet and raising your family here. You could still make that dream come true, you know."

"I don't know, Genny. My life is in Dallas."

"Really?"

With just one searing look, her friend saw straight through the lie and directly into Madison's soul. Deflated, Madison admitted, "Okay, so everyone I care about is in Juliet. Which now includes my children. . . But we're living in my grandmother's house." Even she could hear the whine in her voice.

"There are other houses in town, Maddy. And maybe if you had your own house you would feel more independent, while still having family and friends to fall back on for support."

"But having my own house takes money. And money is another thing I no longer have." Madison made another confession. "Including the money Lily Ngyen paid me to clear her son's name. That's why I had to come out here tonight. I told Mrs. Ngyen I might not be able to do anything, but she put her faith in me. The money is non-refundable and I'm under no legal obligation to return it if I fail, but I have a moral obligation to do my best."

Genesis blew out a long, heavy sigh. Without another word, she grabbed the extra toboggan out of her friend's hands and crammed it onto her own blond head. As Madison scrambled to put hers back on, Genesis asked, "So what's the plan?"

"We'll keep low, walking along the tree line that borders the Thompson place. I think we can get a good look at the backyard of the Muehler house from there. If we're lucky, we'll recognize some of the people there and can turn their names over to Brash."

"And if we're not lucky?"

"Just pray that we're lucky," Madison said as she opened the car door.

With their cell phones on silent, the two friends scurried across the road, crossed through the barbed wire fence, and moved stealthily toward the tree line. The ground was difficult to navigate. Clumps of dried grass, gopher's mounds, and hidden dips made walking across the field not only difficult, but dangerous. More than once, the women turned an ankle or stumped a foot as they found yet another oddity in the terrain. By the time they reached the cover of the trees, they had to stop to rest and readjust shoes.

"What now?" Genesis whispered.

They were within fifty yards of the house now. The old farmhouse was dark and empty, but the sky behind it reflected a faint glow of light. Even from there, they could hear laughter and the sound of a dozen excited voices.

"We need to get around to the back of the house, toward the old barn."

"How are we going to do that without being seen?"

Madison glanced up to the dark sky. There was only a tiny sliver of moon, and it was playing peek-a-boo with the clouds. "When the moon goes behind a cloud, we cross over to the house, then slip around the side of it."

"Too risky. I think we should go further back, cross over to those trees back there, and come up from behind."

Madison debated the plan. "It's farther from the car."

"What if someone is inside the house? Or is stationed out front?"

"Okay, the back it is."

It took fifteen minutes to pick their way toward the back of the barnyard. When there were no trees for cover, they moved with shadows cast by a covered moon. Genesis stepped in a muddy hole and almost lost a shoe. Madison stumbled on a fallen limb and fell on one knee before catching herself. The night around them grew colder and the wind stirred, chilling them both to the bone. They might would have given up, except for the fact that something was definitely happening on the abandoned farm.

The closer they came, the brighter the lights were. Portable work lamps hung along the railings of one of the pens, shining away from the women as they made their way among the shadows. Even if someone looked their way, the glare of the lights offered protection. From the sounds of the farmyard, however, no one noticed their approach. Amid the horrible din of flogging roosters were the men's excited cries of encouragement and disbelief, victory and defeat, all heavily laced with profanity and intoxication.

By the time they reached the old barn, the fight was in full swing. The women did not need a clear line of sight to know what was happening. From the shrieks of the roosters and the cries of the audience, this was a blood sport. Sickened by the sounds, neither Madison nor Genesis tried too hard to see into the makeshift ring.

About twenty men and at least two women gathered around the horrific site, begging for more action, more blood. Most held alcohol in one hand; many had cigarettes in the other. A pungent sweetness in the air hinted at marijuana in some of the joints. Genesis knew she shouldn't be surprised, but she saw three men huddled behind the spectators, most likely conducting a drug deal. While one of the men motioned to the paper bag he held, another was snorting white substance up his nose. She realized two of the men weren't men at all, but teenagers who often came into her café after school. Her heart sank with the knowledge.

Madison scanned the crowd, trying to identify as many spectators as possible. Shadows made it difficult to see exact faces, but that did not keep her from recognizing certain people. Few men were as tall and reed thin as Jerry Don Peavey. No one else in town wore overalls over their extended belly quite like Buster Howell did. And the distinctive crimped brim of Luis Gonzales's cowboy hat revealed his identity, face or no face.

"We need to get closer," Madison whispered, still unable to see at least half the people there.

Genesis shook her head and lifted a finger to her lips. Then she pointed to a shadowed spot in front of the barn. She only saw the back of one man as he stood talking to another, both their faces hidden by the cover of night. Straining, the women could hear snatches of the conversation.

"Good crowd tonight," one of the men said.

"Better than last week. I think Gleason's death scared some of them off," the other man replied.

"Too bad Ngyen's gotta take the fall for something he didn't do."

"Damn fool." The wind stirred again, taking the man's next words hostage and sweeping them away. Only the last of his sentence was audible. "….. but his temper got the best of him." It was unclear which man they spoke of.

A pattern began. The women could hear only bits and pieces of the conversation, a few words at a time.

"- good profits."

"Next week … Havlicek's … good crowd."

"Boss … be happy."

"Greedy bastard. Tried cutting into my take."

"… show him who's…"

Determined to hear more, Madison moved a few steps closer. Her foot connected with an unseen object and made a distinct clink that echoed in the night. She froze in place, her heart thudding so loudly she was certain the men could hear it.

"What was that?" one of the men asked in alarm.

"How can you hear anything over that blood-thirsty crowd? This crowd is…" his words were lost on another breeze.

She heard only part of the second man's reply, but it was enough to know it was time to leave. "Need ….ing out the dogs."

With a frantic hand motion, Madison backed slowly away. She bumped into Genesis before her friend understood the message. Once in motion, the women moved in tandem, keeping their backs against the side of the barn as they slid slowly away from the cockfight.

Genesis waited to speak until they were at the rear of the barn. "What? What is going on?" she hissed in a whisper.

"They're going to bring out the dogs. We have to get out of here!"

In silent accord, they ran across the open field to the safety of the trees. Knowing the dogs would not respect the boundary line, they crossed the fence anyway, onto the back of the Thompson property. If caught, it was easier to explain their presence there than on the abandoned farm.

They moved as quickly as they could in the darkness, stumbling over the litter of fallen branches and muddy imprints left by the Thompson's small herd of goats. When they disturbed a sleeping billy, the goat was not happy. The irritated animal rammed his head into Madison's derriere and gave her a non-too-gentle shove. Her squeal of surprise seemed to satisfy him as he searched for a new place to sleep.

Behind them, they heard the first bay of the dogs.

"We've got to get out of here!" Genesis cried as she began to run.

With only the slightest of limps, Madison followed. Her long legs soon out-paced her friend as she led their frantic race across the pasture.

Their sudden movement frightened the rest of the slumbering goats. Soon all five of the animals were loping behind them in alarm, fueled by the barks of the advancing dogs. The moon came out from behind the veil of a cloud long enough to illuminate the scene below: two figures in black, racing across a rutted field and stumbling now and then, followed by five disoriented goats and, further behind but gaining ground, two large Rottweilers. Much further behind, just coming from the shadows of the abandoned farmhouse, was a man with something in his hands.

Madison glanced over her shoulder as they reached the fence. She stretched the barbed wires apart for her friend to slip through, ignoring the sound of ripping fabric as a moonbeam bounced off something metal in the distance. Instinct told her it was a gun. She shimmied through the wire, yelling for Genny to start the car. The dogs were close now, but the startled goats snagged their attention and temporarily shifted the canines' focus.

The moon was their friend that night, choosing that moment to hide again in the clouds. The car remained hidden in shadows as the women flung themselves inside. Madison did not bother going around; she jumped into the back seat on the driver's side. Her door was still open as Genesis peeled out onto the road and spun past the dogs and goats in a cloud of exhaust.

"Oh my Gosh, that was close!" Madison gasped, collapsing back against the seat. Her breath came out in huffs from their frantic run.

Still trying to catch her breath, Genesis could only nod emphatically from the front seat.

"Are you alright? I heard something rip on the fence."

"Th-That's the least- least of my worries!" Genesis puffed out the words. "Scraped my back. Turn-Turned my ankle. Scared five years off my life."

"My butt still stings," Madison realized, rubbing the offended area.

"Be glad he wasn't really mad," Genesis managed to say between gulps of air. "He wouldn't have stopped."

"Once was enough, thank you very much."

They raced through the empty streets, even though no one followed. Genesis pulled up in the rear parking lot of the café and explained their destination. "We'll take stock of our injuries here, before we have to face Granny Bert."

"With any luck, she'll be sleeping off the margaritas."

"I happen to have the makings for our own margaritas inside," Genesis said, opening the car door and gingerly stepping out. "Come on, girlfriend. You definitely owe me a drink."

18

Madison arrived later than usual at the Gleason farm the next morning, still half-asleep and more than just a little sore after her late night adventures. Minor scrapes and scratches were the least of her concern; her butt was bruised and her knee twisted, making movement slow and painful.

Eddie Menger waited for her in front of House 1, looking none too happy to be kept waiting.

"Hot date last night?" he asked sourly, eying the dark smudges beneath her eyes.

"Something like that." Madison did not feel the need to explain herself to the surly Service Tech as she went about gathering her supplies. Though normally friendly and helpful, the man seemed to be suffering from his own bout of sleepless nights.

His expression changed slightly as he studied her new haircut. She had not bothered to style it this morning, so the ends looked blunt and choppy as they scattered in disarray. With uncanny perception into the origin of her impromptu cut, he squinted his eyes and said almost accusingly, "Hear you're seeing the chief of police."

"What?" That grabbed Madison's attention and her head snapped up. "Where on earth did you hear such a ridiculous thing?"

"Heard he stopped by your house for a late-night visit."

"It wasn't all that late," she corrected sharply. "And he stopped by on an official matter, not that I owe anyone an explanation."

"Hey, just repeating what I heard." Eddie held up his hands in surrender, looking more like his usual affable self.

"Well, you heard wrong," she sniffed.

"Got some other news you might like to hear. Sell date for the flock has been moved up, so today's your last day."

"Really?" Madison asked in surprise.

"Yep. I'll take care of things from here on out."

"Oh. Well, okay."

As strange as it seemed, Madison was oddly disappointed. There was something gratifying about caring for the chickens and watching them grow, almost before her very eyes. In the two weeks she had been there, the birds had grown several inches and put on about two pounds. The target weight for the chickens was eight and a half pounds each, but some of the roosters were closer to twelve. It was amazing to see how they grew and filled out, practically overnight.

"So what happens now?" she asked, almost reluctant to hand over the care of 'her' birds.

"We start selling tomorrow night around ten. Which means tomorrow I have to follow a strict schedule of when to turn off feed lines. We want the birds to empty out the pans as much as possible, but we don't want their guts full of feed when they get to the slaughter plant. I'll have to get the houses ready and all the feed and water lines raised so the forklift can get in here when it's time to catch. The birds came in on two trucks, but it will take at least thirty six when they leave out."

"Do you think I've done alright?" Madison asked worriedly. "I haven't hurt the birds, have I?"

"Actually, the flock looks good. We have a projected weight of 8.75 pounds, so no, you didn't hurt the birds. We still might even win first place," Eddie grinned.

"For Ramona's sake, I hope so," Madison said, and truly meant it. Even if she did not particularly like the woman, she knew how difficult it was to lose your husband and to worry about money. A new worry hit her. "Do you think she'll have trouble selling the farm?"

"Nah, not at all. Last year one of our growers over in Leon County was killed in a car accident right at the beginning of his flock. New owners were already in place by the next flock."

"How long is it between flocks?"

"Growers keep the birds for nine weeks, then have about two weeks to clean out, set up, and maybe take a few days off. That time varies, depending on the market and the demand for chicken. For instance, in the summer, more people are grilling chicken outdoors and so out-times are shorter. In the fall, turkeys are more in demand, so you might have longer out-times," the man explained. "Like everything else, it all depends on supply and demand."

"So how will Ramona find a buyer for the farm?"

"Don't worry, there's a long list of people just waiting to get into the chicken business."

"Really?" Madison asked in surprise. "Why?"

"It's a very lucrative business."

Knowing that utility bills could run into the thousands, farm mortgages were about twenty times that of most homes, and there were dozens of other associated costs that came with running such a massive operation, Madison wondered about the validity of his statement. She kept silent as he continued.

"It's the closest thing you'll ever have to guaranteed success. Growers sign a thirteen-year contract with Barbour, who agrees to buy the chickens at a guaranteed minimum price. If you make upgrades to your farm and place well in competition, the price goes up. What other business do you know that has a built-in buyer and an iron-clad contract?"

Madison frowned, recalling something she had heard. "I thought Barbour could pull your contract if they wanted to."

"Only if you break the rules. They have contracts, too, with restaurants, supermarkets, and the like. They need the chickens from these farms to meet their quotas, so they're only going to pull a contract if the grower does something really stupid."

"Like raise fighting roosters?" Madison was thinking out loud when she murmured the words.

Eddie Menger looked at her in surprise. "Well, yeah. Or any other fowl, for that matter. Ducks are the worst offenders, because they go from pond to pond and can spread disease fastest."

"Do you know if anyone has already put in a bid for this farm?"

"Why? You interested in buying it?" he grinned. "It would only cost 1.7 million."

Madison's eyes widened like saucers. "Dollars?" she gasped.

"No, peanuts. Of course dollars!"

"Wow, I had no idea," she murmured, looking around at the long metal barns with new respect. If a person could go in debt that much and still consider this a lucrative venture, it was no wonder there were buyers waiting in line.

"Regardless of what people say about the industry, we don't work for chicken scratch," the man smirked.

"Apparently not!" Still amazed by the new information, Madison thanked the Tech for all his help over the past two weeks.

"If you've got a few business cards, I'll pass them along when I hear of a grower needing help walking houses," Eddie offered.

"I don't have any with me, but I'll see that you get some."

"Well, best of luck to you."

"Thanks." Madison slipped protective plastic boots over her own rubber boots, preparing to go into the first house. "Oh, one more thing. Would it be all right if I called you in a few days, to find out how the birds did?"

Eddie Menger grinned, understanding her curiosity and sense of ownership. "We might just make a chicken grower out of you yet! You might want to give some serious thought into buying this farm."

Madison laughed at the ludicrous thought of anyone loaning her almost two million dollars, guaranteed income or not. Thanks to Grayson, her credit was in shambles. "Like I could ever get that kind of loan."

Something in Eddie's eyes flickered. Sympathy, perhaps? It looked more like the spark of an idea. "Hey, you never know," he said. "Bankers know a sure thing when they see it. And I have a few connections. If you get serious about it, give me a call."

"I'll call, all right, but just to find out how the birds did." With an amused shake of her head, Madison waved farewell and started to work.

※

Two hours later, Madison wondered why she had felt any remorse at leaving this job behind. Her back ached from picking up hundreds of dead chickens; there were forty-nine in House 5 alone. She had to carry their heavy carcasses to the closest door and set them out to be transferred to the incinerators. She was now hot and sweaty and reeked to high Heaven, but she only had one more house to go.

Four rounds and she would be done.

Deciding she would conveniently forget to give her business card to Eddie Menger, Madison knew she did not want 'walk chicken houses' on her list of offered services. When she started In a Pinch, she had more in mind sedentary jobs, performed in the comfort of climate-controlled offices.

Okay, so the chicken houses were climate controlled. Gas furnaces kept the temperature from dropping too low, giant fans and panels of coils they called cool cells kept the temps from soaring too high. Computers controlled them all to the precise second. But it was hardly the same thing, particularly when the air being blown around was full of dust, chicken dander, and feathers. *And odor,* she added as she readjusted her respirator. The paper filter was designed to keep dust out, doing little to protect her from the noxious fumes in the house. However, it was better than nothing, so she clamped the nosepiece tighter to seal off the tiny gap that allowed the rank odor in.

Madison made her first round, spotting two dead chickens and stooping to pick them up and put them in her bucket. She noted that the cool cell curtains were up.

The chicken houses were designed with heavy plastic curtains on one end, banks of huge fans on the other. When the curtains were opened —and especially in the summer, when water flowed over the cool cells— the fans pulled the air through the houses, cooling down temperatures and creating air flow. It was rather ingenious, Madison mused as she crossed the mid-fence and proceeded to the opposite end of the house. As she passed the first of the fourteen fans, she was startled as its fifty-two inch blades opened and it began to spin. She supposed she was still easily spooked, particularly on the fan-end of the houses where she had found Ronny Gleason's body.

Three more rounds, and I'm done for good, she told herself.

Of course, she would have to replace the exercise she was getting here with a new routine; walking so much each day, stepping over three divider fences in each house and lifting the filled buckets provided an excellent workout. Even the sluggish chickens acted as weights for her legs, as she often gave one a free ride while shuffling slowly among them. Today was no exception. She suspected she might even be getting a better workout than normal, because she seemed to be shorter of breath.

Another round, another five hundred feet closer to her goal.

As Madison passed the fans again, she thought they seemed especially forceful. Her hair flew around her face in wild abandon, and even her t-shirt pulled in the direction of the fans. Were all the fans usually running at once? If all were needed in January, what must August be like? She wondered about that as she made another lap. Her breathing was becoming more labored and the air felt stale. The struggle to breathe made her head hurt.

By the time Madison made it to the back of the house again, she felt markedly worse. The pressure was building in her head, causing it to throb. She felt agitated, like someone was pulling on her and weighting her down. Even the chickens seemed upset. They clucked noisily and were flighty, more so than usual.

"Maybe I need some fresh air," Madison said aloud. She was near the seldom-used side door, halfway between the middle and back of the house. She pushed chickens out of her path and tried to open the door but found it locked. Hadn't she just used it yesterday, to set chickens out? Maybe she had accidentally locked it behind her.

Mindless of the smell, she pulled in a deep breath and tried to fill her lungs. Abandoning the bucket she carried, Madison had the overwhelming urge to breathe in fresh, clean air. She was the same distance to either of the nearest exits, but going forward meant she had to step over the midfence. She suddenly doubted if she had the energy to do so, so she turned and headed to the back of the house. She would step outside, fill her lungs, take a small break, and then come back in and complete her last and final round. Ever.

Wading back through the maze of white feathered birds, Madison realized she had never seen the flock so excited. Even when she found Ronny's body and Cutter Montgomery helped her shoo the birds away, disrupting their habitat, the fowl had not been this worked up. Birds pecked at one another in anger, several flailed against her legs, some flapped their wings and attempted to fly, and all squawked and cackled at once, creating quite the commotion. By the time she reached the back doors, Madison's heart was racing, her head was throbbing, and she could hardly breathe.

She pushed her weight against the door, anticipating the fresh air beyond. To her surprise, she bounced off the door and almost fell down. Shaking her dazed head, she pushed again. Locked! The handle wiggled, however, so she twisted it one more time and tried her best to open the door. It budged the tiniest of bits, but there was too much pressure to make her efforts successful.

That was when it dawned on Madison what was happening. High pressure! All the fans were running —they normally did not, she was certain of it now— and were sucking the air from the house. The displaced oxygen was making it difficult to breathe. The pressure of the air was zapping her energy and making her feel heavy and leaden. The fans were pulling a vacuum on the house, making it impossible to open the doors with the escalating pressure.

Madison's throbbing mind stumbled through a few scenarios, none of them comforting. If Ramona got the high pressure alarm, she would more than likely ignore it, at least the first few times it called. She might eventually call Barbour Foods or perhaps Eddie Menger directly. Assuming he had cell phone service, would he be anywhere in the area? Where had Eddie said he was headed next? Even if Barbour sent someone else out, it might take them an hour or more to get here.

Madison knew she did not have hours. Already the lack of oxygen in the air was making her nauseous and weak. Even the chickens knew something was wrong. She looked around feverishly, hoping to see something that would offer her salvation. A glance at the ceiling showed ceiling seams beginning to pucker. She recalled what Eddie said about sucking the roof in.

"Think, Madison, think!" she demanded, rubbing her pounding forehead.

There was too much air being pulled from the house. If she could get to the control room she could turn off some of the fans, but there was no way she could manhandle the doors. That meant she had to stop the airflow from within, even though all the switches were outside the house.

She looked around again, wondering if there was any way she could jam one of the fans. Blades that big would merely chop up anything she threw at them, even if she had something to throw. Which she did not.

Relief washed through her when she spotted the plugs. Each of the fans was plugged into electrical outlets near the ceiling, but their cords were long and within reach. Madison stumbled over chickens as she pushed her way toward the fans and began jerking on the thick cords. One by the one, the huge blades stopped spinning. She went down the row, disabling every cord she could reach. She was across the house and jerking down cords from the other bank of fans before she felt the pressure in the house subside. With an audible cry of relief, Madison bumbled her way toward the door, tripping once on a chicken and falling to her knees before making it out.

This time, the door swung easily open and she stepped outside into the gloriously fresh air.

And this time, she was not going back inside.

Ever.

19

With a warped sense of déjà vu, Madison called 9-1-1 to report the incident. Once her lungs filled with fresh air and her mind was functioning again, she realized someone deliberately turned on all the fans, knowing she was inside.

Officer Perry came to her aid. Madison vaguely remembered the man from her youth. If memory served her correctly, he was the one who threatened to send her and Genesis to jail if they did not climb down from the water tower immediately. They obeyed, but not before finishing their scrolled version of "Seniors '95" in bright neon pink.

After taking her statement, the policeman mentioned dusting for prints, even though it was a long shot. Between truck drivers, Barbour personnel and Madison, he determined there were too many people with access to the control room to isolate a particular set of prints. He then promised to visit neighbors and ask if they noticed anyone coming or going from the farm, but Madison knew it was merely a token effort on his part.

The best she could do was go up to big house, knock on the door until she woke Ramona from her early afternoon nap, collect her final paycheck, and smile through her teeth as she thanked the woman for the opportunity to serve her. It was all Madison could do to keep from running back to Granny Bert's car and peeling out of the driveway.

Once she was a modest distance from the house, she firmly pressed the accelerator and exited the Gleason Farm in a trail of dust.

If she ever set foot back on the property again, it would be too soon for her liking.

※

"Tonight, we are celebrating," Madison announced to her family. It was a splurge she could barely afford, but if she ever deserved a night out, this was it. "Genny is meeting us at the restaurant. Everyone ready?"

"I am." Blake was the first one out the door. "I'm starving."

"Have you seen my phone?" Bethani searched beneath couch cushions as she spoke.

"It's usually attached to your ear," her mother remarked dryly from the doorway.

"Oh, I remember. I left it on the bed. Be right back!" As she scampered off to get it, she passed her great grandmother in the hall. "Looking hot tonight, Granny Bert!" the teen giggled as she rushed past her.

"I don't know what happened last night at the Aikman's, but it did wonders for her attitude," Granny Bert commented.

"She does seem happier, doesn't she?" Madison smiled after her daughter, belatedly noticing the difference.

Not that she hadn't been understandably preoccupied with other matters today, like the fact that someone had once again tried to do her harm. Much more of this, and she was going to take it personally.

Her grandmother nodded. "She's been downright pleasant, almost like the girl we used to know and love."

Granny Bert drove the short distance to Juanita's, the only Mexican food restaurant in The Sisters other than the opened-again, closed-again mobile taco truck that often roamed the streets. It was a Saturday night and New Beginnings was closed, so the only other restaurant in Naomi was busy. It also had something to do with their excellent food and the fact that tonight was karaoke night.

There was a ten-minute wait before a table was ready for their group of five, but soon they were seated at a large round table and munching on warm tortilla chips and homemade salsa.

"So you are officially done with chicken farming?" Genesis confirmed from her friend.

"So done."

"I'm proud of you for finishing, though. I know it wasn't easy, even under normal circumstances."

"It's the hardest work I've ever done," Madison admitted. "But at least now I know what I *don't* want to be when I grow up!"

"Look, Mom, there's my friend Jamil and his parents. Can I go say hello?" Blake asked.

"Sure, honey, but can you wait until we order? I see our waitress coming back."

As soon as they gave their order to the waitress, Blake sprang from his chair and went to greet his friend. He waved to another friend across the way, making Madison aware of how many locals were crowded into the place.

"I think that's the Thompsons at the back booth."

"Poor Glitter," Granny Bert remarked. "She told me there's been so much commotion around her neighbor's, she can't sleep at night."

Madison slid her best friend a sly look and quickly changed the subject. "Oh, look, there's Cutter Montgomery. And who is that girl he's with? She's gorgeous!"

"That is the infamous Miss Callie Beth Irwin. The one he supposedly is not interested in." Genesis looked over her shoulder at the couple weaving their way through the restaurant. When she caught sight of another diner, she groaned aloud. "Brace yourself for fireworks. This might not be pretty."

"What it is?"

"I just spotted Shilo Dawne, and she just spotted Cutter and Callie Beth."

"You're right, she doesn't look too happy. Wonder what she's saying to them?"

"I don't know, but I'm doubting it's a friendly hello." Genesis cringed as she thought about the possibilities.

Granny Bert piped in. "That poor girl has a hopeless crush on Cutter, but who can blame her? If I was thirty years younger, I might give that cougar-thing a try with young Montgomery there."

Genesis burst out laughing, which drew several eyes her way, including the fireman's. Seeing his opportunity to slip away from a very animated Shilo Dawne, Cutter tipped his hat in farewell, grabbed the other girl's elbow, and steered her toward the table where Genesis and party sat.

"Miss Genesis, Miss Bert, Miss Maddy." Again, he tipped his cowboy hat in greeting, a friendly smile lighting his handsome face. He settled his gaze on Genesis. "What are you lovely ladies doing out this evening?"

"We are here celebrating the completion of Maddy's career in the chicken business," Genesis announced with a bright smile.

"All done? That's great." The young man looked genuinely pleased for her.

"All done," Madison confirmed.

"You know, you should be proud of yourself. The last two weeks of a flock can be a critical time. That's why we were all surprised that Ronny would leave at a time like that, especially leaving a novice in charge." He belatedly offered an apologetic look. "No offense."

"None taken," Madison assured him.

Cutter's eyes strayed back to Genesis and a smile lit his handsome face. "And I guess this is a special treat for you, having someone else do the cooking for a change."

"Always a plus," she agreed.

There was an awkward moment of silence, until Genesis motioned to the girl beside him. She was tall and slim, dressed in a fashionable but very short denim dress with lace leggings, cowboy boots and plenty of blinged out leather. Her pale brown hair was arranged in an artful but messy bun atop her head. "I don't believe your date knows everyone. You might want to introduce her."

The young woman moved to tuck her hand into the crook of his arm, but Cutter pulled away and was quick to say, "Oh, she's not my date!" The girl pouted prettily, but her eyes glittered with poorly concealed pain. "We're here with a group," he explained. "Callie Beth, you know Miss Bert. This is her granddaughter Madison Reynolds, who happens to be Miss Genny's best friend. She's come back to live in Juliet and has opened a temp agency. And this is her daughter-"

"Bethani," Madison supplied.

"- Bethani," Cutter finished the introduction without missing a beat. "And of course you know Miss Genesis, the best cook and pastry chef this town has ever seen, and quite possibly the best in all of Texas. This, everyone, is Callie Beth Irwin." The lead-in to her introduction was noticeably shorter.

After a round of polite greetings, Callie Beth finally snagged his arm. "Cutter, our friends are waiting," she reminded him softly.

"Oh, right." He seemed reluctant to leave, but he finally threw Genesis an apologetic look and allowed the young woman to pull him away, toward a long table near the karaoke stage. Several young adults were already seated and waiting on them.

"What was that look about?" Madison wondered aloud as the couple left.

Genny shrugged. "He probably feels guilty about being here on a date with Callie Beth, since he knows I'm rooting for Shilo Dawne."

"Forget Shilo Dawne. What about me?" Bethani grinned, turning around in her seat to watch the volunteer fireman walk away. "Granny Bert, when was the last time you had your fireplace checked out? Doesn't the fire department make inspections or something?"

"Young lady, you can just pop your eyeballs back inside your head, right this minute," Madison chided. "He is much too old for you."

Granny Bert allowed her eyes to trail along behind him, as well. With a heartfelt sigh, she agreed. "Yes, and unfortunately, he is much too young for me." With a sudden bright smile, she beamed at Madison and Genesis. "But that still leaves you two."

"Us?" Genesis laughed.

"Sure. Like I said, cougars."

"Oh, Granny Bert, with you around, life is never dull!"

"You can say that again." Madison rolled her eyes, but a smile tugged on her lips.

"Wow, everyone is here tonight," Bethani said, spotting the restaurant's newest arrivals. "There's Megan and her whole family, including her dad!"

Madison was not thrilled with the prospect of seeing Brash. After this morning's events, she had forgotten all about last night. She had not given the cockfight another thought, much less the botched kiss episode. But suddenly those awkward moments on the porch swing came rushing back to her. Maybe it was the fact that Brash looked particularly handsome in a striped western shirt and starched jeans. Or maybe it was the fear that Shannon would still be carrying on about her new haircut; when she dropped Bethani off earlier, the other woman seemed intrigued by the change in Madison's appearance. It was probably her imagination, but Madison was certain Brash's ex-wife knew exactly what inspired her new look.

She had no time to worry about it as Matthew Aikman claimed her attention. "Maddy? Maddy Cessna, I can't believe you're back in town!"

His voice boomed in pleasure across the crowded restaurant. When he rushed forward and opened his arms in greeting, there was nothing to do but stand and step into his embrace as the rest of their party watched in varied stages of hilarity. Granny Bert looked amused, Genesis entertained, Megan looked enchanted, Bethani confused. Shannon looked happily unconcerned that her husband embraced another woman, while Brash watched with mild curiosity.

Tugging on her clothes self-consciously, Madison stepped back from the hearty hug to survey her old boyfriend. Matthew was not quite as tall as Brash was, but every bit as toned. Streaks of gray edged his temples and dominated the neatly trimmed mustache that hovered above his lip.

"Matthew, you look great. And it's so good to see you again."

"Talk about great! Just look at you!" He lifted her hand above her head, motioning for her to do a twirl, right there in the restaurant. Feeling like an idiot, Madison offered a half-hearted pirouette. She was thankful she wore something feminine tonight; a long flowing skirt that swished playfully around her legs and favorite boots, topped by a dark blue sweater blouse. "She looks great, doesn't she, Brash?"

From where he stood at the back of the group, Brash's eyes glittered with amusement. He obviously enjoyed Madison's discomfort. "Absolutely," he agreed with the other man.

Blake came back to the table, just in time to see her slow pivot. "Mo-om, not in public!" he jested. To the group, he shrugged and pretended to complain, "We can't take her anywhere." When Megan giggled as his antics, it explained his sudden return. It also explained the bright new gleam in his blue eyes.

"In case you haven't met him yet, this is my son, Blake. Blake, do you know the Aikmans?"

"Apparently not as well as you do!"

"Oh, Mama Matt used to date your Mom," Megan quickly supplied.

Madison raised her eyebrows high. "Mama Matt?"

"She refused to call another man daddy, but she fell in love with Matthew after the first month we were married," Shannon explained, wrapping both hands around her husband's arm and smiling up at him. "'Mr. Matt' was too formal, plain 'Matt' was too disrespectful, so her solution was to call him Mama Matt. And this is our son, by the way. Trouper, say hello to Bethani's family."

After the young boy dutifully obeyed, Matthew patted his wife's hand. "Shannon, I want you to organize one of your famous dinner parties," he said unexpectedly. "All of you are invited. We'll catch up on old times. You ladies set the time and date, and we fellas will show up, right Brash? Blake?" Not waiting for their replies, he tousled his son's hair. "Your momma's famous for her parties, right, buddy? We'll have a great time."

"I'm in," Genesis said with a bright smile.

"Me, too. I'll bring my new juicer and we can make smoothies," Granny Bert offered.

"Uhm, yeah, sounds great." No one seemed to notice Madison's less-than-enthusiastic reply.

Shannon promised to call with details as the Aikman and deCordova family finally shuffled off to their table. Brash, however, turned back and touched Madison on the shoulder, piercing her with his concerned gaze. "You're doing all right after this morning?"

"Yes." She gave an almost imperceptible shake of her head, willing him not to say anything more in front of her family. They did not know about this latest incident and she intended to keep it that way. She plastered on a bright smile. "As of this morning, the chicken business is behind me now."

He understood her message but continued to probe her with keen eyes. Finally satisfied, he nodded and removed his hand from her shoulder. "There are a few loose ends I'd like to go over with you about Ronny Gleason. Could you stop by the office Monday morning?"

"I have to work all day Monday. Can we make it Tuesday afternoon?" It would be the perfect time to tell him about the people she had seen at the cockfight, people with a potential 'beef' against the dead man.

"I'll see you Tuesday." Brash glanced around the table, encompassing the group in his polite smile. "You folks have a nice meal." With a nod, he turned to catch up with his companions.

"Does anyone else think that was a little odd?" Madison murmured.

"What, that he made an excuse to see you again?" Granny Bert asked. She ignored Madison's frown and studied the salsa on her chip. "Or that the hot sauce has a touch too much cilantro? But don't worry, it grows on you after a few bites."

"Not the hot sauce! Doesn't it strike you as odd that Shannon and Matthew go out for a family dinner, and her ex-husband tags along?"

"I think it's nice."

"You have to admit," Genesis said, "it's great for Megan that her parents get along so well. And Brash and Matthew were always such good friends in high school."

"Still, they were always so competitive, and now they've both been married to the same woman... And why does Megan act so infatuated with the fact that I once dated her step-father?"

"She's fifteen," Granny Bert said by way of explanation. "At that age, everything is romantic."

Madison eyed the family as they were seated several tables away. "I don't know. Matthew and I haven't even spoken to one another since we broke up twenty years ago. Yet he hugs me like he's thrilled to see me, and Shannon just stands there and grins, happy as a lark to see her husband hugging another woman. And now all of sudden they're inviting us over for supper?"

"I think you're over-reacting," Genesis said gently.

When Madison glanced their way again, Matthew caught her eye and gave her a thumbs up, darting his gaze to Brash.

"I have a sneaky suspicion it's something more," Madison muttered under her breath. "If I didn't know better, I'd say they were trying to play match-maker."

20

Madison's plans of a quiet, lazy Sunday afternoon did not materialize.

After attending church with her family, Granny Bert insisted on preparing smoothies and sandwiches for lunch. Sipping cautiously on the smoothie —who knew what was in it?— Madison retired to the couch and propped her swollen knee up on a pillow. When asked what happened, she made a vague reference to the uneven dirt floors of the chicken houses; she made no mention of the uneven terrain in the Thompson pasture and the many holes she stepped in while running from goats, dogs, and an illegal cockfight.

Madison started reading on her Kindle, but soon her eyelids grew heavy. After two weeks of extensive physical labor, Friday night's late-night dash across the field, and then yesterday's brush with danger, Madison was exhausted. Snuggling into the cushions, she drifted to sleep for a twenty-plus minute nap.

Her pleasant slumber was disturbed by a dark dream. She dreamed she was trapped inside the chicken houses once again. The pressure was building around her, tugging at her mind and at her clothes, and sucking the air from her lungs. Chickens were flailing at her, pecking on her knee until it throbbed. She managed to push through their white maze and stumbled upon Ronny Gleason's body, all bloodied and torn and sporting only one eye. In her dream, his body smoldered and took on a slightly blackened hue, no doubt from his electrocution. Too true to reality, Madison struggled to get the doors opened. Panic and pressure welled inside her as she fought her way out the exit. Somewhere behind her, a man's voice talked about bets, bosses, and turning the dogs loose. His voice was familiar, but she could not quite place it... When she finally burst from the house, she careened into an excited crowd gathered around two flogging, screeching roosters. Blood and feathers flew as the crowd chanted and raged, begging for more.

"Mom! Mom, wake up!" Bethani shook her shoulder, jarring her from the nightmare.

Madison blinked, staring up at her daughter as she tried to get her bearings. Something tickled her nose and she blew it away, watching as a small feather floated through the air.

"What did you *do*?" Bethani cried, lifting the destroyed throw pillow from her mother's hands. The seams were ripped and the center button missing, with white down spilling out of the frayed edges.

"I- uh – got it confused with a door?" Madison offered sheepishly.

"A door? Really mom? You truly have been working too hard lately." The teen tossed the pillow across her mother's legs and plopped down into the nearby chair. Her voice was more sympathetic as she asked, "Another nightmare?'

"An-Another?"

"We sleep in the same bed, Mom. I know when you have nightmares."

"Sorry. And I'm sorry to disturb you." Madison looked down at the couch, wondering if she could tolerate it for a full night. "Maybe I should start sleeping in here," she suggested.

"Maybe you should stop having nightmares."

Madison gave the teen a rueful smile. "Easier said than done. They don't just go away because I tell them to."

"What was that corny old wife saying Granny Bert used to tell you?"

"You mean an old wives' tale?" Madison smiled. "The one about putting a pan of water beneath your bed to drown the night mare?"

"Yeah, that was it." The girl giggled.

"Oh well, there's no room beneath our bed for a pan of any sort." Madison sighed, picturing the boxes and plastic bins stuffed beneath the mattresses.

"There's no room for anything!" Bethani complained. "Are we ever going to get our own house? Penny Jo Cessna — apparently she's my cousin somehow?— says her Grandpa has a real estate agency and could probably find us a house to rent."

Madison was stunned. Bethani was thinking in terms of relocating here in Juliet?

They were entering unchartered waters. Madison treaded softly, not wanting to disturb the sudden change of current. "Actually, I've been wanting to talk to you about something, honey…"

Before Madison could continue, the teen let out a long, heavy sigh. As her shoulders sank, her face took on a stoic, older-than-her-years expression. "We're not going back to Dallas, are we, Mom?" The words were spoken quietly, more of a statement than a question.

"I-I wouldn't say that," Madison hedged. "Not necessarily. But… it may take a little longer than I thought. How-How would you feel about that, honey, if we stayed here in Juliet for a while?"

"'A while' like through the end of the school year, or 'a while' like through my junior or senior year?"

"I'm not sure," her mother answered honestly.

Again the teen sighed. "Well, I'm still no fan, but I guess it's not *quite* as bad as I first thought. Most of the kids are friendly and the teachers are nice. And some of the girls are trying to talk me into trying out for cheerleader. What would you think about that?" The teen peeked at her mother from beneath her lashes, trying to gauge her reaction.

Madison was torn. The mom in her was thrilled. Being cheerleader in a small school was akin to instant stardom and popularity, meaning Bethani would not only fit in, but would secure her place here in The Sisters; wanting to try out meant she was thinking long-term. But the bread-earner in Madison was worried. She knew being a cheerleader did not come cheaply. There were uniforms, camps, transportation back and forth to practices and games; could she afford it?

Seeing the hopeful expression on her daughter's face, Madison knew she would find a way. Even if it meant adding the dreaded task of 'walking chicken houses' back onto her resume, it was worth seeing Bethani happy and excited once again. Since her father's death, both emotions had been non-existent for the teen.

Realizing the girl still waited for an answer, Madison said, "I think you'll need to practice."

Bethani squealed and clapped her hands, doing a little happy dance in her chair. "You're the best, Mom! And actually, we've already started practicing. Megan asked me to come over this afternoon so we could try out a few new cheers."

"This afternoon?" Madison practically whined. She eyed her own legs, stretched out comfortably on the couch.

Her cell phone rang and Dean Lewis's name showed on the screen. By the time she hung up with him, she was abandoning the couch. "Looks like I can drop you off after all," she told her daughter. "I have to meet a client and pick up a key."

"Cool! I'll call Megan and tell her it's a go."

Envying her daughter's energy, Madison was much slower moving into the bedroom. She traded her comfortable sweats for a pair of slacks and a button-up blouse. She eyed her reflection in the mirror, aware of the fact that the staid blouse was at odds with her trendy new haircut. She had considered buying a new top or two, but if Bethani made cheerleader, her money would go into shoes and tights and colorful shoelaces. It was always the little things that added up and destroyed a budget.

Madison followed Bethani's directions to the opposite side of Juliet, into the newer subdivision that boasted large, sprawling homes and immaculate lawns. She suspected the upscale neighborhood had something to do with her daughter's new approval rating, but no matter the reason, Madison was thankful. She did not relish the thought of fighting her children over the necessity of staying in Juliet.

After dropping the teen off, Madison drove to the insurance office on Second Street. She arrived just as Dean Lewis did, so he ushered her into the building and gave her last minute instructions.

"Mostly I want you to answer phones and handle the mail. You mentioned you didn't mind filing a few things?"

Madison eyed the gargantuan stack of papers on his desk and decided 'a few' was definitely a relative term, but she politely nodded. "No, not at all."

"I do want you to be on the lookout for an envelope from A&O Insurance. It should be the policy on Ronny Gleason's death. If it comes in, could you please call Ramona and let her know it has arrived? I'm sure she'll be anxious to get the money."

"I'm sure," Madison murmured. If rumors were true, it meant she could have another nip and tuck, or perhaps add another cup size to her already-generous bosom.

"Any questions?" Dean Lewis asked.

"No, I don't think so."

"Well, then, here's the key. You remember that you work a full day Monday and Wednesday, mornings only on Tuesday and Thursday?"

"Yes, sir, I remember."

"Fine, fine. We should be in Thursday afternoon, so I'll arrange to get the key after that."

"And you've left your contact information, in case I need to reach you?" Madison double-checked the details as they made their way out the door and onto the sidewalk.

"Yes, it's all there on my desk. Well, Mrs. Reynolds, I trust I'm leaving my business in good hands." He thrust his hand forward for a formal shake.

Madison looked him in the eye and offered a firm, confident handshake. "Absolutely, Mr. Lewis. You have a wonderful convention and don't worry about things here. I have everything under control."

As Madison limped down the steps to the car and her cell phone rang, she was thankful there were no chickens or goats involved with this job.

"Maddy?" Granny Bert's voice crinkled from the other end of her cell phone. "I need you to swing by and pick me up. I have an errand to run."

So much for relaxing today, Madison bemoaned silently, but forced a smile into her voice. "Okay, on my way." She was using her grandmother's car, after all; the least she could do was drive her around on errands.

Sooner or later, she would have to replace her SUV. The insurance company was being stubborn, arguing over the smallest details. Madison was holding out for the maximum payout, but desperation weakened her resolve. She knew it was exactly what the insurance company wanted and she hated playing into their hands, but she needed her own car, and soon.

"Where are we going?" she asked as her grandmother met her at the curb.

"I need to go by the Big House. Hank Adams called and said he thought he saw lights there last night. Need to make sure no one's been inside, messing around."

"It still has electricity hooked up?" Madison asked in surprise.

"Electricity, gas, the whole nine yards. I don't want the pipes freezing or the wallpaper peeling from too much heat."

The Big House, as it was commonly referred to, sat upon an entire city block, on the corner of Juliet's Second and Main. The three-storied structure resembled a wooden wedding cake, with tiers and curves and enough lattice frosting to befit the finest of cakes. A brick pathway lead from the curb up to the house, edged with flowerbeds and small shrubs. Large oak and massive pecan trees dotted the yard, with a few pines mixed in for year-round color. Behind the house was an assortment of smaller buildings: a carriage-house-turned-garage, a gardener's shed, gazebo, and a caretaker's cottage. All could use a fresh coat of paint and a bit of TLC.

"Just pull up here along the street and we'll walk in," Granny Bert said. There was an ornate white iron fence around the property and an electronic gate to keep out trespassers.

"Don't remember the gate code?" Madison teased.

"Of course I remember. I just figured we could use the exercise," her grandmother huffed. "It'll do that stiff knee of yours good."

Madison dutifully followed her grandmother through the foot gate, up the cobbled path, and onto the steps of the first front porch. Three more porches and balconies graced the front of the house, not to mention the long covered porch across the back.

"Be careful on this step. I nearly fell off it last month when I was on the ladder, fixing that loose trim."

"What on earth were you doing up on a ladder? You have no business crawling around like that," Madison immediately chided.

"Don't you dare say a thing about my age."

She raised her hands in innocence. "I didn't use the 'o' word."

"And it's a good thing, too," her grandmother harrumphed. She propped the screen door open with her foot, jiggled a key in the lock, and swung the glass paned front door open with flourish. "After you, my dear."

Stepping through the front door of the Big House was like stepping into another era. Madison had visited museums with less attention to detail than the front foyer of Juliet Randolph Blakely's home. It had been years since Madison had been inside, but nothing had changed, except for the added layers of dust.

"We'll do a walk-through and make sure everything is in order," Granny Bert said, taking the lead. "I'll go left, you go right."

Wandering through the rooms, Madison almost forgot she was on a mission. Each of the rooms had at least one special detail that made it remarkable: burled wood wainscoting, a fireplace with inlaid Italian marble, exquisite stained glass windows, ingenuous pocket doors to make two small rooms function as one large one. For a modern home, the rooms were rather crowded and the layout was awkward, but in its time, the house was nothing less than an extravagant mansion.

Madison stepped on a few squeaky and loose boards, noted wallpaper peeling in the front parlor, and wondered how a kitchen so ill planned and spaced out could ever function properly, but nothing seemed amiss. She met Granny Bert back in the entryway with a shrug.

"I didn't see a thing," she reported. "Should we go upstairs?"

"All the way to the third floor, unless you're afraid of heights."

"Not me," Madison grinned, jogging up the stairs to prove her point. After testing the banister for sturdiness, she even leaned out over the railing in daredevil fashion. She took the right side of the house again, trailing through bedrooms with their own sitting rooms but a sad shortage of bathrooms. Granny Bert was already waiting for her at the carved staircase leading to the uppermost floor.

"I can go up by myself, if you like," Madison offered.

Granny Bert gave her a cool look. "You're implying the 'o' word again."

Hooking her arm through her grandmother's, Madison laughed as they climbed the stairs together. "This house is magnificent. And I understand why you don't live here, but why didn't one of your boys want to? It's a shame a house like this is just sitting here."

"My boys already had homes of their own by the time I inherited it. Your Uncle Glenn built that big house over on Elm, and Joe Bert and Trudy live out on her family's ranch. Darwin lives in Odessa, and your dad lives wherever the wind blows him. Nobody needed this house."

"But it's so gorgeous," Madison said, wistfully trailing her fingers over the smooth banister. They reached the top floor, where only three rooms occupied the space, and all of them empty. The two turrets had once served as sitting rooms for the long narrow room yawning between; that space had been the ballroom, perfect for parties and grand social events.

Stepping into the turret nearest them, Madison looked out the windows and smiled. "Can't you image having a room up here as a young girl? It would be like Cinderella."

"I was thinking Rapunzel," her grandmother smiled. She walked around the empty room, using hand motions to place imaginary furniture. "There would be plenty of room for a bed and dresser. Can't you imagine Bethani up here?"

"She would absolutely love it!" Madison clasped her hands together in delight, trying to picture her daughter in a room such as this. She grinned as she added, "But only if it had good cell phone service."

"It's good to see the girl smiling again."

"You're telling me! Did you know she's thinking of trying out for cheerleader?"

"I suspected as much."

"You did?" Madison asked in surprise.

"She goes around waving her hands above her head and swishing her hips to a silent chant. It was either that, or she was having convulsions."

Madison peered out the window, noting how well she could see the town from there. To the left she caught a glimpse of the railroad track, to the right she could see two blocks down to City Hall and beyond. Directly across the street was a small row of businesses and parking spaces, but the big front lawn made a nice buffer for the noise. Juliet truly was a lovely town.

"At least the twins both seem content with the fact that we'll still be here in the fall. Blake is talking about playing football, and now Bethani is trying out for cheerleader. I just hope she doesn't get her hopes up and then be disappointed if she doesn't make it."

"Tell her to mention my name at try-outs and she'll be a shoo-in," Granny Bert said airily.

Madison paused in mid-air as she started down the stairway. "Granny Bert! That would be cheating!"

"How would it be cheating?" the older woman sniffed. "Mentioning that I'm her great-grandmother wouldn't be cheating and it wouldn't be dishonest. It's a known fact that I was married to a founding member of The Sisters ISD school board, that I personally donated the money to build a new auditorium in his honor, that I'm the mother of a current school board member and grandmother of two of the district's best teachers, and that as former mayor, I encouraged the city to help fund a new elementary playground. Those are the facts, not cheating."

Unease settled in Madison's stomach. "Is that why I was named Homecoming Queen my senior year?"

"You were named Homecoming Queen because you were the prettiest and smartest girl in school, and because you were popular," her grandmother assured her in blunt tones. "My name had nothing to do with it."

As they continued down the stairs, Granny Bert said, "I think I have another job lined up for you."

"Whose dog am I walking now? Or whose medicine needs picking up?" She tried not to sound as despondent as she felt. Other than her upcoming assignment at the insurance office, her temp service was not panning out the way she had imagined.

"Neither. Glenn and Betsy are going on a cruise and need someone to look after the dealership while they're gone."

"I don't know anything about selling cars!"

"What's to know? Either it runs or it doesn't. But luckily for you, they already have a salesman. They need someone to man the phones, make service appointments, do payroll, that kind of thing. Best thing is, it comes with a demo car."

That was all Madison had to hear. "When do I start?" she beamed.

"They leave this weekend and will be gone for ten days, give or take."

"Perfect. I finish at the insurance agency on Thursday."

"See, girl? These things have a way of working out."

They reached the bottom floor without seeing a single thing amiss.

"Guess it was just kids, shining flashlights into the windows," Granny Bert said with a shrug. "That, or Hank was getting a reflection off his lens implant; he had cataract surgery not too long ago."

"To be honest, I'm surprised no one has vandalized the house, considering it's empty."

"Actually, I've been thinking about selling the house," her grandmother confessed.

"Sell the Big House?" Madison asked in dismay. The iconic house had been sitting on the corner for one hundred years. Would new owners honor its history, or would they turn it into condominiums, or worse yet, a funeral parlor? What if they bulldozed the whole thing and built a warehouse in its place? A cheap chain store where everything was a dollar? Her heart ached, just thinking of the dismal prospect.

"Oh, I'd never sell it to just anybody," Granny Bert assured her. "I'd want someone with ties to Juliet's past. But more importantly, someone with ties to her future. I want someone with deep roots and high branches."

"That's a relief," Madison said, putting a hand to her fluttering heart.

"Know anybody that fits the bill?"

"Me? I just got back in town, remember?"

"I know. The question is, how long do you plan to stay?" her grandmother asked with a pointed gaze.

Madison held the door while her grandmother jiggled the key once more and secured the lock. With her eyes fixed on the sleepy street before her, Madison considered the question.

There was something so peaceful about Juliet. Naomi, too. Life in a small Southern town was comforting.

It could also be inconvenient at times. There were no Starbucks, no major fast food restaurants, no malls or Super Centers. However, there was a sense of community and family, a close-knit network that could work for you or against you, depending on the situation. Not a single 'friend' from the city had checked on her since she moved away; almost every single day, someone here in Juliet asked how she was doing or offered to help or gave her some word of encouragement. And the kids were adjusting, even Bethani.

"I'll probably stay around for a while," she finally said.

"Well, when you know for sure, I'll sell you the Big House."

Madison laughed aloud. "Sell it to me? What on earth would I use for money?"

"Oh, I'm sure we could come to a very agreeable price," her grandmother said with confidence.

"Like what?" Madison hooted. "I doubt I could even afford utilities on a house that size!"

"We won't discuss a price until you commit to staying here in Juliet. Then we'll talk numbers."

"Why me? What would your other grandchildren say if you sold the house to me?"

"Joe Glenn just built a house over in the new addition, Hallie lives outside of town in a huge house of her own, and Larry is ranch foreman and lives out on the ranch. Jillian and her husband live in College Station where he's a professor, and all of Darwin's kids live in West Texas. You're the only one who needs a house."

Madison followed her grandmother off the porch, but stopped to look back at the huge, aging structure. It definitely needed some work, particularly on the inside. The kitchen was a nightmare, and the pathetically few bathrooms were small and outdated.

Not that she was even considering the possibility. Madison shook her head to clear the ludicrous thought and laughed away her grandmother's statement. "Not *that* much of a house, I don't!"

She was still laughing when she relayed the conversation to Genesis later that evening.

21

Madison's first day at the insurance company was less memorable than her first day at the chicken houses. She spent the morning filing paperwork and answering phone calls. Two people came by to drop off insurance payments and she collected the mail. By all counts, her newest job was rather boring.

A series of telephone hang-ups kept Madison on her toes. At first, she thought it was someone unfamiliar with her voice and therefore reluctant to speak with her about their insurance needs. Dean Lewis did not have caller I.D. as part of his phone service, so she had no way of knowing if it was the same person calling back. By the fourth hang-up, she knew the calls were intentional. Since she would not put it past Myrna Lewis to call and check up on her, Madison made a game of the calls. Each time silence met her on the other end, she went into a detailed spiel about the many services offered by Dean Lewis Insurance Company. By the end of the day, she adapted part of the pitch into her standard greeting when answering the phone.

When the calls started coming in on her cell phone, she knew someone was deliberately harassing her. She belatedly remembered the vague threats from Friday night's call. With so much having happened since then, she had not given the incident another thought. Should she be worried?

As she locked up at five o'clock, she took note of her surroundings with mild concern. There was an empty store to the left of the insurance company, a busy but closed beauty parlor to the right. Directly across the street was the old theater that now doubled as a gymnasium and dance studio. Beside it was a small engine repair shop and the only business showing any signs of life that afternoon.

Shrugging off the sense of nebulous unease, Madison gathered her coat closer and hurried to Granny Bert's long Buick. Overnight, the unseasonably warm weather had given way to a norther and now temperatures had plunged. There was even talk of snow flurries by the end of the week, but she knew better than to get her hopes up. It seldom snowed this far south.

She was pulling into the driveway at home before the old car's heater kicked in. As she got out and hurried inside to the warm house, she wondered what kind of demo car the dealership offered.

One with a good heater, she hoped.

Tuesday was an abbreviated repeat of Monday. The main difference was that the mailman brought the much-awaited envelope for Ramona Gleason, so Madison called the widow to deliver the news before closing the office at noon.

"You'll have to bring it to me," Ramona informed her.

"Mr. Lewis didn't mention delivering the check. He asked me to call you, so you could drop by at your convenience."

"Well, it is not *convenient* for me to come by today."

"Won't you be in town today?" Madison asked politely. "At least in Naomi, at Talk of the Town?"

She soon regretted mentioning the salon. Ramon Gleason huffed and went off on a five-minute tangent; for the first time in over three-years, she was unable to keep her standing Tuesday afternoon appointment. Not only did her sister-in-law's entire family suffer from the flu, but Deanna had shared the contagious illness with the other stylists. If they did not catch it from her, then surely those bratty kids of Katie Ngyen had spread the germs; they were always hanging around at the salon, even though Ramona had complained about them numerous times. Now the entire salon was shut down for three full days while crews came in to clean and stylists stayed home in quarantine. What was Ramona to do now? She had a trip to Cancun planned for the weekend, and she could hardly go with her nails looking like they did!

Madison finally agreed to bring the check out, simply to break into the other woman's rant. She was closing the office early today anyway, and could deliver the envelope after she stopped by to see the Chief of Police.

The depot-turned-police-station was a pleasant mix of old and new. Wooden benches still lined the walls of the historic building and the large old windows allowed in plenty of sunshine from outside. On this overcast winter afternoon, the light filtering in was weak. The antique ticket counter was still in use, a functional yet preserved relic from the past.

Beyond the counter, the twenty-first century kicked in with full gear. A sea of electronic gadgets beeped and blinked on the wall behind the desk, and black and white images flashed across multiple surveillance monitors.

"May I help you, Mrs. Reynolds?" the ever-efficient Vina Jones asked from behind the desk. Like the depot itself, the woman was a treasured relic. It was impossible to determine her age. Her black-as-night skin was still smooth and almost wrinkle-free. The tiny crinkles at the corners of her eyes, detailed in sharp white contrast to the rest of her skin, was the only hint at her advanced age. Her buzzed hair was like a tight skullcap of fuzzy gray; it had been the same style, and same color, since her early thirties. It was anyone's guess how long ago that had been.

"Is the Chief in?"

"Let me see if he is taking visitors." Her words were neither sharp nor cool, but they were definitely professional.

"He asked me to stop by." Madison felt compelled to add the tidbit as Vina spoke discreetly into the earpiece on her cropped head.

Within seconds, she nodded her approval. "The Chief will see you now."

"Thank you." Madison tried her best not to skulk. There was something about Vina Jones that made her feel woefully inadequate and bothersome. If she could just slip past her, she would be out of the woman's way...

"Mrs. Reynolds?" Vina's voice stopped her halfway across the room.

Madison turned with all the enthusiasm of facing a firing squad. "Yes?"

Vina flashed a bright white smile. "You tell Miss Bert I said hello, you hear?"

An invisible weight fell from her shoulders. "I'll do that!" she said, straightening her posture as she returned a bright smile.

Brash's office was in the far corner, the walls made of glass as much as they were wood. The blinds were all open and he could see her approach, so there was no need to knock. He stood to greet Madison when she entered, coming around to offer her a chair.

"Her bark is much worse than her bite," Brash chuckled, nodding in Vina's direction.

"I bet she's wonderful at interrogation," Madison murmured, sitting in the chair he held for her. "She terrifies me, and I haven't done anything wrong!"

"The day Vina Jones retires will be a sad day for The Sisters Police Department," he agreed. "That woman has been here as long as anyone can remember, and she runs this place like a well-oiled engine. Without her, we'd all fall apart," he admitted with unabashed candor.

Brash settled into the chair beside her, foregoing the more formal place behind his desk. His sharp eyes roamed over her, taking in every detail of her appearance. Madison squirmed uncomfortably, afraid he would see too much. "So how are you doing?" he finally asked.

"Fine."

"That was the answer you gave me in front of your family. Now I'm asking when it's just you and me." His voice dropped with a serious note. "How are you, Maddy?"

It was time to be honest, even with herself. "I don't think 'frightened' is the right word, but I'm not far from it," she admitted. "Between being rammed by another vehicle, getting shut up in the chicken houses, and now all the phone-calls, I'm starting to get skittish."

"Wait, you've had more phone calls?" he asked with a scowl. "When was this?"

"All day yesterday and today. I had ten, I think, at the insurance office, another four or five on my cell phone. No one says anything, just calls and then hangs up."

"Insurance office?"

"I'm filling in for Dean Lewis this week while he and Myrna are away at a convention." She saw the surprise on his face and laughed before he said anything. "I know, I thought the same thing. But there was also some gardening show, and she wanted to go badly enough to let me work. As far as I'm concerned, it's a win-win. I get paid, and the Hadley's can walk down the street without being harassed."

Brash nodded thoughtfully. "Which explains why she wanted us to do a daily drive-by. She wasn't so much worried about her house, she was worried about her yard," he realized.

"Sounds about par," Madison agreed.

"So tell me about the phone calls."

"I did. They call, they hang up. No call-back number."

"And last Saturday? Officer Perry says you didn't see anyone or notice anything amiss?"

"Other than all the switches changed to create high pressure with me inside, there was nothing unusual about the day. I met with the Service Tech from Barbour and then went about my day. I was in the last house when it happened."

"We spoke with Menger; he said everything was in working order while he was there. He didn't meet anyone on his way out or see anything unusual. But there have been odd occurrences around the farms before, just as you and I have discussed."

"So it has to be someone with some knowledge of the farms. And they had to have known my schedule, to know that I would be inside."

"Have you noticed anyone following you lately? Anyone hanging around the house?"

Chills popped up on Madison's arms. "No," she said slowly. "But when I left the office yesterday, I had the oddest sensation of being watched. I just thought I was on edge, with the phone calls and all."

"I want you to be extra vigilant, Madison. Someone is harassing you. Either they think you saw something when you found Ronny's body, or you have made someone nervous with all your questions around town. I've told you once and I'm telling you again, leave the detective work to me."

"That reminds me. I have a list of names for you." She rummaged through her purse until she found the neatly folded piece of notebook paper.

With a crinkled forehead, Brash read off the names. The list had a familiar ring to it. "What is this and where did you get it?" he demanded.

"It's a list of people you need to interview. One of those men may have been the one to actually murder Ronny Gleason."

He generously ignored the fact that she was telling him how to do his job. He concentrated on more pressing matters. "Where did you get this?"

Hedging the question, Madison redirected his attention by saying, "I have it by good authority that the next cockfight will take place at Bernie Havlicek's, sometime this week."

"Havlicek's? Again?" he asked sharply. Then he narrowed his eyes. "And you know this, how?"

"I –uh- may have overheard it somewhere."

"Where?"

"I was … out walking… the other night –" She chose her words carefully.

"What night?" he barked.

Madison hesitated before giving her reluctant answer. "Friday."

"Friday? You mean … after?" The words went unspoken, but they settled uneasily between them.

After I tried to kiss you? After you accused me of being a scoundrel and a cheat? After you destroyed what we were slowing building?

"Yes."

"What did you do?" It was an accusation, as much as a question.

Madison was reluctant to give him all the details. She did not want to implicate her friend in her shenanigans. Technically, they had been trespassing.

"I was feeling restless. So I went for a walk."

"Where?" His questions were pointed and direct, leaving little room for wiggle.

Still, Madison managed to twist her way through her answers. "Just outside of town," she said vaguely.

"You went walking at night on a country road. In late January. In the dark. All by yourself." From the sound of his voice, he did not believe a word of it, any more than Genny had. Reading the expression on her face with startling acuity, Brash corrected himself. "Ah, of course. You took Genesis along with you."

"There's safety in numbers," Madison mumbled.

"Where did you say this walk took place?"

Knowing he would not relent until she spilled the whole story, Madison sighed. "At the very end of Sawyer Street. Out near the old Muehler place."

"Where there are absolutely no street lights or even house lights, for that matter. One of our most popular late-night destinations for walking," he said dryly.

"It's near the Thompson's. I'm friends with their dogs, so I knew they wouldn't bark at me."

He called her on her lie. "That is the lamest and most ridiculous excuse I have ever heard."

Madison waved the words away. "It doesn't matter why I was there. All that matters is what I saw and what I overheard."

"Which was?"

"They were holding a cockfight at the abandoned farm. I saw those men on that piece of paper-" she used exaggerated hand movements to emphasize her words, "-placing bets and engaging in illegal gambling. Which means that any one of them could potentially have reason to want Ronny Gleason dead. And I distinctly overheard two of the men say that Don Ngyen was taking the fall for something he didn't do!"

Her smug look of triumph crumbled under Brash's simple question. "Who were the men?"

"Well, I – I don't know. I couldn't see their faces. One of their voices sounded familiar, but I don't know who they were."

Brash closed his eyes and pinched the bridge of his nose in an obvious effort to control his temper. "There are so many holes in your story, I don't know which one to crawl through first," he grumbled. "Apparently you feel I should release Ngyen, based solely on the fact that you overheard some unknown man claim he was innocent."

"No, not solely for that reason."

"Oh, that's right. These other men might have a motive, too, so obviously that let's Ngyen off the hook."

"You don't have to be so snarky."

To her surprise, Brash looked slightly amused. "You're afraid of our coordinator, but you don't mind smart-mouthing the Chief of Police?"

"She's scary," was Madison's only defense.

Because she was right, Brash moved on. "You were trespassing on posted property."

"I didn't see the sign."

"Did you happen to notice the fence?"

Madison chose not to comment. With a determined glint in her hazel eyes, she said, "I also overheard them talking about the boss, someone obviously higher up than Ronny Gleason. And I think you're right. I think this is an organized gambling ring."

"I'm so glad you approve of my theory. I suppose your years of watching Matlock and CSI qualify you to offer your glowing endorsement?"

With great effort, Madison resisted the urge to stick her tongue out at him.

Brash continued. "Of course, the biggest problem I have with all of this is that you were witness to illegal activity, yet failed to call it in. By failing to report it, a smart Assistance District Attorney could argue your silence makes you an accessory to crime."

Madison had a quick comeback, along with a charming smile. "A smart Chief of Police would recognize I have valuable information to share and would never dream of pressing charges."

She knew he was having difficulty maintaining his stoic expression. His eyes glittered with appreciation, but his voice remained gruff. "You should have reported it, Maddy. We might could have caught them in the act."

She shook her head. "Once they turned the dogs loose, I'm sure they packed up and scattered."

"Dogs? They turned the dogs out on you?" White showed around his surprised brown eyes.

"Luckily they were distracted by the goats, but not before one slightly irate billy had his say." She could not help but rub the offended area.

"Let me guess. You're friends with the Thompson's dogs, but not their goats."

"Actually, I am now quite fond of those goats. If not for them, the dogs would have caught us."

Brash surprised her yet again by tossing back his head and laughing. "I never knew you were such a firecracker," he said. The words sounded suspiciously like a compliment. "Miss Bert must be rubbing off on you."

"Heaven forbid." Madison pretended to shudder, but a smile hovered around her lips.

"Look, Maddy, you have to stop this nonsense. You are not a private investigator and you have no business snooping around dark country roads and spying on illegal gambling operations. You are very lucky you did not get caught."

"Yes, I do realize this," she said wearily.

"Someone has tried, more than once, to cause you serious bodily harm. Someone is harassing you and most likely monitoring your every move. If you won't stop this nonsense for your own safety, do it for your family. Think of your kids. What would they do if they were to lose both of their parents?"

Stricken by his words, Madison's face lost its color. "That- That's a low blow, Chief," she finally managed to say.

"I don't think you realize how serious this is, Madison. You could have been killed, any of those times. Including at the farm, if anyone had seen you or if the dogs had caught you. This isn't some little my-bird's-bigger-than-your-bird bragging match. These people play for blood."

Thinking of all the blood she had already seen, Madison shuddered for real.

The radio on his side crackled as Officer Schimanski requested back up on a possible arson. Madison heard the tone-out for The Sisters Fire Department as the dispatcher rattled off an address.

"I've got to go," Brash said, already up and grabbing his jacket.

"Sawyer Road?" Madison repeated the address given on the radio.

"Yeah," Brash said, cramming his cowboy hat onto his head. "It's the old Muehler place. Someone set it afire."

22

Madison watched as fire trucks pulled out from the station with their sirens blaring. The old cotton gin housed the fire station and was directly across the track from the depot where she sat. Waiting for all the emergency personnel to leave, including Brash in the police cruiser, she watched a pick-up slide into the station and a man dressed in a suit dash inside. In less time than it took her to put on a pair of pantyhose and shoes, the same man came barreling out of the station in full bunker gear and jumped into the backseat of the last departing fire truck.

Assuming it was safe to proceed, Madison pulled out of the parking lot and onto First Street. As she crossed the track into Naomi, two more pick-up trucks pulled out to pass her. Flashing emergency lights identified them as personal vehicles for members of the volunteer fire department.

The trucks zoomed ahead and were soon out of sight, even before Madison turned and headed toward the Gleason Farm. There was little doubt the fire set at the Muehler place was directly related to the cockfight she and Genesis stumbled upon. What struck her odd was that the arsonist waited until today to destroy any evidence left behind. Was it just a coincidence? Perhaps they needed the few extra days to gather the pens and roosters and whatever else needed to conduct their illegal operation. But something told her it had more to do with the fact that she had gone to see Brash today. Someone was watching her, and they knew the moment she went to the police.

The thought was sobering. It gave her a creepy sensation to think that someone was spying on her, watching her every move. But who? Who was watching her? Why hadn't she seen them? And why would someone want to watch her in the first place?

Madison went back over the sequence of events in her head, examining each piece of information she had gathered.

Ronny Gleason died of electrocution. Since there was no evidence of accidental shock at the farm, it was safe to assume he died somewhere else and someone moved his body. There was the possibility of his death being an accident and someone — possibly a man who spoke poor English?— trying to cover it up for fear of being accused of murder. Madison tucked the thought away as one theory, but she favored another; someone had killed Ronny Gleason because of his gambling and then dumped his body in the chicken house, where they hoped the chickens and the heat would destroy all evidence of foul play. If not for an autopsy and the sharp eye of the medical examiner, the scheme might have worked.

Ronny Gleason definitely had a gambling problem. Frequent trips to Las Vegas pointed to a serious addiction, particularly one this late in his flock. According to Cutter Montgomery, the grower planned this last trip during a critical point of the operation and was even willing to leave it all in her incapable hands. That was a sure sign of desperation if she had ever seen one.

What would make a man do that? she wondered, turning onto County Road 452. Did he owe someone a large sum of money again? Was he that desperate to make some quick cash? Or was it his addiction overruling common sense? Maybe there was a big poker game taking place in Vegas; she would check that out when she got back home, since she had nothing else to do this afternoon. Or, she considered, maybe he was meeting 'the boss' and making more plans for his illegal gaming operation. From what she gathered, Ronny Gleason bought the fighting cocks from other people, set up the fights, and took a nice share of the profits, win or lose.

He could have easily made someone angry. Her imagination took flight, wondering if it could be someone more important than a local gambler who lost this month's rent. A bookie, perhaps, worried about someone cutting into their own territory of organized gambling. *Oh, wait, the mafia!* she decided. They were more dangerous and more likely to commit murder.

Madison was feeling quite pleased with herself and her keen sense of detective skills until a staggering thought hit her: according to her theory, that meant the mafia was the one watching her every move! Fear slithered down her spine and she quickly shook the idea away. So not the mafia. Surely, there was someone else.

Her eye slid over to the file folder on the seat. One obvious suspect was Ramona Gleason. The envelope she was delivering suggested Ramona's husband might be worth more to her dead than alive. But was the woman capable of murder? And of the physical strength involved in moving her husband's body? Maybe she had an accomplice. Granny Bert said she never heard of 'the plastic widow' having an actual lover, but certainly everyone thought it possible, if not downright probable. Maybe she had talked her lover into helping her kill her husband and move his body to the chicken houses for decomposition and eventual discovery.

Not that this theory brought much more comfort. Madison twisted her lips in thought as she pulled into the driveway leading up to the Gleason home. If her latest theory was right and Ramona was responsible for Ronny's death, she was putting herself in danger by coming here. No one knew where she was. The police, the fire department, and probably half the town were two miles away at the Muehler fire.

She told herself she was over-reacting. The truth was, she was no private detective, just like Brash was always insisting. She could come up with dozens of theories —the mafia, a cheating wife, disgruntled gamblers who lost the shirt off their backs in one of Ronny's fights, even townspeople he owed money to— but they were merely hypothetical. She had no proof. She did not even know the identity of the men she overheard at the fight, the ones talking about the 'boss' and Don Ngyen's innocence. She could scare herself silly with supposed murderers and the fear of being watched, but it might just be coincidence that the abandoned Muehler place caught fire today. And, she reminded herself, Ramona Gleason went to Talk of the Town every Tuesday, so she had an alibi for the time Ronny was killed. Madison was over-reacting.

Still, she shot off a quick text message to Genesis, letting someone know where she was. And she would make the visit brief. She would drop the check off at the door and be gone.

Feeling much more confident, Madison stuffed her cell phone into her pocket, grabbed the envelope from the seat, and pulled her coat around her as she stepped from the car.

The Gleason's exuberant puppy ran up to greet her as she rang the doorbell. Despite the dog's large size, she knew the black Labrador was friendly and posed no harm. It pranced around her and alternately barked and whined, begging for attention. Madison laughed as the overgrown puppy jumped up and twirled mid-air, trying his best to impress her. Her laughter died when the dog's foot came down onto a bowl of milk sitting on the porch. As his huge paw hit the edge of the bowl, the liquid splashed up and got all over Madison's outstretched hand as she tried to calm him.

"Kujo!" Ramona cried out the dog's name as she swung open the door and saw the mess he had created. "Go on, Kujo, get! Get away!"

"He was a little excited," Madison said needlessly, slinging milk from her hand.

"Sorry about that. You can come in and wash your hands, if you like," the other woman offered.

Madison hesitated. She told herself she was being ridiculous. And her hand was already feeling sticky and cold. It only made sense to step inside and clean up. Besides, the milk had splashed on her coat and she needed to wipe it off before it stained. She could not afford to send it to the cleaners.

"Thank you," she said, stepping through the door Ramona held open.

Ramona spotted the check in Madison's other hand, the one spared from the splash. Without a word, she whipped the envelope out of her grasp as she passed by.

"Finally!" the new widow said with dramatics.

"I actually thought it was rather quick," Madison murmured. "When my husband died, it took the insurance company weeks to pay the claim."

"Well, thank goodness that is not the case here. I need this money," she sniffed.

Madison resisted rolling her eyes. Talk about needing money! *I needed money to exist, not to fluff up my appearance!*

"The bathroom is that way," Ramona said distractedly, flinging one arm behind her as she peered down at the envelope in her hands.

The hall had a series of closed doors. The first one Madison opened was a coat closet. She glimpsed real fur and at least two designer leather jackets before she quickly shut the door. She tried the next one, only to discover an office. *Maybe she should hire me as a housekeeper,* Madison thought as she surveyed the messy room. She moved across the hall to another closed door.

Ah, finally. The bathroom. Madison slipped into the room, immediately appreciating the large space. A huge Jacuzzi tub with dozens of jets dominated the back corner. The room had a classic black and white theme, including the white marble of the tub splashed with ebony. Designer monogrammed towels proclaimed one 'His', the other 'Hers'.

The bathroom at Granny's was small and cramped. Madison idly wondered if the bathrooms at the Big House could be modified to resemble this one. She shook her head and turned away from the tempting sight, but not before visions of bubble baths danced in her head.

She slipped off her rings and lathered her hands with soap from an ornate dispenser. After washing the sticky substance from her hands, she went to work wiping down her coat. When she was satisfied there would be little or no stain, she rinsed her hands again and reached for her rings.

A thought rambled through her mind. Why was she still wearing Gray's ring? Their marriage was over long ago, a good two years before his death. She owed him no loyalty, not after all he had done to her, but somewhere in her broken spirit, the rings offered a sense of belonging. If nothing else, they reminded her that once upon a time, a man had wanted her enough to give her his name.

Her wedding ring slipped from her fingers and hit the tiled floor. It bounced a few times before rolling across the room. Madison chased after it, but it disappeared under the plant stand at the foot of the tub. As Madison got down on all fours and crawled beneath the cascading fronds of a Boston fern, she wondered if this was some sort of sign. Here she was on her knees again, groveling to keep the ring on her finger.

"Maybe it's time to take it off," she murmured aloud, just as her fingers touched the cool circle of white gold.

A dark place on the wall caught her attention and Madison pushed more fronds aside to get a better look. A black smudge scorched the wall around the electrical plug, indicating a recent flash of fire. A thin black mark sullied the white tile of the floor, resembling a cord.

With sick realization, Madison turned her head and confirmed what she already knew: the tub was directly beside the plug. It would be all-too-easy to plug in a small appliance, drop it into the tub while Ronny bathed, and electrocute the defenseless man. Hadn't Genny said something about Cutter having to reset a breaker for Ramona Gleason? Apparently she did not realize the plug had shorted out and played havoc with her breaker box when she killed her husband.

Stuffing her ring back onto her finger and backing out from beneath the plant, Madison nearly overturned the small table in her haste. A stubborn stem caught on her coat collar and tagged along for a ride as she pushed herself upright on wobbly legs.

"Think, Madison, think," she whispered.

She had to get out of here. She could not let Ramona know she had seen anything amiss or that she even suspected her. She would have to act calm, cool, and collected as she said her goodbyes and hurried out as fast as possible.

Madison stared at her reflection in the mirror with dismay. Her eyes were wide and frightened. Her skin, always light and kissed with peach undertones, was particularly pale and pasty. One look at her, and Ramona would know something was wrong. "Pull it together, girl. Suck it up and get out of here."

She gave herself the pep talk before taking a deep breath and reaching for the door handle.

Madison was thankful for her long stride, which carried her quickly down the hall and into the living room. She came to an abrupt halt when she saw the stormy expression on the other woman's face.

"What is the meaning of this?" she fairly shrieked, tapping her high-heeled foot onto the plush carpet.

Madison darted a guilty gaze toward the bathroom. "I-I don't know what you're talk-talking about," she stammered. She eased a few feet away, closer to the door.

"This check," she screamed. When she flung her arm out to flash the paper in front of Madison's face, Madison instinctively ducked. Ramona scowled deeply but did not let the move distract her. "This tiny, paltry, hardly-worth-the-ink-it-took-to-print-it check! What is the meaning of this?"

"I-I don't know what you're talking about," Madison said, but this time her voice held a note of confusion.

"Would you stop saying that?" Ramona spat. "Of course you know what I'm talking about! You just delivered this check to me, sad amount that it is. What I want to know is why this check will hardly pay for a new pair of shoes, much less for my husband's funeral!"

Madison felt a prick of guilt. Ramona was using the insurance money to pay for Ronny's funeral? She just assumed it would go for a new face-lift or tummy tuck, or an island getaway for her and her lover.

Ramona was still ranting. "I wanted the best for my Ronny! I know what people say, but they just didn't understand our marriage. I wanted him to have a nice casket, a new suit of clothes, a granite headstone! This check won't even pay for the flowers!" She paced across the room, flapping the check in the air as she whipped around and marched back to where Madison stood. "What I want to know is where the rest of it is! Why isn't this check for more?"

"I have no idea," Madison said in all sincerity. "I didn't open the envelope; I just delivered it to you."

"Then I suggest you call that boss of yours and find out what the hell is going on here!"

Madison saw her opportunity to escape. "I-I will," she promised. "I'll go right now and call him."

Ramona followed her to the door, mumbling beneath her breath. According to her, the day had gone from bad to worse. She had to break her standing appointment at Talk of the

Town —a three-year tradition, down the sink drain!— and now she had been cheated out of what was rightfully hers. Poor Ronny deserved better, she wailed. He deserved the fine funeral she gave him, without it sending his widow into debt.

Madison only heard half the lamented tale as she hurriedly bid goodbye and raced to her car. She threw the car in reverse and tore out of the driveway, flinging the papers from her seat into the floorboard. Her only concern was putting as much space as possible between her and the murderess.

When Madison's phone rang, she was almost off the Gleason Farm and close to freedom.

"Well, congratulations!" a cheerful voice greeted her.

Madison pulled the phone away from her ear and glanced down at the caller ID. "Eddie?"

"Yes, ma'am. I'm just calling to tell you what a fantastic job you did on the chickens. You not only won first place, you kicked everyone else's butt!" the Service Tech happily announced.

"Really? That's fantastic. I was so afraid I was going to hurt the flock!" Madison could not help but feel a measure of pride in the accomplishment, even though she knew she had little to do with the flock's overall performance.

"You should be proud of yourself."

"I am," she admitted, sitting up a bit straighter in the seat of the borrowed Buick. She was discovering all kinds of hidden talents today, from detective skills to chicken growing.

"To show their appreciation, Barbour is offering a very rare and unusual bonus. I wondered if you could meet me at the farm so I can deliver you a check."

"A check?" she asked in surprise.

"As I said, you did an excellent job. I'm headed out to the farm now. Think you could meet me there in about ten minutes?"

"I can be there in two," Madison said, already making a U-turn in the road.

"See you then."

A smile lit Madison's face as she turned onto the farm road. A bonus! Even if it was just a token amount, it was more than she expected. Probably more than she deserved, her conscious railed, but she ignored the sarcastic little voice in her head. She texted Genny as she drove down the gravel road; surely, texting on such a secluded path was allowed.

Big news! Know who killed Ronny. Meeting tech to pick up bonus $$ for chickens. Be there in 10.

She pulled up between the first two houses to wait for Eddie. She had a moment, so she bent to retrieve the papers flung across the floorboard. With a few still out of her reach, she put the car in park and went around to open the passenger side door, slipping her phone into her pants pocket as she did. When a bottle of water fell out on the ground, she stuffed it into her coat pocket and bent down to retrieve a small envelope, almost identical to the one she delivered to Ramona. It was stubbornly wedged beneath the edge of the floor mat. As she freed the envelope, the neatly typed name on the front caught her eye. She frowned in confusion.

"I believe I will take that now, thank you very much."

The man's voice startled her. With her back to the unseen man, she realized she knew that voice. It was the same one she heard at the cockfight, the one discussing the boss's greed that cut into his own profits.

As Madison held the envelope over her shoulder with one hand, she used the other to press 'send' on her phone. With any luck, Eddie Menger, the last person who had called, would pick up and know she was in danger.

23

"You couldn't leave well enough alone, could you?" the man taunted as he snatched the envelope out of her hands. "You had to go poking your nose into places it didn't belong!"

Madison heard a buzz and feared it might be coming from her head. *You cannot faint now!* she chided herself, feeling lightheaded.

Behind her, the man snarled. "What the hell are you doing calling me? Get your phone out here where I can see it!"

Belatedly, Madison placed the voice. Eddie Menger! It was his phone buzzing on vibrate. How could she have been so stupid?

"Turn around and show me your phone," the irate Service Tech said, roughly jerking her arm and spinning her around.

"I-I dropped it," she lied. "That's what I was looking for."

"Then get in there and find it." He shoved her forward but held one arm behind her back. "And don't get any ideas about trying to get away. Kill the motor and give me the keys."

Bending over into the car, Madison did as he demanded, visually searching the car for something to use as a weapon. All she saw was two empty water bottles, a half-eaten taco from her lunch (whose other half was now settling heavily upon her stomach), a bobby pin, a handful of loose change, and a crumbled brochure advertising cremation services.

Granny Bert is planning her funeral? Madison blinked in surprise. *And she plans to be* cremated? Madison suppressed a horrified shudder, wondering why anyone would want their body to be burned.

"Did you find your phone?" Eddie Menger demanded, bringing her out of her stupor. "Hurry it up!"

"I don't see it."

"Oh well, doesn't matter. I'll find it later."

Later? He jerked on her arm, just as she saw the ballpoint pen. She barely managed to slip her fingers around it as he pulled her away from the car. As she deftly worked the pen up the sleeve of her shirt —she might need it later, if this plan did not work— she suddenly flung herself backwards, throwing her full weight into the startled man. He stumbled back and almost fell, but he never lost hold of her arm. His grip was like a steel vise and every bit as painful.

"Here, now, none of that!" he told her sternly. His voice was oddly calm, which only managed to frighten Madison even more. She suddenly understood the term 'cold-blooded' killer.

He slammed the car door shut and pushed her to walk in front of him.

"Wh-Where are we going?" she asked.

"Shut up and walk. And keep your hands where I can see them."

"I-I'm cold."

"You'll be plenty warm where we're going," he said with a smirk.

She stumbled along the white rock road, toward the rear of the houses. "Why?" she asked after a moment. "Why did you kill Ronny Gleason?"

"Damn fool threatened me. *Me!* After all I had on the man, he actually thought he could double-cross me! The fool got what was coming to him."

"What did you have on Ronny?"

"For starters, he was keeping game roosters, which was against Barbour rules. He was fighting them and taking bets, which is against Texas law. Plus the man was bribing a Barbour Service Tech to falsify records. There was a reason he always placed at the top of competition, and it wasn't because the man knew how to raise chickens!" Eddie Menger barked out a bitter laugh.

"A Service Tech?" Madison asked in surprise. "How could another Service Tech falsify records for this farm?"

"Who said it was another Service Tech?" His sly grin was laced with evil.

"You? He was paying you to rig competition?"

Eddie Menger looked at her with a smug smile. "I've got me a sweet little system going. All my growers are in the top ten percent of the company's best performers. Not only does it look good on my part, but it brings me in a nice bonus paycheck and some sweet incentive awards. I've won season tickets to the Houston Texans, an all-expense-paid dove hunt down in South Texas and a fancy new laptop. That laptop sure has come in handy, too, especially when I want to control things on the farm without stepping foot on the property."

Madison gasped and forgot to take a step. She stumbled to a halt as she stared over at him. "That's how you did it!" she cried. "That's how you made all those strange things happen, how you made the house go dark with me in it, and how you created all those alarms! You-You manipulated me into going out that rainy night. And you tried to bring the house down around me by creating high pressure with me inside. You tried to kill me!"

"Don't act so surprised. You were getting too close. Instead of minding your own business and just walking the houses like you were hired to do, you had to go butting your nose in where it didn't belong." He jerked on her arm again, spurring her back into motion.

"What-What did I do? Where did I poke my nose?"

"deCordova started sniffing around, asking questions, looking into Ronny's gambling problem. Soon he'd be looking into his finances and see a few inconsistencies. Before long, Barbour would get wind of the cockfights and start asking questions of their own. The Ngyens pay me to keep quiet about their part in all this, but Barbour would want to know how I let something like that slip past me. If they shut down the Ngyens, I'd lose commission on a farm. If they shut down the fights, I stand to lose a lot more."

"I heard you tell that other man the boss was getting greedy, cutting into your profits."

"You-? Where? Where did you hear that?" Eddie demanded.

Pleased that she was able to offer at least one surprise of her own, Madison gloated. "At the Muehler place."

"That was you?" the man snarled.

"You turned the dogs out on me!" Madison said with indignation.

"That was Harold. If I'd have known you were there, I would have snapped your neck."

His matter-of-fact tone caused a new chill to race down Madison's already shivering spine. She blanched as she absorbed the knowledge that he planned to kill her now. He would not admit his guilt to her if he planned to let her live.

"Who is your boss?" she asked, trying to stall the inevitable.

"Don't you worry about that. You have other things to worry about."

She had to keep him talking. She did not know where they were headed, but she knew it was to her death. "So you killed Ronny because he threatened to go to Barbour about your little scheme?"

"It's hardly a 'little' scheme," Eddie bragged. "It goes far deeper than rigging feed conversion and placing first in competition, deeper than earning hush money to keep a few secrets. I own a farm in Leon County, too, did you know that? It's not under my name, of course, and I don't run it. I have people to do that for me. And thanks to this envelope you just brought me, I'll soon own this farm, too."

"The grower who died in Leon County," Madison murmured, recalling a previous conversation. "The car wreck."

"Funny, how a brand new car like that can suddenly develop mechanical problems."

"So you somehow blackmail the growers into naming you beneficiary on their life insurance policies?" Madison guessed.

"Just an added little detail in keeping them at the top of competition."

"So you make money all the way around. You earn a paycheck from Barbour, a bribe from the grower, a bonus from Barbour when that grower performs well, hush money from the farms growing fighting roosters, money off the bets placed on those roosters, plus you collect life insurance when you kill off a grower or two?"

"Technically, there have only been two. It was just a lucky coincidence that Larry Botello died of a heart attack shortly after he signed over his policy."

"Let me guess," Madison said dryly. "They have different insurance companies so no one has ever made the connection. But what about Ramona Gleason?"

"What about her?"

"She's not at all happy with her check. Why haven't the other wives complained?"

"What's to complain about? Most banks require that growers have a life insurance policy. I have nothing to do with who they name beneficiary. My policy is completely separate." He frowned as he said, "I'm not completely heartless. I don't want to leave their families with nothing."

"Just without a husband or father."

The Service Tech shrugged. "The right amount of money can ease a lot of heartache."

"Apparently Ramona didn't receive the right amount."

"That's her problem, not mine. The damn fool husband of hers took out a second mortgage on his farm last fall. I imagine most of his policy went to cover that."

"So that's how he paid off all his debts," Madison murmured aloud.

"Yeah, but he placed some sucker bets and he was right back in debt again. Only this time, it was with the wrong people. We had a sweet little operation going on down here, until he brought in the big boys for a piece of the action. First thing I knew, they were taking over." Eddie spit on the ground, as if to rid his mouth of a foul taste. "That's the second time Ronny's screwed me over, but I made damn sure it was the last. First time he cost me my teaching job at the school, then he cut into my action on the fights. When he threatened to squeal on me, I knew I'd had enough."

"So you killed him, just to keep your job at Barbour?" They had reached the end of the rock road and were at the back of the farm, near the incinerator.

"Not the job."

"To stay out of jail?" she guessed again.

"I killed him to stay alive. It wasn't Barbour or the law he threatened me with."

Realizing Eddie Menger was more frightened of the 'big boys' than he was of the legal system or job security, ice settled into Madison's veins. That could only mean that the men controlling the game roosters were powerful and extremely dangerous.

"Did-Did they tell you to kill me?"

Eddie laughed. "Don't flatter yourself. You aren't important enough for them to even notice. No, killing you is completely my idea."

"So how did you kill Eddie?" She thought about the blackened wall in his bathroom. "Was Ramona in on it?"

"And break a nail?" Eddie scoffed. "No, all that broad thinks about is herself and how she looks in the mirror. While she was off to her usual Tuesday afternoon beauty appointment, I slipped inside the house and waited for Ronny to take his bath. I knew he had a bad back and always sat in front of the Jacuzzi jets after he walked houses. I tossed a radio in with him, pulled him from the water, then took him to the chicken houses where the chickens were supposed to peck away all traces of foul play. Then you came along, and messed up everything. My plan started to fall apart."

"And now?" Madison asked bravely. "How are you going to get around it all now? And how are you going to explain my death?"

"Don't have to." He grinned at his own ingenious plan. "You're going to disappear. There will be talk that you and Ronny were lovers before you moved here. Maybe you were the reason he was always slipping away to Vegas."

"That's crazy! I have children who can vouch for my whereabouts! And I was married, you know."

"But not happily. I looked into your life, Madison Cessna Reynolds. I discovered Little Miss Heiress has some dark secrets in her past. All I need to do is plant the seed of doubt. I'll let them make their own assumptions after that." He gave a nonchalant shrug. "Maybe you were heart-broken. Maybe you were the one to kill Ronny Gleason in the first place, then pretended to find his body." He grinned again. "Yeah, I like that one. You killed him when he refused to leave his wife and marry you. Maybe you even had something to do with your own husband's sudden death, trying to clear the way for the two of you to be together. But now that you have to live with the reality of what you've done, you can't face your children. You'll run away, never to be seen again."

"And just how are you going to make that happen? No one will believe I left my family behind. And surely they'll find my body." It was amazing how calm she sounded when discussing her own demise.

"No, I promise you, no one will ever find your body," he said smugly. "And if you want your family to be safe, you'll do exactly what I tell you to do."

"Leave my family out of this!"

"Your son is a pretty good ball player." Eddie Menger's eyes had an evil glow. "And your daughter is coming along nicely with her cheerleader practice. I'd hate for something to happen to either one of them. They're cute kids, and have their entire future ahead of them."

"No! You can't hurt my kids!" Madison made a grab for his arm, imploring him to keep her family safe.

"I can do whatever the hell I like," he informed her coldly. "But luckily for you, I have no desire to hurt kids or old ladies. Your grandmother actually took my side at the school board meeting when I got fired for fighting with Ronny on school grounds," he mused. "She's a cool old broad. But make no mistake. If you don't do exactly as I say, I will kill every one of them."

"Anything!" Madison cried without hesitation. "I'll do anything, just promise me you won't hurt my children!"

"What about your Granny?" he smirked. "You'd let me hurt the old lady?"

"You-You said you wouldn't. Not if I went along with whatever you have planned."

Eddie seemed to consider her words for a moment, judging her sincerity. He finally nodded. "Just to ease your mind, I promise not to harm that best friend of yours, either. It would be a darn shame to lose the best baker this town's ever seen."

"Genny," Madison whispered, her knees now weak. Whether it was from relief or fright, she could not say; probably both.

"So get going," Eddie said, nudging her forward.

There was an open field beyond the incinerator. Madison looked at him in surprise. "You're letting me go?"

His laugh was short and humorless. "No, silly. Of course not."

"So-So where am I going?"

"To the incinerator, of course."

24

Madison's eyes grew wild. Not that! Surely the man did not plan to burn her alive!

"I don't have all day," he said with exasperation. "I have to get rid of the car and take this check to the bank. I have accounts in several towns, in case you're wondering, so that no one gets suspicious. Can't use a local bank because everyone's so damn nosy around here." The very thought aggravated him and he took it out on Madison, shoving her none too gently. "Go on. Get inside."

Madison's legs were leaden. She was rooted to the spot, unable to move. Fear washed over her and left her feeling cold and weak. Again, she thought she might faint.

"I said to move!" Eddie Menger snarled, shoving her with enough force to make her stumble.

"I can't," she whispered. "I can't get in there."

"You can, or I can start with killing your son. He has baseball practice right about now, doesn't he?" Eddie asked, consulting his wristwatch. He then pulled a detonator from his coat pocket and waved it in Madison's face. "Too bad the entire baseball team will suffer because of your stubbornness."

Madison's whispered plea was hoarse and raw. "N-No. No, don't do that. I beg you."

"Then get in." He lifted the heavy cast iron door of the barrel-shaped incinerator.

Tears streamed down Madison's face. She couldn't do it. Her legs were like limp noodles when she tried to move forward. Her stomach lurched and she was certain she would lose her lunch. She couldn't make herself crawl inside the cast iron oven to a certain death.

But she had to. If she wanted to save her son's life, she had to do it.

Her movements were slow and awkward as she climbed onto the upturned bucket Eddie provided. She lifted her leg and clumsily started to crawl inside the narrow opening of the oven. One leg was already on the grating when she stopped and looked back at her murderer. Her face was ashen, her eyes large and frightened and swimming with tears. "How-How do I know you won't… you won't… kill them anyway?"

"I'll give you my word."

His ludicrous statement, spoken so earnestly, brought out a hysterical laugh. "And I'm supposed to believe you?"

He shrugged in total unconcern. "Up to you. But I tell you what. If you'll get inside without causing me any more trouble, I'll give you the detonator. That way you'll know your kid is safe and you can die with a clear conscience."

She had no choice. She curled her long body into a ball and crawled completely inside the cold tomb that reeked of burnt, decomposed chicken flesh and putrid ashes. The smell alone was enough to gag her, without the horrid knowledge of what was yet to come.

"Always wondered how long it would take to cook a human body," Eddie said conversationally as he poked and prodded her long leg to make it fit inside. "I'll come back in a few hours, make sure you're burning alright."

"The-the detonator," Madison begged, snaking her arm out to reach for it.

He tossed the device inside without care to how it landed. Madison made a wild grab for it, but there was little room inside the cramped confines for her long, flailing arms. The devise fell to the bottom of the incinerator with a clatter. With a sense of cold panic, Madison looked down to see how the detonator had landed. When she saw the red button facing up at her, she went weak with relief.

Her relief was short-lived. Eddie lowered the hatch door, closing her inside the pit of death. When she tried to push against the door, he laughed from the other side and told her it was useless. "Don't bother. I'm wiring it shut. And you can forget screaming, because there's no one around to hear you. The fire department and police are conveniently out at the Muehler place, so your boyfriend or that Montgomery kid won't be coming to your rescue anytime soon."

"Eddie! Don't do this! You can't leave me like this!" she screamed frantically, pounding on the sides of the roughened cast iron until her hands were chaffed and raw.

Inside the pit, light filtered in around the vents and through the cracks. While Eddie worked a piece of wire round and round the handle to insure it stayed tightly shut, Madison forced herself to calm down and look at her surroundings. She was on the wide grating shelf where the chickens were thrown to cook, much like in a barbecue pit. Below her were uncooked bits of chicken and ashes littered with bones and feathers. Swallowing back the bile that rose in her throat, she turned over, so that she lay on her back. The blackened walls loomed around her, threatening to suffocate her with claustrophobia. Once Eddie turned on the gas valve, the temperature would be two thousand degrees and hot enough to roast flesh, but right now the dark interior of the cast iron pit was empty and cold. Wind whistled in through the cracks, increasing the sensation.

Nothing, however, was as numbing as the ice inside her heart. Madison knew she was about to die, and there was nothing she could do to stop it. In a matter of minutes, fire would flame into the pit and cook her alive.

Her eyes zeroed in on the ceramic igniter and the gas line that fed the inferno, situated just above her head. There was a similar igniter on the gas furnace at Granny Bert's. Sometimes it failed to make connection and would not spark. Without a spark, there was no flame.

Knowing her only hope of survival was to disable the igniter, Madison pounded at the small electronic probe with her fist. Nothing happened except to rip her skin. She thought of turning around and kicking it with her feet, but she could hear Eddie walking around the incinerator. If he was done securing the handle, he would be lighting the furnace soon.

She was running out of time.

Madison knew it was a long shot, but she had to try something. She tugged off her coat and worked a piece of her sleeve into the narrow gas line. Remembering the pen stuffed up her shirtsleeve, she used it to push the fabric as far into the line as possible, packing it tightly. She knew it would probably do no good, but it was worth a try. When the body of her coat hung heavily onto the grating, she remembered the water bottle. Grabbing it from the pocket, she doused the igniter with water, then used the cap-end of the bottle to pound away at the probe.

Outside the incinerator, she heard Eddie banging and clanging around as he prepared to start the furnace. She worked frantically, sobs hiccupping in her chest.

Madison heard him flip the switch, heard the rush of gas swoosh down the pipe, waited for the powerful surge of heat to blast against her skin.

A small 'click' echoed in the empty chambers as the igniter failed.

Gas fumes filled the air around her before quickly dissipating, but not before she inhaled the noxious vapor. Nausea roiled in her stomach and made her head swim, but she kept steadily banging on the probe, lest it finally kick in.

She heard Eddie curse at the failed attempt to light and braced herself for another burst of propane. This time, she held her breath and buried her face against her arm until the fumes evaporated. As Eddie tried to start the burner for the third time, Madison finally delivered the fatal blow that permanently disabled the igniter. If he still planned to burn her alive, he would have to find another way.

Madison knew it was only a temporary reprieve. Eddie Menger could not let her live, not after telling her everything he had done. She only had a few moments to think of another plan.

Lying back down on the grate in the cramped space, Madison fished in her pocket to find her cell phone. Afraid he would hear her if she called for help, she decided to text. She did a group message to all her family contacts and to Brash, shooting off a text message that was inadvertently altered with auto-correct. Not bothering to double check the interpretation, Madison pushed send.

At New Beginnings Café, Genesis felt the cell phone buzz in her pocket as she poured Tom Pruett another cup of coffee. She glanced up at the clock, wondering why Madison had not arrived yet. Her 'be there in 10' time estimate was up about ten minutes ago. It was probably her texting now, saying she was finally on the way.

"The people doing the documentary want to focus on my time in the Navy." The old man continued to talk as she refreshed his cup.

"I thought you said you were in the Army," Genesis frowned.

"Oh, no, no, the Navy. I flew a fighter jet. Let me tell you something, it was quite a feat landing those babies on a mere three hundred foot runway." He went off into the technical details of aligning dashboard sights with deck markings, back before the process was automated by computers. Genesis only half-listened. She was beginning to suspect that Cutter was right about Tom Pruett; most of the man's stories were too outlandish —and too often changed— to be true.

After several minutes, she sneaked a peek at the message on her phone.

Bond at bb field. Eddie men get. I'm incinerator. SOS.

Genesis frowned, wondering what on earth it meant. She hadn't heard anything about a bond. And besides, the baseball field was only a few years old. Why would there be a bond to build a new one? And who was this Eddie that would get the men to build it? But most importantly, what did she mean by *'I'm incinerator'*? Did she mean she was furious? Burning mad? It didn't make sense.

"I'm in the process of building a new helicopter prototype right now," her customer went on. "I'm waiting on a shipment of parts to get here from Canada. You would not believe how much this project is costing me, but if I sell the blueprints to the Navy as planned, I should pocket a cool million, plus royalty rights."

"Mmm, that sounds nice," Genesis murmured in distraction, her mind still on her message.

'*SOS*', it said. Help her because she was angry, or help her because she was in trouble?

"Excuse me, Mr. Pruett, I have to go." She walked off in the middle of his inventory list of parts, but he never seemed to notice. He continued to rattle off items as Genesis sent a message back to her friend.

What's going on? Where are you?

Seconds later, her phone buzzed.

Mom, what's up? Strange message, even for you. LOL.

The reply message for the group text came from Blake's phone. As an afterthought, he added another.

You okay? Text me back. LYB.

A new message popped up from Madison.

911! Send help to fat m!

Shilo Dawne passed by as Genesis frowned down at her phone, trying to decipher the crazy messages from her friend.

"What's wrong, Miss Genny?"

Genesis looked up with a stricken expression in her blue eyes. "I keep getting these weird messages from Madison. Something about a bond at the baseball field and somebody named Eddie. Now she wants help at the fat m, wherever that is. I think she's in trouble, but I have no idea where she is!"

Looking over her boss's shoulder to see the screen, Shilo Dawne read the messages. "Spell check," she guessed. "'Eddie men get' is probably Eddie Menger, the Service Tech for Barbour."

"Oh my gosh, you're a genius!" Genesis gasped. "And that's a bomb. A bomb at school! You call 9-1-1; I'm headed out to the Gleason farm!" She was already halfway to the door, texting as she ran.

Hang on on my way!

25

Eddie Menger tried to light the furnace several more times. With each effort, enough gas leaked around the packed fabric to make Madison light-headed. She knew it was important to stay awake and alert, but she was growing groggy. She lay back and rested her weary body, trying to formulate a plan in case no one answered her text message or could not get here before Eddie implemented his own Plan B.

She thought of her children and a drowsy smile came to her face. They were both such good kids. Blake had been turning girls' heads since he was twelve, and every year he seemed to get taller and broader and more handsome. He had a quick wit and a funny sense of humor, and his father's blue-gray eyes. And Bethani. Dear Beth, with her tender heart and big baby blues. She had taken her father's death so hard; how would she react to losing her mother, so soon afterward? Both twins would be devastated.

Pictures of the past flashed through her mind, tiny little snippets in time that warmed her soul and made the thought of death somehow easier. The twins' first birthday party. Blake, learning to ride his tricycle. Bethani chasing after him on foot. Funny things they said and did, the handmade cards they made her each Mother's Day, the way they still kissed her goodnight before they went to sleep each night.

"Love you bunches." Madison whispered their trademark saying aloud, her voice faint.

Her thoughts flitted to Gray. They had been so happy on their wedding day. Even happier the day the twins were born. Her mind wandered through those happy years, lingering on pleasant memories of a picnic in the park, their vacation at Disney World, a special Valentine dinner, a passionate night of making love. A dark memory intruded, but she pushed it away. Not now. Not her last thoughts of the man she once loved.

Her mind grew fuzzier. Granny Bert would take care of the children. Granny Bert and Genny, dear, sweet Genny. The best friend anyone could ever have.

She heard her phone buzz and she lifted it with a weak hand, trying to read the screen. Genesis wanted to know what was going on.

Shaking her head to clear it, Madison realized the gas was taking its toll on her. She couldn't give up, not now. With new determination, she worked to stuff the jacket sleeve tighter into the gas line. She opened the water bottle and took a long sip to clear her mind, then crawled around until she could put her face against the filthy black wall of the incinerator and breathe fresh air through the cracks. Within just a few minutes, she felt her mind clear and her body awaken.

The first time Eddie struck the outside of the incinerator with a pipe wrench, trying to force a connection so the furnace would come on, she absorbed the blow with staggering force. The walls of the cast iron oven quaked as he banged metal upon metal. Madison fell away as surely as if he dealt her a direct hit, her cheek immediately smarting. Tears of pain pricked her eyes and she covered her ears with her hands as the sounds echoed within the hollow cavity.

Hope sprang in her chest when she heard the rumble of a truck and the crunch of approaching tires on the white rock.

"What the hell is a feed truck doing here?" she heard Eddie roar. Judging by sounds and the shadows she could decipher through a tiny slit in the corner of the oven, she knew he dropped the wrench and hurried away.

He would stop the truck before it came any closer. Once he got rid of the driver, he would come back. And when he did, he would kill her. There was no doubt in Madison's mind.

She picked up her cell phone and dialed 9-1-1.

It took a moment for her to convince the operator that she was not playing a prank on her. Yes, there was a bomb on the school baseball field. No, she did not set it. Yes, she was truly trapped inside an incinerator on a chicken farm. Yes, someone was deliberately trying to kill her. No, she would not hold the line until help arrived.

She hung up and called each of her children, knowing they were both at school and could not answer, but leaving voice messages saying that she loved them both very much and that she was proud of them. Then she called Genesis.

Another voice mail box.

"I probably don't have long to talk. Eddie Menger killed Ronny Gleason and some grower in Leon County, and he's in on the cockfighting. He set the fire at the Muehler place to lure the police out there so he could kill me. I managed to disable the incinerator but I know he'll find another way. Genny, take care of the kids for me. I know you'll love them and raise them the way I would. Make sure they go to college and don't get mixed up in drugs. Bethani needs extra help in math and Blake wants to go to the Valentines dance. Remind them that I love them, and don't ever tell them the truth about their father. Thank you, Genny, for always being there for me. I love you, my friend. Take care of yourself."

Madison was quite proud of herself for getting through the conversation without breaking down. Not wanting to risk Eddie coming back and hearing her talk and know that she still had her phone, she texted her next message. She wrote a detailed message to Brash, outlining Eddie's criminal deeds and warning of the bomb on the baseball field. Even if the man killed her, he would not get away with the murders.

After a final text to Granny Bert, thanking her for her guidance through the years and her undying love and support, Madison slid the phone back into her pocket and waited for Eddie to return.

Her only weapon was a ballpoint pen.

༄

She did not have long to wait. She heard him return with shuffled feet, cussing and grumbling the entire way. She heard the truck come nearer, circle around the end of the nearest house, and all too soon roar away, leaving only silence.

"Damn piece of junk!" Eddie yelled, tossing something against the side of the incinerator's wall. "Ronny kept saying it wouldn't light half the time, but he was too cheap to fix it, that sorry –" The words faded as Eddie apparently bent over and mumbled them toward the ground. She heard a scraping noise, then a clang. She realized he was undoing the wire he had wound round and round the handle. Soon he would have the hatch open, and it would be her best chance at escape. He probably expected her to be half-drugged from the noxious propane fumes.

Madison forced herself to lie still. She kept her lids all but closed, relying on only the tiniest sliver of sight to implement her plan. She felt the blessed rush of cold air swoosh in when Eddie opened the hatch door, but schooled herself to only take tiny, inconspicuous breaths.

"You still alive in there, or did the gas do you in?" he asked, poking at her arm. She forced herself not to flinch. She pretended to be unconscious, even as he leaned closer and pulled on her eyelid. She dared not allow her eyes to focus, not until he lowered his arm.

The moment he pulled his arm back, his face still bent close to peer at her, Madison's fist flew forward, the pen gripped tightly in her hand. She aimed for his throat, at the tender dip of his jugular notch.

As the tip of the ballpoint pen sank into the soft flesh, angled downward, blood spurted in all directions. Madison was instantly horrified and appalled, and wanted nothing more than to jerk her hand away, but she drove the pen in with all her might. It was his life or hers.

Eddie Menger staggered backwards, reaching for the pen with both hands as he gasped for air. Madison did not wait to see if he succeeded in pulling the makeshift weapon from his throat; she pushed her legs free and wiggled out of the small space as quickly as possible. She heard fabric rip and felt her knees give way as she landed on rubber legs. She fell to the ground, only inches from where Eddie sprawled out on the white rock, his entire body twitching as he grappled for air.

Assuming she had crushed his windpipe, Madison wasted no pity on the man. She skirted around him, trying to make her escape, but one long leg darted out, catching her foot as she ran past. She tripped, landing hard on her palms and collecting a few small pebbles beneath her skin. Mindless to the pain, she half-crawled, half-scampered away, finally pulling herself to her full height as she gained ground.

Madison ran like the wind, not bothering to look behind her. He could be already dead or just inches behind, but she wasn't slowing down long enough to confirm either. She raced up the gravel road, past Granny Bert's car that Eddie still held the keys to, and was just turning the corner when she saw Genesis's car flying onto the farm.

Genesis slammed on her brakes, skidding to a stop ten feet beyond Madison. By the time the dust settled and Genny was out of the car, yelling her name and pulling her into a fierce hug, Madison could hear sirens in the distance.

Help had arrived.

26

Eddie Menger died on the way to the hospital. Madison found some small measure of relief in knowing he actually died from a heart attack, rather than from asphyxiation.

There was no bomb at the high school and the detonator was fake, but it looked real enough to make Madison willingly crawl into the furnace to face her death. When Blake heard that part of the story, tears came to his eyes and he threw his arms around his mother, hugging her extra tight.

There was no getting out of a trip to the hospital this time. Even though Madison insisted she felt fine and had only a lingering headache from the propane fumes, no one would listen. Only after a doctor checked her vitals, cleaned her scrapes and cuts, and bandaged her hands did they believe her. Once they got her home, her family hovered around her, almost afraid to let her out of their sight. Bethani fluffed the bed and brought her magazines to read, Blake kept vigil from a bedside chair, Granny Bert made her a vegetable smoothie, and Genny snuck in some Genny-doodle cookies.

The weather turned overnight, and by morning, a fine dusting of snow lightened the landscape of The Sisters. The overpass out on the highway had just enough ice and sludge on it to proclaim school closed for the day. With most of the town shut down —snow, no matter how minuscule, did that to a small Southern community— and with her mind and body still aching, Madison opted not to go into work at the insurance agency that day. When Myrna Lewis called the office to check up on her and discovered it closed, she tracked Madison down at home and chewed her out, insisting that both their business reputations had been ruined. Myrna promised that by the time she was through, not a soul in town would hire In a Pinch Temporary Services.

Myrna Lewis had to re-think her position when she and Dean returned early the next day, only to find the insurance office not only opened, but actually crowded. With the snow thawed and the weather already warming up nicely, people came out in droves to see the woman who had single-handedly caught and killed a murderer. Some pretended interest in insurance policies, while others came by to offer their appreciation, others to bring a casserole or a plate of brownies. Dolly Mac Crowder blatantly asked for a picture with the local hero. When Myrna tried to dock Madison's pay for the missed day of work, her husband firmly overruled. He handed Madison a check for the full amount due, plus a fifty-dollar added bonus.

Don Ngyen was released from jail and all charges dropped. By the time he returned to his family's farm, not a single fighting rooster nor any evidence of their existence could be found. By the time Barbour Foods got wind of extracurricular activities taking place at the new Ngyen farm, there was no physical evidence to support the allegations. Ramona Gleason came to the farm that same day and offered to sell to the young Vietnamese. She wanted no part of the chicken industry and planned to move away.

For at least the time being, the cock-fighting ring in The Sisters was broken, or at least warped. With no one to organize the fights and one less grower to provide birds, the gambling ring drifted to the next town, with the identity of 'the boss' still undiscovered. Considering the immediate threat removed, Brash deCordova moved the case to the back burner, so that he could concentrate on more pressing matters.

Within days, life in The Sisters settled back to normal.

According to Granny Bert, normal was, after all, only a setting on the dryer.

✒

Halfway into the ten-day assignment at her uncle's car dealership, Madison met Granny Bert for a late lunch at New Beginnings. Genesis joined them for the meal, while Shilo Dawne took care of the other customers.

"Shilo Dawne, I want to thank you for all you did last week." Madison took a moment to thank the girl personally.

"I didn't do much."

"You called 9-1-1 about the bomb, and then you called Cutter."

"The minute he heard Miss Genny was heading out there to help you and that you were trapped, he left the fire and headed your way."

"He got there the same time as Brash did," Madison confirmed. "Thank you for calling him."

"It was nothing," the dark haired beauty insisted, but a flush of pleasure colored her cheeks.

"Most importantly, you deciphered the text message!" Genesis beamed at the girl. "It would have taken me a while to finally make the connection, and Madison had no time to spare." She looked over at her best friend and squeezed her hand affectionately. "Even though, in the end, she rescued herself."

"I'm just glad it all worked out." Shilo Dawne smiled before moving on to take another customer's order.

Madison propped her still-bandaged hand onto the table and gave a rueful shake of her head. "Who said nothing exciting ever happens in a small town?" she murmured, not for the first time.

"I think you did," Granny Bert reminded her.

"I stand corrected."

Genesis changed the subject with a bright, "So, you're still liking the new assignment?"

"Actually, I do. I'm very impressed with the car dealership. It's such an odd little mix of mostly-used-but-a-few-new cars." Madison used her hands to juggle the words and the overall 'feel' of the business. "And I really like the little car I'm driving. I'm thinking of buying it when Uncle Glenn gets back."

"Think it will do well in the city?" Granny Bert asked, slyly watching for Madison's reaction to the innocent question.

Madison toyed with the rim of her iced tea glass. After a pregnant pause, she made a quiet decision. "I don't think I'm going back to the city. I've decided to stay in Juliet permanently."

Genesis squealed in delight and tapped her hands together, while Granny Bert sat beside her, looking quite pleased.

"I was afraid we might have scared you off," the old woman admitted. "You've had a rough introduction back to the community."

"That's true. But everyone has been so kind and supportive. People are still bringing food by. Last night when I was eating that homemade potpie Gladys Peavey dropped by — which, by the way, would not be good in liquid form, so don't even think about it— I realized I would never get that sort of love and support in the city. Last week's event would just be another blurb on the news, forgotten as soon as the next crime happened. If nothing else, my brush with death reminded me how precious life is, and how important it is to spend it surrounded by the people and the things I love."

Genesis lifted her own tea glass for a toast and said, "Hear, hear."

After they tipped their glasses together, Granny Bert asked, "So how do you think the kids are going to take the news?"

"We discussed it last night, and they're good with it," Madison reported with a smile.

"So it's official?"

Madison turned to gaze out the window, at the small town of Naomi beyond the glass pane. On the other side of the railroad track Juliet looked much the same, only prettier. The towns and the people were not perfect. There was a long-standing rivalry between the two towns, but the lines of animosity were beginning to blur. Those lines had certainly been non-existent this week, as people from both sides of the track came out to greet her and offer their condolences and best wishes. In a community where everyone's personal business was a topic of public discussion, it was also a public concern, and treated accordingly. At least she knew people cared.

Taking a deep breath of courage, Madison nodded her head and turned back to face her grandmother and her best friend.

"Yes, it's official," she said decisively. "I'm staying."

NOTE FROM THE AUTHOR

Thank you for reading!
    Please take a moment – right now!— to write a brief review on Amazon, Goodreads, or the platform of your choice. You may not be like me, but if I don't do something *right now*, I will somehow manage not to do it at all. Please don't let this happen to you. Your reviews and personal response are the only way I know if you like (or hate) what I'm doing. Your opinion matters! Give it voice!
    You may contact me in any of these methods:
    www.beckiwillis.com
    beckiwillis.ccp@gmail.com
    https://www.facebook.com/beckiwillis.ccp?ref=hl
    I hope you enjoyed this book and have an opportunity to read some of my others. Thank you for allowing me to entertain you through the pages of my imagination.
    Happy Reading!

ABOUT THE AUTHOR

Becki Willis has been writing since grade school, though her earliest works are best left unpublished. Her original goal was to write romance novels, then it was historical fiction. Before either could happen, she got sidetracked with life... marriage to her high school sweetheart... raising their two children... careers she loved but that had little to do with writing... In 2013, Becki brushed off her old dreams and resolved to become an author. She published her first book - a mystery - in November, sold her gift shop/restaurant in December, and dedicated herself to writing full-time.

An avid history buff, Becki likes to poke around in old places and learn about the past. Other addictions include reading, writing, unraveling a good mystery, and coffee. She loves to travel, but believes returning to her home in rural Texas is the best part of any trip.

Visit Becki's website at www.beckiwillis.com, or contact her at beckiwillis.ccp@gmail.com. She loves to hear from readers and encourages feedback!